ALDRIC: A SCI-FI WARRIOR ROMANCE

JANE HENRY

Copyright © 2017 by Jane Henry

Published by Stormy Night Publications and Design, LLC.
www.StormyNightPublications.com

Cover design by Korey Mae Johnson
www.koreymaejohnson.com

Images by Period Images and Bigstock/petar djordjevic

All rights reserved.

1st Print Edition. March 2017

ISBN-13: 978-1544991375

ISBN-10: 1544991371

FOR AUDIENCES 18+ ONLY

This book is intended for adults only. Spanking and other sexual activities represented in this book are fantasies only, intended for adults.

CHAPTER ONE

R-482

I watch the violet fingers of the sun tinge the horizon as I crouch, hidden behind the large, flat green leaves of the bush in front of me. My breath comes in gasps, having just hastened from the portal to where I now stand. The entrance to the portal—one of the few connections I have to my home planet—is now shut fast, and I am left alone on a foreign planet, the tiny communication device tucked into my bag the only connection to my home and my people. When the last streaks of light have diminished, it will be time to make my move. My heart thunders in my chest but I ignore the unease. If I must succeed in my mission, then I must not succumb to fear. I must assimilate into the throngs of people, the savages who line the streets of Avalere like wild beasts.

If I am to save my people, I must pretend to be an Avalerian. My hand goes to my side, checking once again for the slim silver weapon I've tucked into the band at my waist. I wish I had more time to study the people to whom I now go, to truly immerse myself in their culture, but time has been pressing. I am left with little more than threads of rumors I heard as a child. I am unsure what is fact or fiction.

The Avalerians are unlike the civilized, progressive planet of Freanoss, to whom I belong. I am told the Avalerians are barbaric. During the day, it's warm here, and even now they're dressed in simple, scant clothing. This piques my curiosity, as I've never seen a human dressed in anything but regulation white, the uniforms given to us in our youth. The barbarians still eat food cooked with heat, from animals they breed and slaughter. I cringe as I envision what it must be like to partake in meals with them. I will long for the cleaner, sterilized methods I am used to. I lift my chin and inhale deeply. If I do not pretend to be one of them, I cannot save my people.

But there are baser traditions that I truly fear. The mere thought of being forced to engage in their uncultured ways makes my stomach twist in knots, the palms of my hands unnaturally damp. They believe some of their people contain a greater life force than others, and thus they have an imbalance of power. There are no equals. And I am told—though again, I have no verification of such rumors—that the savages of Avalere believe in *coupling*. I shudder, and under my breath mutter the words that I've grown with, while the comforting repetition of our mantra stills the shaking of my limbs.

We are one body. We are one people. Together, we will conquer darkness and rise as one.

The glowing rays of the sun now gone, the black of night surrounds me. I move slowly, careful to make my way toward the throng without arousing much suspicion. It is time for me to dress in the clothing of the savages. I have a small bag with the clothing I will need. The regulation white I still wear has protected me from the elements while I traveled to the foreign planet. I have never felt real cold or heat, but only the controlled climate of Freanoss. It's cooler here now that the sun has set. Little bumps on my arms raise, and I shiver.

In front of me now, I see them, moving to the music,

drums being beaten with what looks like sticks. I shudder. *Barbaric.* Part of me finds the music appealing, the rhythmic *thump, thump, thump* primal and loud. But I quickly denounce such thoughts, eager to rid myself of any sympathy toward the barbarians. My breathing accelerates as I advance, watching now from my hidden position. The women are dancing, swaying their hips and moving their hands in time to the deep, thunderous beat of drums. Small children squeal as they chase one another, but as I watch, my attention is drawn elsewhere.

In front of the crowd are what look like ancient thrones, gilded and carved, and upon the thrones are a dozen fierce men—warriors, I surmise. They look vastly different to the men of Freanoss. These men bulge with muscle, bare from the waist up, black slashes of tribal markings along their arms and their large, muscular necks. Their hair is not shaven short in familiar regulation length but rather longer, thicker, framing their faces. Some have it tied back at the nape. The man I am most riveted to—the largest, fiercest looking one of them all—has long black hair. His eyes gleam like obsidian. His strong jaw is heavily bearded, his arms folded across his muscled chest. He is watching the dancing in front of him with a trained eye, his head slightly nodding as his gaze travels over the crowd.

I pull my eyes away. I must hasten to change my clothes if I am to assimilate. My safest chance of avoiding notice is to look like one of them.

As I remove my uniform, I will myself to ignore the discomfort of the cool night air. I remove the small tunic in my bag with trembling hands, and pull it over my head. I blink in surprise at myself, my own bare arms looking oddly out of place in the dark of the forest, my legs bare but for the hem of the tunic that hits just above my knees. Even if I *look* the part, how will they ever believe I am one of them? I shove my uniform to the bottom of my bag, placing it next to the tiny communication device I've removed while changing, but I tuck my weapon in the waist of the tunic. I have no idea what will transpire in the next few hours. Once I've gleaned the information I need, I will be able to return to my people and leave the savages for good.

With a deep sigh, I tuck my bag beneath the shade of the largest bush I can find. Removing my weapon, I hit the button on the side, and at once a silver blade emerges. I mark an *X* on the side of the branch. Once I hit the button on the side of my bag, it will vanish from sight. I must remember where I have put it. Without it, I will not be able to return easily to Freanoss.

It is a breach of our founding fathers' pact for me to be here now. I am not troubled by my choice to break the law. I have justified my choices, because the Avalerians were the ones who instigated our dispute. I glance at my weapon. Is it wise to enter the crowd armed? Leaving my weapon behind would be like severing a limb, so though my bag will remain invisible, the weapon comes with me. I draw closer to the crowd.

Ahead of me now, there are dozens of women together, huddled, laughing and swaying their hips in time to the music. I direct my steps toward them, recognizing that I will most safely be hidden among them. My hair is dark like theirs, and though my skin is soft and pale, unlike their golden-toned skin, it is my hope that I can hide among them as I get my bearings.

I feel utterly naked, but walk with purpose past a couple in front of me with a few small children, beyond the vendors selling something that is fragrant but turns my stomach. I tuck my head and pretend to sway my hips with them, though I cannot pretend to laugh with them. I remind myself all that is needed is one night to pretend to be one of them, and I will glean the information necessary for my mission. Avalere has been stealing from Freanoss. Though we are a small nation, we are a thriving one, due to the abundance of natural resources the Avalerians have taken at will. It is my job to infiltrate them and report back to my people what I find.

The music is reaching a crescendo now, the drums booming, the sound near frantic to my ears. Excitement seems to grow as the laughter of the women increases in volume. I begin to wonder if I've made a mistake. Why is this throng so raucous?

The large man sitting in the center of the circle now rises, and to my horror, he begins to advance toward our group. I am transfixed, looking at him up close. His hair is black as night, hitting the sharp angle of his bearded jaw. He is so unlike any man I have ever seen, I stare. On Freanoss, women grow their hair slightly longer than men, and the length is a matter of personal taste. However, bodily hair on both men and women is clinically removed once one reaches puberty, and the men from Freanoss are always clean-shaven. I cannot avert my eyes from the man in front of me now, his form towering over the crowd, his muscles rippling beneath the flickering light of torches. When he moves, his strength is magnificent to behold. I half expect him to speak in growls, rather than the commanding voice that now rings clearly, so deep it reverberates through my being like the drums.

"Come to me," he says, curling a finger toward the group. "It is time."

Time for what? My stomach twists in fear. I have made a terrible mistake. This is not an anonymous group of women, but rather a group being taken to the circle of men. I turn, stepping away from the crowd with my head down, hoping that if I avoid eye contact, I can escape my plight, and move back toward the people to my right. I need to get away from this group, as the women are now moving to the center of the circle of men. If I duck quickly between the women to my left, the man herding the women up front will perhaps not see me. I must not get too close to him. But as I skirt to the left, he advances. I increase my pace, but now I fear my swift movements will alert him to my plan to escape. Does he know now I am not one of them?

As I step left, two women block my way, seemingly

unaware of me standing in front of them as they advance forward. I am shoved to the right, closer to the man who beckons. I must move. I duck between two women, but he sidesteps, and I find myself planted right in front of the man. He looks at me curiously, before placing both hands on my shoulders. His voice is firm but gentle when he speaks to me. "Now, now, little one," he says in a low growl, and though he's smiling, his eyes are fixed sternly on me. "You know what we expect. Go, now." He turns me around and gives me a little shove back toward the mob of women. I begin to panic. I do not want to be on display like this. Will they find me out? What is this ring of men going to do? No, I will not go willingly.

I move to escape, but he grabs me, his large hand spanning my waist. He spins me around, and to my utter shock, he delivers a hard slap to my scantily clad bottom. My reaction is instinctive. I move swiftly, my elbow connecting with his hardened stomach. His head snaps back in shock and he utters a sharp gasp before he reaches for me. I could kick myself. *Damn* my trained instincts. I have now done exactly what I am not supposed to—drawn attention to myself. I look quickly to see what he will do in response. His eyes narrow, his lips thin, and I'm aware that a hush has come over the crowd.

"Be still, woman." His voice rings out, and I look to see that all men are now on their feet, weapons drawn. Why are their weapons drawn? Yes, I've drawn attention to myself, but their reaction confuses me. It is then that I see the gleaming silver a few feet in front of me. My knife has fallen from my waist in the skirmish, and shines in the center of the ring.

The man releases one arm from me just long enough so that he can reach for my weapon. His left arm tight around me, I am helpless to move. *Curse* me and my carelessness. He turns to me, his voice a low growl. "She brought a weapon in our presence," he says. I glance to the side and see he is now tucking the weapon into his own waist.

"Woman, are you aware of the law of our nation, that bringing such weapons in the midst of a village celebration is a punishable crime?"

I blink. I wonder if I have heard him correctly. Numbly, I shake my head. How could this have gone so wrong so quickly?

The warrior's grip returns to my shoulders. "I am within my rights to punish the woman for her offense against me, before she's brought to justice." My heartbeat quickens as he continues, addressing the crowd. "Though she's earned a stern chastisement for striking me, perhaps given the festival of the half moon, we should consider her second transgression mercifully." He pauses. "We've not had a foreigner defile our presence with barbaric weapons since the New Dawn. Perhaps mercy is in order."

I cannot breathe.

His voice lowers so that only I can hear him speak. "Though it will be my duty to bring you to justice, it will be my pleasure. It seems a gift from the gods has graced our presence."

Gift? I must escape. I *must* go home.

He steps back and raises his voice, addressing the crowd again. "The festival of the half moon brings with it a cry for mercy. Tonight, I shall serve a dual purpose, and execute both mercy and duty. Though I accept my duty to chastise the woman for her transgression, I accept her as my chosen mate from the circle." He bows to the women still in his presence in the circle, who return his bow. Some look disappointed, while some have trained their eyes on the other warriors. My head spins.

King?

Mate?

The crowd *cheers*. I struggle, writhing against the man's grip, but I cannot escape.

The man holding me pulls me closer to him. His chin lifts and his eyes focus on the crowd. "You have my word," he says. "I will see to her properly."

And with those final chilling, parting words, he pulls me away.

·······

I will not go quietly. I *will not*. They can call this man *king* or whatever it is they like, but I am no servant of his. He does not own me, and now that my identity is revealed, I will fight with every ounce of strength I have. I pull, push, and writhe in his grip. Though I am no weakling, I am unable to break free. I am small, but I am strong, and I will fight. I lift my foot and stomp as hard as I can on his. The breath hisses out of him and his grip slackens, but he does not release me. It is all I need, though. With a swift move, I once again elbow him as hard as I can, and the distraction gives me room to wriggle out of his grip, one arm free. I must hide. It is imperative I get away from him. I will *not* be captive to this savage. With one final yank, I pull my second arm away from him.

But the moment I turn to run, a piercing pain radiates down my scalp. I howl. The brute has me by the *hair*.

"That is enough, woman!" he bellows. My head is yanked back, and his eyes are no longer amused or kind, but furious slits as I'm once again pinned in his iron-like grip. "You will be thoroughly chastised for your display of temper," he hisses in my ear. "Do you wish to be disciplined in public as well? I will save you the mortification even now, if you but apologize and beg my forgiveness. Then you will face your punishment in my chambers, rather than here."

"You savage," I hiss. "How dare you!"

He arches a brow. "You will not apologize, I surmise?"

I narrow my eyes at him and glare. His lips part into a wicked smile and he tilts his mouth to my ear. "This is your last chance, little one," he says. "I am stronger than you, and you shall not win. But you will leave with a scrap of pride if you but do as I say. Do you wish to be punished in front of my people?"

I frown. Will he truly chastise me in such a mortifying manner? One look at his stern countenance, and I know he speaks the truth.

"I..." I begin, stuttering and faltering. I do not know what to say. He gestures for someone to bring him something. I watch, mortified, as the eyes of the crowd focus on me. A man approaches, holding a length of rope. My captor twists the rope about my wrists and pulls the length taut, frowning at me. "The proper response is, 'I'm sorry, Master.'"

I grit my teeth and defy him with my silence. *Master!*

I *cannot*. I *will* not! No man is master of *me*.

His jaw clenches. "Very well, then, little one," he says, and to my surprise, I hear a pang of regret in his voice.

He drags me to what looks like a marketplace, where there are tables and chairs, barely visible in the darkness. A crowd has gathered around us, and some follow us now, as he pulls me to an area that looks like a temple of sorts. It is simple but magnificent, golden-domed and flanked with panels of ivory. But now I see where I am being brought. It is a wide-open area that looks almost like an arena of sorts. There is a large, flat platform and several wooden posts... *whipping* posts. This entire area is designed for public punishment, where those who misbehave are publicly flogged. My stomach drops. I have heard such places once existed, but whips, chains, and jails no longer exist on Freanoss. Criminal behavior has been carefully bred out of my people as we progress toward sameness. We've eradicated deviant behavior, and have no need for cruel punishment.

He barks out a few orders. Torches flame to life, quickly placed along the edges of a platform.

I begin to fear the chastisement I've brought upon myself.

When we reach the platform, he drags me to the furthest corner of the arena, for I do not walk willingly. He takes my bound wrists, and ushers me up against what looks like a table. It is narrow, like a small desk, and when he pushes me over it, my belly is flat against the surface. With one swift move, he yanks my wrists, and he deftly lifts the length of rope, securing it on a peg at the opposite end of the table. I am now effectively stretched out, my arms flat in front of me, my torso flush with the surface of the table. The position I hold makes the small tunic I wear rise, and I am no longer covered. To my shame, I feel the cool night air across my backside and lower back. I am mortified, tears threatening to fall. As he adjusts my restraints, I cannot help but whisper, "Please. Don't."

He stands at the table in front of me, bending down so that his eyes meet mine. He is deadly serious as he leans in close to me.

"Please don't?" he says. "I gave you a chance to repent, and yet you chose defiance." He reaches one large hand out and brushes back a strand of hair that has fallen across my face. Though his tenderness takes me by surprise, I cringe as his finger grazes my head. Physical human contact is unfamiliar to me, as we on Freanoss recognized long ago how such animalistic tendencies spread disease and illness. We do not *touch* one another.

His eyes roam from mine, down the length of my body stretched across the table before he speaks again. When he does, his voice has deepened. Though not harsh, it is corrective and unrelenting. "You disobeyed me. You have broken the laws of Avalere." As he speaks, his eyes darken, and it's almost as if he has convinced himself of his purpose. "Need I remind you that according to our laws, you ought to be executed? I feel compelled to protect you from our harshest penalty." He stands, his lips a thin line, his eyes narrowed and fixed on mine. His voice lowers, and now only I hear it. "The stripes I will lay across you are given in my mercy." I close my eyes. I have no choice but to accept my fate.

He is speaking to the crowd but I do not hear what he says, as the blood rushing in my ears is near deafening. My cheeks are aflame, my eyes shut tight, as I am mortified by my predicament. I jump as a warm hand presses against the bare skin on my lower back. I brace myself for the first searing zing of the whip, or whatever he'll use to punish me, and jump in surprise when it is his hand that connects sharply with my bare skin. I gasp, the blow searing my flesh. Again, he strikes, the ringing sound of his hand connecting like a gunshot.

"You will obey me, little one," he says sternly. "You *must* obey me." He pulls back and I brace myself for another blow. "You ought to be whipped," he says, as another strike of his palm hits my flesh. "And if you raise your hand to me again, you shall be." Another stinging swat. I can hardly breathe for the pain, his large hand like a thousand bee stings, falling hard and fast. It hurts far more than I anticipate. He now spanks me in earnest, one blow falling after another. I feel his foot push against mine, spreading my legs, before another harsh blow lands on my inner thighs. My skin is on fire, every strike seemingly harder than the one before. He pauses. For a moment, I wonder if he is done. His voice raises as he addresses the crowd.

"The woman is small, and she is unfamiliar with our traditions. She is now mine to correct. She will learn obedience and subordination. Tonight, as I punish her, I mark her as my own."

Fear spikes in my chest, as I wonder what he means by marking. Is he referring to the marks of his hand upon my skin, or something else? I am terrified, gripped with fear at the coupling the barbarians partake in. Is there 'marking' involved in coupling?

He turns back to me, his voice dropping as his hand rests on my neck briefly. "Disobedience will not be tolerated." He pulls back and resumes spanking me, one hard swat after another. My backside burns from the blows, and each punishing swat atop my flaming skin makes me cry out. As my feet barely grace the floor, I writhe in pain.

"Now, now," he chides. "A girl who is brave enough to

strike the Warrior King ought to be brave enough to take her chastisement."

Another searing swat lands. Is he mocking me?

His voice lowers again. "Six more blows," he says. "And with each strike of my palm, you will count out loud. "There is a brief pause. "And if you do *not*, then I shall resume your punishment with my sword belt until you do."

I close my eyes and brace myself. His palm lands firmly.

"One," I hiss.

"Very good," he says, before delivering the second searing swat.

"Two."

Another hard smack falls, harder than the last, and I go up on my toes. "Three," I whisper, trying to maintain my dignity. Thoroughly punished in front of a crowed that is cheering, shouting, and whistling has stripped me of my pride. I want them to go away. I want to run.

The fourth swat lands on my thighs again, and I cry out from the pain. "Four," I choke, tears burning my eyes, my throat strangely clogged. I cannot begin to sort through the emotions I am feeling right now. I just need this to be done.

I am ready for the fifth swat, and take it bravely. "Five," I say, mustering up all my courage.

The last swat is the hardest of all. The crack echoes around us. "Six," I whisper, slumping against the table.

My punishment is over. But my imprisonment has only just begun.

• • • • • • •

The rough, firm feel of his palm massages my stinging skin. My eyes are shut tight, but I feel him lift my bound wrists from the peg.

"Come here, little one," he says. I am lifted in his arms. My eyes fly open in surprise. I am not used to being touched by a man, and certainly have never been carried by one, since physical touch like this is forbidden on Freanoss. The pairing of mates has been outlawed for decades, ever since the New Dawn. I have also been trained to believe I am resistant to the desire for human contact, capable of rational thought not colored by archaic notions. I have been bred to be stronger than my ancestors and not susceptible to the weakness they succumbed to. And yet... something within me yearns for his touch. My body likes the feeling of helplessness I get when in his arms. I tell myself it is merely exhaustion coloring my feelings. When I am rested, I will think rationally again.

I shiver from cold. I am not used to feeling such things. I lift my head and turn from him, arching my body to keep myself distanced.

"The little one defies me even now," he murmurs to himself, still holding me firmly while marching with purposeful strides. Oddly, I notice people are quieted, bowing to him as we pass. All around us I see brightly lit torches held high. Servants, perhaps? He speaks to me again. "It will be my duty and pleasure to teach you obedience. You will see."

I will see what? The man is *mad*. I am not staying here to be taught anything. I will escape from him, after I find what my people need. But I shall not make the mistake of defying him so brashly, not again. For now, I will submit to him as he *is* stronger than I.

And I will escape.

CHAPTER TWO

Aldric

I carry the little one in my arms as if she were a small lamb, tucked against my chest to keep her warm from the night air. I have punished her, and now it is my duty to comfort her. She has learned her first lesson from my stern correction. At first, she pushes against me, and I am not quite sure why she is fighting. I ponder for a moment whether her chastisement was thorough enough. But as a trained warrior of the highest order, I know how to read her *prana vitae*. I inhale deeply, interpreting her scent. As I walk between the flickering torches held by my servants, I feel her both tremble and cringe. Her defiance is bred of fear. The little one is uncomfortable and frightened.

I do not regret the discomfort. It was with mercy I administered her punishment, saving her from a harsher sentence. She does not yet know that she is mine, but soon she will. It was my duty to choose a woman from the ring as my mate, and she made my choice much easier than I'd anticipated. She is lovely, her petite stature fetching and quaint, her eyes dark blue like the sky at dusk. Her hair gleams in the moonlight, her skin creamy and unblemished, but what draws me to her above all else is the scent about her, both mystifying and enchanting. I have never met a woman like her before. Is she an enchantress? Does the blood of the gods flow in her veins?

As mine, the little one must learn to obey. But the smell of fear is strong, and it is the fear I must address.

"Relax against me," I order. "You will not get away by pushing or fighting me."

She still pulls away from me, turning her head.

"If you continue to resist me, I shall be forced to punish you again in my chambers." I speak slowly so she knows I mean what I say. "And I will *not* hesitate to punish you again." She needs to obey me. It is for her own benefit.

She struggles against me and without thinking, I growl, low in my chest, a warning that she must obey. Her movements cease, and she looks to me with wide eyes.

"You growl like an animal," she says, her brows furrowed.

"We are brothers with the animals, little one," I say.

She wrinkles her nose in disgust, before asking me a question. "Why do you call me that?" Though her question is interesting, I like that she has stopped resisting me for the moment. We are now only several yards away from our destination.

"You are little," I say in explanation. "And I do not yet know your name. Do you dislike it?"

Her eyes flicker away from mine for a moment. No. It is not that she does not like it. She likes it very much, and it is her attraction to my name for her that troubles her.

The little one is complex. I smile to myself. I have chosen well.

"I have never been called such things," she says, her eyes going back to mine. "Among my people, I am not *little*."

"Among *my* people, you are," I say. "And this is where you have come." But I am puzzled by her insistence. "There is nothing wrong with being little," I say. "I like that you are little."

"Easier for you to overpower me," she says, her eyes, the color of the fathomless ocean, flashing at me. Her skin is fair. I wonder if she's ever been kissed by the rays of the sun or if it's the stark contrast of her raven-colored hair that makes her look so pale. Though she is lovely to behold, the expression on her face is not. She is scowling. As much as I enjoy her feisty spirit, I cannot allow even the slightest thread of disrespect. I frown at her.

"Yes," I say firmly. "It *is* easier to overpower you, and I do not regret for a moment doing so."

"Of course not," she mutters, turning her head away, muttering under her breath. "*Savage*."

I lift my right hand, holding her solely with my left, as I administer a sharp swat to her backside. "That is enough," I say. She closes her mouth and turns her head to the side. This little one will need a very firm hand. I am not afraid of my task. I have trained women in obedience before, though none have been mated to me. I will enjoy seeing her transformation.

"We are nearing our home," I say. "I have carried you, for you have been punished. And now that I have punished you, I must see you are well cared for. It is the way of Avalere. There will be time for me to show you the home that is to be yours. Tonight, you need rest."

"I am capable of walking," she says.

I am nearing the end of my patience. "And I am capable of taking you across my knee," I growl. She quiets.

We pass the final bend in the forest, and now approach the castle. It is a simple yet elegant abode. When my father deferred headship of Avalere to me, he willingly forfeited all property. As my father chose to remain at the large, stately castle of Avalere for his retirement, I chose a smaller abode. It is large but simply furnished, with fewer servants to manage, and fewer entrances to guard, the castle proper being maintained for the day I shall return with my wife, who will bear my children. For now, the little one will stay with me in my more intimate home.

I pass the arched stone entrance and walk swiftly to my chambers. The fire has already been lit, the bedclothes turned down, the table by the fire laden with a small platter of fruits, cheeses, and nuts aside a flagon of wine and a pitcher of water. I bend and gently set the woman on her feet.

"Sit, little one," I order, pointing a stern finger to the chair, but as she moves to obey, she winces. She is not used to being chastised, I see. Perhaps my punishment was sufficient after all. I watch her sit gingerly upon the hard surface of the chair. Her face contorts in pain as she sits. This will not do.

"Come here," I instruct. She looks at me in confusion, but I beckon to her. She frowns for a moment, and I inhale, trying to remain patient. I am not used to such defiance. Servants obey my command without delay. "Woman, when I give you an instruction, I expect prompt and respectful obedience. *Always*. Now come here."

She slowly rises, coming to me, frowning all the way. When she is within arm's reach, I grasp her waist, spin her around, and lift her tunic. She lifts her hand to smack me away, but I deftly grab her wrist and pin it by her side, ignoring her protests as I inspect her.

"You have not been chastised before?" I ask. How curious.

"Never!" she near wails. "We do not partake in such barbaric acts on my planet!"

"That is evident," I murmur, "as well as unfortunate. I am displeased with your lack of obedience."

She looks over her shoulder at me, trying to get away, but I hold fast. "We have no need for your methods," she hisses.

"Young one," I say sternly. "It seems you have *much* need for my methods." I ignore her protests and mutterings, as I inspect her punished bottom. She is reddened, and there is one very small bruise forming. Though I only used my hand, I struck firmly, and her unblemished skin was not used to such treatment. I lower her tunic and spin her around to face me. "I must tend to you," I say. I lift the small silver bell upon the table and give one quick shake. In moments, I hear a knock at the door. "Come in."

My head servant Lystava enters. Small, thin, and graceful, with dark skin and dark hair gone gray around the temples piled atop her head, she eyes the woman with curiosity. No doubt she has heard from the crowd that I have taken a claimed woman to my chambers. For years, Avalere has waited for the day I would take a mate, and are likely gleeful I've finally made a choice. Lystava smiles politely and bows to me.

"Yes, my lord?"

I smile at my most faithful servant. "Greetings, Lystava," I say. "I wish to have the silver *salvete*. Will you fetch it?" Her eyes widen before she hastens to obey. The silver *salvete* is of great expense, and used sparingly. But this woman is my mate, and will have duties to perform. She will need to be healed, and quickly.

Moments later, Lystava returns with a small vial, and hands it to me with a bow.

"Thank you," I say, dismissing her with a nod.

"Come," I say, pulling my woman by the hand to the bed. "Lie face down across my bed, and lift your tunic."

Her eyes widen, and I am puzzled by her reaction at first, until I realize she may suspect I am going to punish her again, or perhaps violate her in some way.

"I need to apply this salve," I say. It is the last bit of explanation she will get from me. "Now do as I say." I point, my patience waning.

She obeys, standing but laying her torso on the bed now, her face flush against the bedspread, and lifts her tunic. She trembles.

I place my left hand on the small of her back. "Shh, now, little one," I soothe. "This will feel very nice. And when we are done, we shall eat." She closes her eyes and nods. A warmth floods my chest as she finally acquiesces, and I stand taller, proud of her small act of submission. Though I will punish her soundly for acts of defiance, she will be richly rewarded for her obedience. Thus will her training commence.

I tip the vial into my palm, the liquid silver gleaming in the flickering light of the fire. The vial is fashioned so that only small drops seep onto my palm. It is all that is necessary with a potent salve. I gently smooth my hand over her bare skin. Her bottom is hot to the touch, and she winces slightly when my palm touches her. But as I continue the massage, she sighs. I smile softly to myself as I look, and see the markings upon her have now faded to a deep red.

"I have punished you in front of my people," I say. "You were marked with my skin against yours." I pause, my voice dropping, as my hand massages her skin. She must know how important this is. "You will learn to obey me. Now come here." I pat her bottom gently, and she stands up, turning to face me. Her cheeks are flushed, her eyes lowered. I reach, embracing her, and pull her against my chest. She fits there as if she was created for me. My arms instinctively encircle her. She is warm, and I inhale deeply. It is no longer defiance I now detect, but something else. Something primal and undeniable. If my limited knowledge of Freanoss is correct, her knowledge of coupling is nonexistent. I smile.

It will be my pleasure to teach her.

• • • • • • •

The little one sits upon the stool by me. I eye her warily. Though she is now under my watchful eye, I cannot trust her. I do not know why a woman of Freanoss is not only here, but came bearing weapons from her home planet. Though I will tend to her needs and demand her obedience, I will keep a trained eye upon her as I discover her purpose. For now, her basic needs must be met.

"Are you hungry?" I ask. After the evening's ordeal, she

must need sustenance. To my surprise, she looks at me in confusion.

"Hungry?" she asks.

I blink. "Yes. That is what I asked. Are you hungry?"

She shrugs. "I do not know. I have heard of such things as hunger, but I am unfamiliar with the feeling." I must be frowning, for she quickly amends her words. "I know of such things. I have been educated enough to know that others experience hunger. But the Freanossians have eased such primitive urges, and we now circumvent hunger with methods to nourish and sustain without having to encounter unpleasantness or discomfort. We take supplements and nutrient-rich bars that sustain energy and provide the necessary nourishment."

How very odd. The differences in our cultures after the New Dawn are remarkable, of this I am aware. Though I know the modern methods of Freanoss are different, until now I had no reason to truly contemplate the disparity in our cultures.

"Unpleasantness of hunger?" I ask. "Hunger is a natural human experience. It is deep within our *prana vitae*." But I am not going to argue with her. I am weary and hungry, and the little one *will* eat. She eyes the plate on the table with trepidation. She frowns, as if the wedges of cheese will somehow leap off the plate and nip her fingers.

"Hunger feels like an emptiness. Sometimes it is painful. It twists and gnaws, the body's natural reminder to feed." I reach for the flagon of wine and pour the rich crimson liquid into a tapered glass. I lift it to my lips, and quench my thirst with a long, steady pull. I sigh in contentment as I place the glass on the table. The heat of it warms my chest, the slightly sweet, slightly sour taste sharpening my hunger. I take a large triangle of white cheese and place it wholly in my mouth. She watches me, frowning.

"I have taken my first sip and morsel of food," I say with a nod. "So now, you may eat with my permission."

She frowns first at me, and then the food. "I am not

allowed to eat until you do?"

My eyes widen in surprise. I have much to teach this young one. "Certainly not. I am the king, and you my woman. You will eat when bidden to do so." I frown at her. "If I were a cruel master, I would have you perform your acts of service with no nourishment, and consider sending you to bed hungry. However, I wish to be neither cruel nor cossetting, so I will allow you to eat." She will not appreciate the kindness I am showing her if she does not understand the methods of Avalere.

Her little lips turn downward. "While I thank you for your generosity," she mutters, and I detect a strong thread of disrespect in her voice, "I prefer not to eat." She turns her head away disdainfully.

I take another wedge of cheese and eat it, followed by several plump purple grapes. I swallow my food, then take another long pull from my glass of wine before I speak to her.

"I asked if you were hungry," I say sternly, making sure she heeds the tone of my voice. "I did not ask you if you wanted to eat. Now answer me. Do you feel an emptiness, pain, or discomfort that might indicate hunger?"

As if in answer to me, her stomach growls. She crosses her arms over her belly, trying to silence her traitorous body. She turns her face away from me. She has not answered me.

I lean forward and grasp her chin with my fingers, turning her eyes to focus on mine. "When your king asks you a question, you are expected to answer. Now answer me. Do you feel hunger, or no?"

She nods, her eyes focusing on mine. "I do." A brief pause, then, "But I do not wish to eat." She wrinkles her nose in disgust.

I release her chin and nod. "I see. But I am not giving you a choice in the matter, you see. If you are hungry, you must eat. Now do so, or I shall be forced to feed you myself, but not until I've taken you across my knee for your defiance."

Her eyes widen. I do not wish to punish her again, but I must teach her to obey me.

She eyes the food on the plate. Her bravado wanes a bit, and her voice is small when she speaks. "I don't know what it is, or what I like," she says. "I..." Her voice falters before she continues. "It is unfamiliar to me."

Ah. She is not defiant, but afraid. I nod. "Come here," I say. Though apprehension colors her eyes, she stands, shuffling her feet as she slowly walks over to me. When she is by my side, I gently push her to sitting upon my knee. "You will try one bite of everything," I say. I take a small purple grape in my fingers and lift to her mouth. Like a good girl, she opens for the first bite as I put it in her mouth. "Chew, little one," I say. "This is a grape. It is juicy and sweet, and can be eaten whole without being peeled. We crush and ferment them to make wine." She obeys, and as she does, her eyes widen.

She swallows. "That is... I do not have a word," she says with surprise. "What do you call something that tastes wonderful?"

I smile. "Delicious?"

She nods in wonder. "Delicious," she says, savoring the word as much as she savors the fruit. I am pleased. My kingdom is well known for their flourishing vines.

I pick up a small wedge of cheese. "Again," I instruct. She obeys, opening her mouth, and I carefully insert a small corner of the wedge. It is a sharp cheese, tangy and salty. She closes her mouth and chews. "As is that. What do you call it?"

"This is cheese."

"Cheese," she murmurs. "Delicious."

She reaches for another grape. Surprised at her boldness, I swat her hand away. I am feeding her now, and she must defer to my leadership.

"No, little one," I chide. She tucks her chin and her eyes cast down. She is chastened. That is a far better response than the flashing eyes and defiance. She is learning quickly.

I continue to admonish her. "When your king feeds you, you will wait patiently."

"You are not my king," she says through gritted teeth.

I spin her around so that she is straddling my lap, facing me, and I grasp her firmly, my fingers cupping her jaw. The temptation to punish her again is strong, but I must keep in mind that she is ignorant of our ways, and it is my job to teach her. "You listen well, woman," I say. My voice is low, a near growl, as I convey my displeasure at her disrespect. "That circle of women that were brought forth were woman who are subservient to the *Hisrach*. They voluntarily gave themselves to the military leaders of our planet. You entered our presence as one of them. *You* made that choice. Thus, choosing you out of the ring, I was given headship over you. I marked you publicly. I *am* your king."

"You are not," she whispers, shaking her head.

I am baffled at her defiance. Does she not know what I am well within my rights to do to her? I could have her flogged and imprisoned. I could mount her at my leisure, morning, noon, and night, and call each of my men to do so in turn. I could have her beg at my feet, caged by my bed, and fed the scraps from my plate.

Lesser men have done this, and more.

I lean in closer to her, my eyes meeting hers squarely as I speak. "Little one," I say. "I am not *merely* your king. I am your master. You would do well to remember that."

CHAPTER THREE

R-482

I am angry with myself for undertaking this mission. I insisted I would be able to handle the brief, anonymous job. There were others who thought my idea to infiltrate the barbarians as a spy was preposterous. They were perhaps correct. How could I have ever suspected that I would find myself where I am now, sitting upon the knee of a savage who fancies himself *king*. Bile rises in my throat, and I'm sorely tempted to kick the shin behind my heel. But I am smart enough to know assaulting his majesty again will earn me another *chastisement*. And he promised me that if I struck him again he'd whip me. Oh, the *shame* of it all.

I allow him to feed me, and this is not quite a hardship. Really, after the salve he applied to my battered skin, the only thing that now hurts is my pride. His touch is gentle, his voice soothing, as he speaks to me of the food, what various items are called, from where it came. I nod, feigning interest. What I'm really doing is marking where I am, taking note of possible escape routes, and trying to formulate a plan to get back to my bag. I need to observe the king and his people, and garner the information I need. I must obtain my communication device.

After a few more bites, he pushes the plate away. I would like more. This is my first time tasting such delicacies, and I do not wish to stop quite yet.

"Please, may I have more?" I ask.

"No, little one," he says with gentle sternness. "Eating too much rich food when you are very hungry could make you ill. The cheese of Avalere is rich and flavorful, but strong. You've had enough. Now, you may sip some wine before we retire for the evening, but that is all. I shall call off the servants for the evening so we have our privacy, and then you will sleep by my side."

I am utterly horrified at the notion of sleeping beside the savage. I've never slept beside another person. I shiver. The savage stands, gently pushing me to my feet, as he leans over and rings the bell beside him.

What if he decides to violate me while I sleep? What is to prevent him from making free with my body? I've only ever slept alone, in the privacy of my bunk, in the sterile, uniform environment to which I've become accustomed. I shiver. Within seconds, the silver-haired woman who fetched the salve for him returns.

"Yes, my lord?" she asks, her hands folded behind her back.

"It is time we retire. See we are not woken early in the morning. The little one will need a change of clothing and a basin of warm water with which to wash. Tonight, I prefer she stay with me rather than prepare herself. She will remain in my chambers."

The woman nods. "Has she no name, my lord?"

He raises a heavy brow to me.

I shake my head. "Name? My reference number is R-482. We are regulated according to our numbers, and find names to be old-fashioned." I turn and toss my head at the *king*. "Though *he* seems to think my name is 'little one.'"

She arches a brow and her mouth opens in a little 'o' but the savage laughs a deep, bellowing laugh.

"She has fire, this one," he says. "It was why I wanted her from the moment I saw her. I cannot abide spineless servitude in my mate, Lystava."

She turns to him, her mouth still pursed. "My lord?"

He nods with a chuckle, stroking his heavy beard. "Make no mistake. She will still learn to obey." He nods. "She will also have a name."

I turn to look at him curiously. Will I, then? If the almighty king says I will, I suppose I will.

Lystava merely smiles and nods her head. "Very well, my lord." She brings me what I need shortly, and takes her leave. I am now alone with my king… my supposed *master*.

• • • • • • •

All lights have been extinguished. I tremble in the darkness. I look to the window, and see it is large enough for me to get out. But how high is it from the ground? We took a small staircase to get here, and it's very likely that we are far too high for me to escape that way easily.

"Come," he orders. His deep voice carries through the small chamber. It is time. I have little choice but to obey at this juncture. If I obey, I may find it easier to escape when the time is right.

I have cleaned myself, and prepared myself for bed as best I can. I have no idea what their bedtime rituals are like, but I do know that I am tired. My eyelids droop, my body weary from the exhausting day I have had. Just this morning, I was preparing to embark on a mission to save my people and our planet. Now, I am not sure where I will go or what I will do next. But it only makes sense that I will be better prepared for my task ahead if I can rest first, if he will let me, but I fear the unknown. I know there is nothing he cannot do to me, if he desires. Who will stop him? There is no other choice now but to obey, and plot my escape. I climb into the large bed. It is resting on a wooden frame of sorts.

This man claims mastery over me. What will he do now that we are alone? His large, hulking frame takes up a good deal of the enormous bed, but there is plenty of room for me as I am much smaller than he is. On Freanoss, I am considered tall. Here, I feel like a mere child.

Regulation sleeping habits are vastly different from the primitive methods of Avalere. In my climate-controlled environment, I have need only of a small, thin blanket that I use when I rest. I take my regulation supplement for sleep, and shortly thereafter, sleep comes to me easily. I sleep the required amount, and wake as I've been trained to. It is a straightforward affair. Now I wonder if I can rest, lying beside the barbarian.

I feel shy next to him, as he is stripped of nearly all his clothing. Before he extinguished the light, I observed his bare chest in the flickering candlelight. He is strong, this king, his shoulders broad and wide, the hardened muscles in his abdomen rippling when he walks. Somehow the slashes of markings on his shoulders and neck make him seem even more fearsome. Even his hands are so large, he can span my entire waist easily. When I sat upon his knee, I expected to feel like a child, yet I felt anything but childish. I felt the warmth of him surround me, and strange stirrings took root in me in response to his innate power and strength. I did my best to ignore that his touch was gentle, his hand around my waist warm and protective, but as I lay in the dark, the memory returns with vivid clarity.

It seems I am to wear my light tunic to bed, as he has not instructed me to do anything different. I move to the very edge of the bed, as far away from him as I can get and quietly crawl beneath the covers, my back to him. I am practically falling off the edge. Though I suspect my act of defiance will not be tolerated, I enjoy the brief moment I am apart from him. Will he touch me? I wait in the darkness. He has positioned himself between me and the door.

"Now, now, little one," he says. "You will not sleep apart from me. Come closer, please."

I begin to tremble, both from fear and cold. He has allowed the fire to die down in the room, and my body is unaccustomed to self-regulation. I wonder what he will do to me. What recourse do I have? I have heard tales of barbarian violations, and the prospect frightens me. What will he have me do? If I disobey him, I will be punished. I suspect he has actually been somewhat lenient with me, and is capable of harsher, more cruel punishments. The pain from my earlier spanking no longer hurts, but the memory of being bent over the table and chastised is still vivid. Reluctantly, I move closer to him, but apparently it is not close enough. His large hand encircles my waist, and he pulls me so that I am flush against his body. I gasp.

It is his warmth I feel first. It is unlike anything I've ever experienced. Heat exudes from him, the length of his legs against mine, his bare chest against the fabric of my tunic, his arms over me. I am puzzled by my response. Though I am still afraid, the feeling is not altogether unpleasant. It is nice to be warmed, I tell myself. And that is the only reason why I'm almost enjoying the warmth of his embrace, and why my breath has begun to come in shallower gasps. I am losing control of myself, finding that I am eager to be held even tighter by him. I try to move away.

His arms tighten, his mouth nestles in my hair as he whispers, "*No.*"

I close my eyes. I have little choice. Disobeying will earn me punishment.

He inhales deeply for a moment, and it surprises me when one large hand lifts from my waist and goes to my hair, stroking gently.

"You are afraid," he says softly.

I close my eyes. I do not want to admit fear. Fear is weakness. I am strong.

"There is no need to hide your fear from me. As your master, it will be my duty to not only teach you obedience, but to see to your needs as well. One led in fear is not as useful to me as one who embraces her submission."

I am shocked at the audacity of his words. *Useful* to him? *Embrace* my submission? I will never! Though I do not respond, he chuckles, again stroking my hair.

"You will see," he says. "Now, come here. Roll over on your back so that I may see you up close."

My eyes have now adjusted to the darkness as I reluctantly obey. Moonlight filters in through the window on my side. He reaches out a tender finger to my hairline, tracing the edge of my hair. "Our women have lighter hair than yours," he says. "The darkness of your tresses gives you the appearance of an enchantress."

I stiffen. I know not of what he speaks, and he will not garner a response from me. His finger trails down, over my cheekbones. Though his finger is rough, a warrior's hands, his touch is gentle.

"Such soft skin," he murmurs. It is an odd remark, I think. On Freanoss, nutritional needs are met, and genetic alteration has removed imperfections. Thus, we all have clear, soft, unblemished skin. His finger trails to my lips, as he traces them. Strangely, my heartbeat accelerates. It is an intimate touch. I am torn between wanting to hide, and wanting him to touch me even more.

"Such full, lovely lips," he says softly.

I swallow, as his hand travels lower, to my chin, then down to my neck, as he traces my collarbone. I shiver.

"Little one," he says. "Have you ever known a man?"

I shake my head, unable to speak. I have never been touched by people, let alone a man.

"And yet you are not a child."

I shake my head again.

He smiles at my response. When he speaks, it is to himself. "She is a gift from the gods. A gift I will treasure." But I barely pay attention to his words, as I am wholly preoccupied with where his touch is leading. My breasts feel full and strange. I have never felt this before, and it frightens me.

"Your breath is shallow, little one," he says. "From fear,

or anticipation?"

I know not, so I do not respond. He leans in and my breath catches in my throat as his mouth comes to my forehead. His lips are warm and soft.

"Hush. It's just a kiss, little one. And a chaste one at that. Tonight, we must rest." He sobers, the teasing glint in his eyes fading. "You came to me with no name. That must change. As you are mine, you shall be named by me." He takes my chin gently in hand and tilts my face to look up at him. "In my people's tongue, *Carina* means little one. Henceforth, you shall be called *Carina*." He gently pushes me back on my side. He keeps one hand on my hip. "Sleep now, Carina," he says.

My mind is filled with many thoughts. My new name. His touch. My fears. As I lay in the bed of a savage in a strange land, I feel the unfamiliar pull of my primal instincts, my breasts tingle and my thighs clench together. It is unsettling to me. I swallow. I cannot allow myself to be seduced by him.

"And, Carina?" he says softly in the darkness. "Put thoughts of escape to rest. I have trained men at the door, and guards in the garden beneath the window. They have been alerted to your presence. Be sure you do not entertain thoughts of defiance." He pauses. "You know what will happen if you defy me." A chill creeps through me.

I stare in the darkness for a very long time, wishing for the familiar tablet I take before bed at home that beckons sleep, before I finally, pressed up against his warmth at my back, succumb to slumber.

CHAPTER FOUR

Aldric

When I rise the next day, my little one—*Carina*, she is now called—is still fast asleep. She is tucked against my chest, and my flank is pressed up against her warm, shapely backside. I feel myself begin to harden, and close my eyes. I must be patient. Though she will learn utter obedience to my will, I wish to earn her trust as well. I have not gotten to where I am without learning self-control. It is time I exercise it.

The light is just beginning to creep through the window near Carina's side of the bed, the light gracing her cheek. I am thankful I thought to have my servants refrain from the standard morning ritual. Normally, they'd have brought me my breakfast and helped prepare me for the day ahead. But today, my Carina and I have much to do. Though I will tread lightly in some ways, she has questions to answer. I sit up, tucking the blanket back around her, and rise.

She will begin by telling me why she is here. Freanoss is a small planet, but if she is someone of high rank, she might be sought after by her people. If it were my daughter or sister in a foreign land, I would stop at nothing to get them back if they were taken. I wonder why she comes here now, and if she was sent here by the Freanoss leaders. Though I am confident of my legal lordship over her, I wish to prepare myself for battle if need be.

I like the idea of taming this outlander. She shines above all others, her beauty ethereal, and even her audacity to defy me draws me to her. She is courageous, and when I have trained her, she will serve as a fitting queen. I wonder what she dreams of when she slumbers.

She shifts on the bed, and stretches her arms up over her head, yawning. I smile to myself. She is delightful, her little mouth opening wide as she stretches, like a little kitten waking from slumber. Her moment of peace is short-lived, though. Seconds after waking, she sits straight up in bed, snatches the blanket up over her chest, and stares at me with wide eyes. I wonder what has frightened her so.

"Stay away," she whispers, pointing her finger at me.

Though I recognize she is afraid, my little one is not allowed to give me instructions. I frown, and though I move slowly, I approach her side with firm steps so that her eyes are riveted on me. "You may not instruct me, woman," I say. "It is not your place to do so."

She frowns. "Leave me alone," she growls. Ignoring her protests, I approach her and sit by her side.

"I shall tell you one final time," I say, with as much gentleness as I can muster. I am already prepared to spank her, but I would like to give her an opportunity to correct her behavior. "You may not instruct me. As your king, I demand respect and obedience. If you speak to me again in this manner, I will punish you."

She looks at me as if pondering whether it is worth continuing in this vein. She frowns, her eyes roving the room. There is much I wish to learn of her. But first, she must be taught obedience. "The correct response for your transgression is 'I'm sorry, my lord.'" I wait. Though I will be patient, she will learn to obey. I pause a beat, waiting expectantly. Did she learn nothing yesterday? Must we begin every day anew? To my shock, she pushes the blanket off herself and moves to the other side of the bed, away from me.

I stand and follow her. What is the meaning of her defiance? She is grumbling to herself, scowling. It seems my little one rises in poor spirits.

I cross the room to her in swift strides, grasping her forearm firmly. She pulls away from me, but I am prepared for her to fight, and she is no match for my strength. I easily subdue her. With one hand, I pull out the wooden chair by my desk. It is armless, and made to support a man as large as I am. I sit down quickly and yank her across my knees.

"No!" she screams, waving her arms back at me furiously, but I will not be deterred. This little one must be taught a lesson. I take her wrists and pin them to her lower back with my left hand, while with my right, I administer her first smack. Yesterday, I was lenient with her. Today, I shall not be so understanding.

With her over my lap, I have much more control over her punishment than I did before. She screams with the second blow of my hand, but I do not waver in my punishment. The sounds of my hand slapping her bare bottom resound in my chambers, intermingling with her wails.

"You barbarian!" she screams, wriggling herself partially off my lap. This will not do. With my right hand, I bring her back to my lap, lift my leg, and restrain her with my leg over hers so that she cannot escape my grasp. Now her small, bare backside is vulnerable to my correction. I lift my hand high and bring it down with purpose. She howls as her spanking continues, and to my surprise, expletives color her language. I am shocked. I have never heard a woman use such language. It is unacceptable for a woman to speak in such a way, and she will learn that lesson as well.

"You may rail against me," I say, underscoring my words with sharp swats. "But you will not treat me disrespectfully." The slap of my hand against her bare skin resonates in the room. She howls and writhes but cannot escape my firm grasp. It is well that she cannot. I am nowhere near done correcting her.

I administer one sharp blow after another, feeling the sting of my hand on her skin. I intentionally swat the sides of her thighs, vulnerable and tender. "You will speak to me with respect," I insist. "You will not utter oaths unbefitting a woman in my presence." Another sharp blow has her wailing.

"Leave me alone!" she shouts, her voice catching. "You are a *savage* people!"

I frown. It seems I shall have to stay the course further than I'd anticipated. Perhaps the next time my little one needs a lesson, I will help advance her education with my strap.

"Savage though we may seem, compared to you," I say, as I keep a steady rhythm of smacks, "women in our culture know their place. They would not dare to utter words of disrespect to their masters. Those who fail to surrender to their masters face very serious consequences."

"Masters!" she utters, gasping with each hard blow I administer. "There are no masters of the human race! We are all equal!"

I pause, my hand raised over her reddened, fiery hot backside. "Is that so?" I ask. "Though your theory is interesting, it seems at this particular moment, there is only one of us receiving correction, and one *administering* correction." I deliver another pointed smack but then I sober. I dislike having to correct her, and I haven't yet managed to convince her to submit. "And I shall continue punishing you until I've made my point." I give her another slap, then another. I've punished women before. I've taught them obedience. But the punishments I've administered were far shorter than this, as merely incurring my displeasure has typically made the women under me repentant before correction began. This little one is far more tenacious. Though I must have her obedience, I like her spirit. I like her fire. And my body does as well.

Beneath her, my erection presses hard against her as I continue to hold her. Having to teach this little one has aroused me. I long to have her beneath me, ruled by her master, eager to obey my bidding. But before we continue, she must learn to obey. I grit my teeth, determined to persevere until I have made my point.

"Please," she begs, while I continue to spank her. "Please stop."

I will not stop until she has demonstrated repentance.

I pause, my hand on her fiery bottom. "I merely asked for you to speak to me respectfully," I remind her. "Your people's belief in equality has no bearing on your subordination to me as your master on *my* planet. I explained to you already that I am your king and your master, yet you do not seem to have grasped the import of my words."

I do not wish to continue her punishment. I *do* wish for her obedience.

My hand still on her hot bottom, I question her. "Will you apologize for your rudeness?"

Her shoulders slump, but she does not respond. I raise my hand and bring it down with a resounding *slap*.

She jerks and howls. "Yes, yes! Heavens above, *yes*."

Good. I pause again, my hand raised above her. "Well, then?"

"I'm sorry," she mumbles, her words barely coherent.

"Say again?" I ask.

"I'm *sorry*," she says, but I am not sure she truly is. We do seem to be making some progress.

"Will you speak with respect to me, as your master?"

She groans out loud. I barely stifle a chuckle. Her reluctance to submit is quite fetching.

"Yes..." she pauses, and I can see what an effort it is for her to swallow her pride, "...my *lord*." The word is hissed, but I hear her. I place my hand on her warmed bottom and squeeze. She bolts up, saying louder this time, "Yes, my lord!

I am... sorry." Her voice trails off at the end, a mere whisper, as if she is trying to compose herself. I wonder if she is. If she wept now I would know I had moved her, but she was trained to be strong on Freanoss. I would teach her to rely on me.

I shall not punish her further. I smooth my hand over her bottom, as red as if she's been burnt by the summer sun. My little one will feel my correction for some time.

"Are you... going to use that salve on me?" she asks tentatively.

I chuckle. I've just spanked her soundly, and already she's hoping for a reprieve from her chastisement?

"The salve I used last night is a precious commodity, and is used sparingly," I explain. "Since you've defied me again, it seems I was hasty in alleviating your discomfort last night. We've only just begun the day. I prefer you feel your correction as the day continues." My voice lowers. "You will obey me, Carina. I will not falter in my duty if you fail to do so."

She simply nods her head, but does not speak. She is so small, so lovely, her curves womanly and attractive. And she is mine.

I caress her bottom. She winces at my touch. Massaging her will help prevent bruising, though as I take my little one with me about my day, I am not terribly concerned for her modesty. If others see she has been marked by me, it will reinforce to them that I am her master.

Now that her punishment is complete, I must take care of her. My little one will learn that repenting of her naughty behavior will be richly rewarded. Slowly, I caress her soft, warm skin, my large hand easing the discomfort of the spanking I've just given her. She lays still over my lap, the fight gone from her, allowing me to bring her comfort. Unable to restrain myself, I lower my mouth to her reddened skin, and kiss her tenderly.

"Ah, Carina," I murmur. "You have taken your punishment and learned from your transgression." My hand moves from the small of her back, slowly down and then back up again. A second time, my hand travels lower, over the curve of her bottom, to her sweet thighs. Her body is exquisite, and my desire for her increases. As my hand moves over her skin gently, she shivers with a low moan. Could it be that even though she's been disciplined over my knee, she is aroused? Slowly, I move my hand lower to her inner thigh and firmly push her legs apart. She gasps, but does not protest, as I spread her legs and my large fingers gently explore her feminine folds.

"Ohhhh," she says. "Oh, no, you... ohhhh."

I smile to myself. I bet my little one is thankful her face is still turned away from me. Given the way she is squirming and writhing beneath my touch, it is likely her cheeks are as crimson as the bottom I've just punished. My breath catches as I explore her further, and find her slick with arousal. Gently, I touch her, my fingers seeking to pleasure.

"Please don't," she says, while even still, she is arching her body, her words asking me to stop while her body begs me not to. "You... it's not... you cannot touch me like that," she whispers.

Cannot? I can touch her in any way I desire, but I will listen to what she has to say.

"Why not, Carina?" I ask, moving my fingers so they are on the very tops of her inner thighs now, no longer touching her folds, gently massaging the tender skin.

She gasps, moaning, as her hips writhe over my knee. "I... it is not sanitary. It is not *clean*. One must never touch those parts!"

I cannot help myself. I chuckle, deep and low, the rumble of my laughter causing her to tremble on my knee.

"Do not laugh at me!" she protests.

Instinctively, I swat her backside. "Tsk, tsk," I chide. "You will learn how to speak to your master, Carina. Perhaps we shall continue our day with you across my knee. Shall I call my servants to come and feed you, while you are still in such a position? I can situate you with a pillow and chair so that you are more comfortable, while I leave your pretty little backside bared over my lap, ready for correction when you decide to be disrespectful." I give her a firm squeeze to emphasize my point.

She squeals and wriggles. "Oh, no! Please, no," she says, pleading now. "I don't mean to be disrespectful. I will try to do better."

"Very good," I say, eyeing once again her tempting folds. "Now where were we?"

"I was trying to explain to you that you cannot touch me the way you... were," she falters.

Burying a smile, grateful she cannot see, I stroke one finger through her core. "You mean, like this?" I tease.

"Ohhh... no, no!" she says.

I stop. "Tell me again why not? You are mine to do with as I will. And it seems this is far more enjoyable for you than a spanking, is it not?"

She squirms again. "On Freanoss we know that touching one another in such a way is a base, unclean thing to do. Unhygienic."

Unclean? I question the very sanity of her people. I have a basic knowledge of the Freanossian ways, and I'm aware they do not couple, but the reasons behind such customs are enigmatic to me.

"I care not for what your people think, Carina. Now shall we continue this discussion over my lap, or would you like to be let up?"

She sighs. "Please let me up."

I am happy to do so, especially since she's now lost the biting edge and is attempting to be respectful. I lift her up and swing her legs around, so that she is now sitting on my lap. She holds herself stiff and upright, apart from me, but that will not do.

"Come here, little one," I say. I pull her close to me, so that her head lies now upon my chest. After a stern chastisement, it is my duty to comfort her. "Your people's ways are not my ways," I say. "I will listen to what you say, and consider what you wish. But I shall do what I feel is right. As my property, I may touch you when and how I wish."

She tenses in my arms. I lower my voice to her ear to whisper, "Carina. Though I may touch what belongs to me, you will enjoy this."

She shakes her head, trying to move her head away from me. "No," she says. "It is wrong, and vile, the basest humiliation."

I take her inane assertion as a challenge.

"Do you mean to tell me," I say, "that within a civilized planet like yours, a full-grown woman, as lovely as you are, has never been pleasured by a man?"

"Pleasured?" she asks, her head still upon my chest. "If by that you mean defiled, certainly not. I am an upstanding citizen. We do not give in to such base actions."

This puzzles me. I have heard rumors that the Freanossians have scientific methods to populate their race, but the thought of removing the intimate act of coupling is shocking to me. At the same time, I am thrilled. Upon my knee sits a woman who now belongs to me, and she is wholly unblemished, a virgin. She is mine to teach, correct, and pleasure. Before long, she will be begging for my touch.

"The ways of your people are mysterious. And I care not for them. You will be pleasured, be it *hygienic* or not."

She turns to face me, her eyes wide. "You would take me against my will?"

I smile. "No, Carina. I will not. I will have no need."

I will feed and clothe her, then we will pay a visit to Isidor, the ancient sage, keeper of great wisdom. I will need wisdom in conquering this little one.

CHAPTER FIVE

Carina

If I could trust myself to sleep, I would wish to return to slumber, but the sleep I have just wakened from is nothing like what I am accustomed to. It was not rested. My dreams were vivid and disturbing. I dreamt of the savage who slept by my side, and in my dreams, he did vile things to me. He touched me with his hands and his tongue. I shudder at the memory. He teased me and pleasured me, and when I woke I was near frenzied with... something. I know not what it is that my body longs for. Without my regimented nightly supplement, my body has begun to do strange things to me.

I welcomed sleep on Freanoss. When I slept, the worries of the world ceased. I slept dreamlessly, restfully, and woke refreshed and renewed. Today, I woke teeming with foreign feelings. I feel the swelling of my breasts, and pulsing between my legs. I squeeze my thighs together, desperate to stop the longing. I have been taught that impulses are untrustworthy. Before the New Dawn, people died from coupling. I do not wish to partake in such barbaric acts. But the savage has other plans, including, apparently, *beating* me into submission.

He places one of his large fingers under my chin and lifts my eyes to his. "We have much to do today, Carina. I have many questions for you, and you must answer. But first, it is time you were prepared for the day, and well fed."

I am still sitting upon his knee, and I wish to get up. Beneath my sore bottom, I feel the strength of his legs, and his muscular, powerful thighs. Up against my chest, I feel him, hardened and muscled. His arms around me are formidable. Even his voice and stature are commanding. Yesterday, I could see him as the savage that he was, and I could think clearly. Today, my body yearns to be touched by him. The desire within me is growing stronger, threatening to make me lose my mind. I wonder if he somehow enchanted my sleep.

When I woke, I was furious at the unfamiliar thoughts and feelings that took possession of my body. I allowed my fear to dictate my actions. I regret having earned further chastisement according to his barbaric custom. I shall cooperate with him now, as I keep my head about me.

He reaches across from me and lifts the small silver bell. He rings it. The tinkling sound of it is lovely, and I wish to hear it again. I have never heard such a thing before last night.

"Ring it again," I say.

He quirks a brow at me. I realize the error I have made at his immediate change in stature, and correct myself. "Please," I amend. "Ring it again?"

With a smile, he shakes his head. "One ring means for my servants to come. Two will make them fear they've angered me. If I call them and they fail to come promptly, I consider their actions to be disobedient. None have earned my disfavor, so I shall not ring a second time."

I frown. His servants bow to his command, of this I am clear. Is he a ruthless master?

"How many servants do you command?" I ask.

He sobers. "Several hundred, little one, though all in this kingdom obey me."

I swallow, my mouth suddenly dry. What means will I have to escape if the legions of savages obey him?

"If you are in command over your entire nation, then why is it that you allowed the circle of women to come forth? Could you not simply choose the one you wanted?"

He smiles. When he smiles, his dark eyes appear a bit lighter, his heavy brows less severe, the lines about his face softer. Despite his savage look—his full beard, half-clothed body, bare but for the soft folds of leather trousers—I find I long to be closer to him. There is an enigmatic pull. "The circle was an ancient ritual, Carina," he explains patiently. "As for choosing the one I wanted?" He pauses, his smile fading as he sobers. "That is precisely what I did."

I blink, unsure how best to respond to him. My heart beats rapidly, my breath coming in shallow gasps.

A faint knock comes at the door. His servants have come to do his bidding.

It seems so shall I.

· · · · · · ·

My second partaking of the savage's food comes sooner than I am prepared for. For the first time in my life, I am sitting upon a very sore backside. I've never experienced punishment like the barbarian has put me through. Children in Freanoss are taught obedience in the controlled environment of the Institute. Their needs are met by the nurses, assigned women who feed, clothe, and train the little ones. I knew as a child not to disobey the rules. Disobedient children were removed from the community rooms, and not allowed the privilege of socializing, but it was very rare. We never knew what happened to those who disobeyed, but it did not matter. As defiance was bred out of the populace, we became an advanced people. We are genetically engineered to value the sameness of our generation, and sameness breeds obedience. At least I've been taught so, until now.

My insistence on testing the savage and the boundaries he's given me surprises even me. Though I've never been one to be terribly afraid, or easily cowed, I've not been a disobedient type. Even my coming here was sanctioned by the Freanoss commanding lieutenant.

I eye the savage as he eats. After taking his first sip of the white liquid they give him, he takes a hefty bite of some type of spongy food. I eye him warily, and he quirks an eyebrow. "I have now eaten," he says with a wave of his hand. "You may do so." I am not sure how to feed myself. They have such an interesting method of nourishing themselves. I long for the clean method of Freanoss. I eye the food, but do not wish to have it. I shake my head, and I know, even as I do, it is not simply because I do not wish to eat. There is something deep within me that responds to his stern, commanding nature, as if defying him is somehow necessary. I squirm upon my chair and eye him. When he frowns, one brow lifting as he slowly puts his own food down and looks purposefully at me, I feel within me my heart beat a little faster. Is it fear, or something else? Perhaps a primal attraction to… danger? I swallow, my mouth suddenly dry, as he leans forward on the table and speaks in a low, deep voice.

"Little one," he says. "You must take nourishment. Avalere is unlike Freanoss, and those who do not eat become weak." He pauses a beat as his eyes darken a bit, and he reaches a large hand to my bare thigh, massaging. "And you know what I expect when I command you to do something."

The pulsing between my thighs intensifies at his touch and his stern words. He is so very different from the men of Freanoss. In our efforts to promote sameness, the contrasting masculine features with feminine have been modified, no longer in stark contrast as they once were. I have never seen such large hands, such strength of body, or such enormity. His mere presence is commanding, the deep timbre of his voice arresting.

Even now, as I sit upon a punished bottom, I am almost eager to push just a bit more. I want to feel the pulsating, near-pleasurable feeling deep in my belly and between my legs, when he commands me. I swallow, mustering up my courage. I lick my lips. When I speak, my voice is strangely husky. "And if I choose not to eat?" I ask, feigning braveness as I thrust out my chin. I am not prepared to intentionally defy him. I simply need to see what his response will be.

His hand on my thigh pauses, as he stares curiously at me for a moment. "Are you prepared to disobey me?" he asks. *Disobey.* The word causes my heart to stutter a steady rhythm within me.

I shake my head. I truly do not wish to experience his wrath again. "Was there a command to follow?" I ask. "You simply said I *may* eat."

His lips twitch, his eyes twinkling at me. He nods. "Quite right," he says, his hand moving slowly up my leg. I gasp. The pulsing between my legs throbs. "I have not given you a *command* to eat. However, it is my desire that you do so." Gently, his fingers dip further up my leg. He's tracing soft circles upon my skin, the heat of his palm somehow transferring to the heat of my body. How could this be happening? I have never felt such urges before. My body is begging him to go further up, continue whatever he is doing, and not to remove his touch. He is so close now, his breath is a mere whisper. "Will you obey me, Carina?" he asks in a low rumble. "Or shall I take you across my knee again?"

To my shock, my heart skips a beat in my chest, somehow tied to the pulsing vibe as I shift my legs. I want him to touch me more, for his hand to slip beneath my tunic. A little voice in the back of my mind tells me *no*, this is unsanitary, that his touch alone is defiling me, but the corrective inner voices in my mind are slowly becoming fainter, as the primal urges within me drown them out.

"I will obey you," I whisper. But I am not sure how. My hands are trembling. I am lightheaded, as I look at the table in front of me. I do not know what to eat. He removes his hand, and takes a piece of the sponge-like substance, tearing off a small piece. He offers it to me by holding it in front of my mouth. Obediently, I open my mouth and he gently places the morsel of food on my tongue. The appearance of this food is misleading. It does not taste like a sponge at all. It is soft and sweet. I want more.

"Drink your milk," he says. "Kourabie is rich, and your body will absorb the nutrients if you combine it with milk."

I lift the glass he hands me, the opaque white liquid foreign to me like nearly everything else in this land. I lift my eyes to his, and he nods encouragingly. I take a sip. The liquid is smooth and rich, creamy and fresh. It is delicious. Next, he lifts a small, round fruit from a platter. It is unlike what he fed me the night before. This is a deep red, and the skin gleams in the sunlight that streams through the window. With his left hand, he holds the fruit, and with his right, he takes a knife and cuts a wedge for me. My lips purse and I squint my eyes. He must find my reaction amusing, as he chuckles.

"Very good," he says. "It is both sweet and sour, but you were brave enough to try what was foreign to you. Good girl."

I am surprised at my reaction. I ceased being a child when I passed the age of eighteen several years ago. I do not wish to be thought of as a child. But when he expresses approval for what I've done, I am strangely pleased. I smile softly, continuing to eat small bites of the kourabie, fruit, and milk. After a time, I wish no more.

"Have you had enough, little one?" he asks.

I nod, placing my hands in my lap.

"Then I will have my servants clear our dishes." He smiles softly. "Are you ready to hear the bell again?"

I nod eagerly. He chuckles as he rings it. Moments later, servants arrive and clear the remains of our meal. Lystava stands in the doorway, directing the others, who enter with bowed heads and hastily do the king's bidding. I assume she must be a sort of head servant. She turns to the savage. "My lord, is there anything you wish me to bring for your bride?"

Bride. It is a strange word, and I am not entirely sure of its meaning, at least not in this land. Why has it made him peer at me strangely? A look crosses his face as he eyes me, but he quickly dismisses it and addresses her. "No, thank you," he says. "I've acquired her clothing and what little she will need for today. I will take her to the market shortly. Later, I will meet with my commanding officers. But until then, we have a few places to visit, and I wish for her to sample the wares of Avalere."

I am standing, and I see her eyes fall to the hem of my dress. Her brows raise, but she quickly turns away from him and nods, as she exits. "As you wish, my lord."

She leaves. I wonder at her amusement, but then I remember the marks of his punishment upon my bottom and legs. She no doubt sees them. His bringing me to the market is perhaps two-fold: both to parade me as his possession, and to show me his native land. I frown, not wishing to be displayed to his people.

"What is it you'd have me wear?" I ask, impatience threaded in the tone of my voice.

He hears it and frowns, but does not reply as he walks away from the table to a wooden wardrobe that flanks the wall at the foot of the bed. He opens one door, and I gasp at what I see. Small, simple tunics hang on wooden pegs, many vibrant shades of blue. "Blue will match the color of your eyes, and it is the color of the king," he says, as he removes a garment. It is short, similar to the tunic I wear now, and it looks flimsy in his large hands.

He moves to the foot of the bed and sits. "Come here, Carina," he says in his deep voice.

There is something about being commanded to come to him that causes me to look at him shyly. Why must his imperious nature do such unpredictable things to my body? I drag my feet to him, as I have begun to fear what my body will do when I draw close. But I must obey him. He is impatient, and I fear I have pushed his patience far enough. When I am within arm's reach of him, he plants his hands on my hips and pulls me between his thighs. The warmth of his legs presses against the outside of mine. His eyes are heated, and he is almost frowning, but not quite. I reach for the dress. It is shimmery, reflecting the light that streams in through the window, a lovely, vibrant blue. I am not surprised at the length and weight of it, light and airy, as the heat of the day has already begun to rise. I do wonder what it will cover.

"No, Carina," he chides. "It is my duty to dress you."

My arms instinctively cross on my chest. He is to see me stripped? He has only seen my nakedness when he has bared my bottom to him. I tremble. What choice do I have but to submit? Resisting him now will earn me a punishment. And part of me—though I do not wish to admit so, and will not to him—wants to be bared to him. His eyes are fixed on mine, no doubt watching my reaction to his command. I know already that he is prepared to punish me if I disobey.

"Uncross your arms, please," he says. I swallow, slowly obeying him, trembling at the loss of protection I feel with my arms crossed. He places one large, warm hand on the small of my back, and pulls me even closer to him, so that we are practically embracing. When I am near, he moves his hand up further so that he is now grasping the back of my neck. He threads his fingers through my hair. My heart is thundering so that I can hardly hear myself think, his near proximity intoxicating. I like the smell of him, though I could not describe it. He smells clean, strong, and powerful. With his hand on my neck, he leans in to me, bringing my face so close to him I can see the depth of his dark eyes, and I realize just before our lips meet what he is going to do. I begin to pull away, scared of my mouth meeting his, but his touch grows firmer, almost forceful upon my neck, and I cannot help but allow him to have his way.

I don't know what to expect, but the contrast of his sharp whiskers and soft lips take me by surprise. His mouth is warm and soft, his lips full and urgent. Though I do not know how to react, my body responds of its own accord. My knees grow weak. I am thankful he is supporting me with his legs. I am not sure I would remain standing.

My pulse beats rapidly, warmth spreading from the top of my chest down to my feet. The throbbing quickens between my thighs, as one of his hands holds my neck and a second lifts the edge of my tunic and engulfs my bare bottom, the sting at his touch oddly welcome. He continues to kiss me, his mouth moving over mine, and I begin to respond without knowing what I am doing. I both feel and hear his responding growl.

After a moment, he pulls his mouth off mine. "Do not try to pull yourself away from me again, Carina," he instructs. "You are mine to do with as I will. Am I to assume that you have never kissed a man, much less coupled?"

I close my eyes briefly. My mouth is dry from discussing such things with him! I feel a faint flush creep to my neck and cheeks. "No," I whisper. He raises a brow. "No, my lord," I quickly amend.

He nods slowly. "Your failure to respond properly will only be allowed for a brief time, little one. The next time you fail to address me correctly, the flat of my hand will remind you."

Again, the prickle of excitement pulses between my thighs. I nod. "Yes," I stammer. "Yes, my lord."

What has this barbarian done to me in such short a time? I am obeying him meekly, no longer the independent, aloof woman of Freanoss, but a weak, helpless female. I am disgusted with my descent into the barbaric ways, though I had little choice. Fighting him would only earn me punishment.

He pulls away from me and the back of one finger caresses my cheek as his eyes lock into mine. "I am not a patient man, Carina," he says in his deep voice.

My breath catches as I nod.

His eyes flick below my face as he takes both hands and

reaches for the hem of my dress. "I will disrobe you now," he explains. "And you shall not protest, or stop me."

I nod, marveling at my ability to move. I am transfixed by him.

He nods, then I feel a brush of cool air as the tunic is removed. The hem rises above my bottom, then the small of my back. I want to pull it back over me and run from him. What will he think of me when he sees me naked? What if he dislikes what he sees? If women are no more than property on Avalere, and he is lord and ruler of them all, what will happen if he doesn't like me as I am? Will he reject me, and trade me for another?

And why am I suddenly afraid, fearful of his rejection of me?

Do I not wish to escape him?

This, and more, flit through my mind like leaves whisked about on a blustery day. I cannot grasp them or stop them. Instead, I focus on staying still and obeying him. The tunic is being raked over my head now, and I close my eyes, panting in fear and anticipation, as all clothing is removed. With my eyes closed, I can only hear the rustle of the fabric, and him shifting his large frame as he pulls me closer to him. Silence descends as I am now bared.

"Open your eyes, lovely," he says, his voice a low but commanding whisper. *Lovely.* He is calling me lovely? Swallowing hard, inhaling deeply for courage, I obey.

His eyes are locked onto mine for one brief minute, as he nods his approval of my obedience, and then his gaze lowers, taking in every curve of my body. He swallows. I shift, uncomfortable under his gaze. He lifts his hand and strokes a finger from the smooth curve of my shoulder, down my chest, to the swell of my breasts. Gently, he traces the fullness, before he moves both hands to my back, drawing me close to him. His warm, whiskery mouth meets my skin and he kisses first one breast, then the other. To my shock, I feel the warmth of his tongue begin to encircle my breast, and when he reaches my hardened nipple, his tongue flicks lightly along the edge. His tongue is softer and warmer than his fingers. I gasp from the sudden intensity of the feeling between my thighs, pushing my legs together. He grasps my nipple gently between his teeth. I gasp at the sensation, his eyes burning through me, as he takes me fully in his mouth and sucks. My head falls back, and I moan, unable to stand the intensity of my desire. He places both hands on my bare backside, still throbbing from my punishment, torturing me with alternating nips and licks to my nipple. I cannot speak. I cannot *think*. All I do is feel. What witchcraft is this?

He releases my breast. To my shock, I utter a little groan of disappointment. But he has only released me so that he can focus his attention on my other side. Again, the sweet, seductive torture of his teeth and tongue, as he anchors on to my aching bottom. Between my legs, I am on fire, and though it goes against all that I believe, all that I've been trained to know is right, I know that I need him to touch me there. If he doesn't, I don't know how I will cope. Does he know I want him to touch me?

His mouth meets the bare skin of my navel. His tongue flicks out and laps at me, as he murmurs, his low voice husky. "So sweet," he whispers. "You are so beautiful. I wish to devour you."

Devour me? My heart hammers as his tongue flicks out and he licks me, before his mouth opens and his teeth nip my side. I gasp from the jolt of pain quickly followed by warmth and increasing arousal. Will he hurt me? Though my body yearns for more of his touch, I am shaking with nerves. I pull away from him but he holds me tight as he sucks the place he's just bitten. I am panting now, fighting for little gasps of air, as my body is enchanted by his touch. He releases me. I marvel at the little marks he's left. He is a *savage*, an animal. Then why does my body lean in closer to him, hoping for more of the sweet, seductive torture?

His touch reaches lower now, and as he sits on the bed, his fingers probe, one hand still gripped on my waist while the other spreads against the warmth of my inner thigh. I am reminding myself how to breathe. I know not what he will do next. I am completely undone.

His hand moves higher up my thigh, so now the top of his hand barely touches my sex. I close my eyes. This is wanton, uncivilized, so wrong. Yet I couldn't stop him now if I wanted to. He pinches and squeezes my thigh. A near sob of desire escapes my lips. His eyes lift quickly to mine.

"Do you want me to touch you, little one?" he asks.

Why is he asking me? He is already touching me. It is his touch that has undone me. I cannot speak. I have no words. I am at his command. Swallowing hard, I nod. I *must* feel him touch me more.

He nods soberly. "Hold onto my shoulders," he says.

I obey, my arms encircling his wide, muscled shoulders.

He grips my bottom with one hand, the warmth of his palm cupping the pain he put there, but the touch is welcome. His other hand moves from the inside of my thigh, further up. "You are bare," he says. "Bare and beautiful."

What an odd thing to say, I muse. I have been bared and barren of hair since I reached womanhood. It seems the savage likes it.

One finger travels higher. I take in breath in shallow gasps. His finger is so close, so *close* to where I want it. When his finger dips between my folds, my knees buckle. I am raw, nothing but nerves, as his gentle yet firm touch encircles my womanhood. The sweet, blissful, torturous feeling consumes me, and I focus on his touch, his caress. I know I need more. What will happen if he keeps touching me? His steady rhythm increases, and he's moving faster now. My heartbeat is accelerating, my need to breathe forgotten, the strength of his shoulders beneath me, my breasts against his head, my need intensifying with every stroke of his hand.

"Do you like that, Carina?" he whispers, his voice a harsh breath of air against my breasts.

"Mmmm," I moan, incapable of coherent thought or

words.

His hand stops. *No*. He cannot stop now. I do not know what will happen when he continues, but I do know that he *must not stop*. No, no, this cannot be. What is he doing to me?

He sits upright, firmly moving my arms off his shoulders. His eyes stare at me soberly, not a trace of amusement now as he eyes me. "It is time for you to be dressed," he insists.

"No," I whisper, shaking my head, moving closer to him. "Please."

"Not now," he says, his eyes stern as he looks at me, as if challenging me to disobey him.

He cannot stop now! How dare he? "You must," I insist, moving against him as if to make him touch me. "If-if you don't… touch me… I need you to touch me!" I am angry now, my need so intense I want to hurt him. "If you do not touch me, I will!"

I am shocked at the words that have come out of my mouth, but I am near frenzied with desire.

His eyes darken. He reaches for my hair, grasping a fistful of it in his strong hand, pulling back so that a prickle of pain stings my scalp. "You shall not," he orders. "Your body is mine, and mine alone. You forfeited your right to pleasure yourself when you became mine. I own every inch of you, from the little lashes that frame your eyes down to the swell of your hips, to the apex of your thighs, to the toes of your feet. Your pleasure is mine to command. I am master of you, of every inch of you."

I groan out loud. I am going to die from the want within me, and his denial of my needs. His grasp on my hair flexes. I cry out from the pain of it, but he holds fast and continues. "If you obey my commands and behave yourself, the time will come when I will culminate your pleasure," he says. His voice is harsh, almost angry. "But until then, you will do as you're told."

He is waiting for my response. I want to hurt him, knee him, and smack away the hand that is holding my hair. I even entertain the thought for a moment, before I banish it. What would my violence against him incur? He is stronger and bigger, and I will be punished.

He promises if I obey he will pleasure me… eventually.

I swallow and exhale. "Yes," I say, barely biting back the curse words that I wish to utter. His reaction surprises me. He releases my hair, both hands going to my waist as he pushes me over his knee. I realize a split second before he spanks me for the error of my ways.

"Yes, my lord!" I say quickly, but not in time to stop his palm from descending. The blistering swat has me up on my toes, and I squeal out loud from the pain of it, but to my shock, pressed up against his thigh like this, my desire throbs.

What has he done to me?

CHAPTER SIX

Aldric

I inhale deeply. She is ripe with arousal, though she claims ignorance of her sexual desires. I want to take her on the bed, master her body thoroughly. I long to feel her trembling beneath me, shuddering under my thrusts, keening with a yearning so intense, she is at my utter mercy. I long to taste her, to slip my tongue through her sweet folds, ravaging every inch of her body, mind, and soul, until she is split open to me. She has awakened in me the fire of desire. But she shall not taste pleasure until she has learned that her ecstasy belongs to me alone.

I have much to teach my Carina.

"Raise your arms above your head, please," I instruct. Her lower lip sticks out a bit, a near pout, though not quite disobedient enough that I need to correct her again. I understand her frustration. If I am correct in my understanding, she has never experienced sexual release. She will feel release unlike anything she could imagine. But she will learn to defer to me, and I have many methods I will employ to instruct her. Making her wait for pleasure is only one of many tools.

When she obeys, I lift the blue garment I've chosen for her and slip it over her head. It falls over her shoulders, past her breasts, and drapes lightly so that it hits her well above the knees. I turn her around, and inspect to be sure the marks I've left her are visible. I frown. They aren't quite to my liking. Turning her around again to face me, I push her lower back firmly so that she is bent over my knee. She must be marked, but she must also be reminded of her place. I can feel the tension within her, and I do not trust that she will obey. My men are a possessive people. They must know that she belongs to me, and to me alone.

"I have not disobeyed!" she says, already understanding that I am about to lay a few more stripes on her. It is good she has learned so quickly.

"You have not," I say. "But we are about to move from my chambers, and I want it clear that you belong to me. I can do so with a chain around your neck, but that is not my preference. I prefer you choose to obey without physical restraint. I can be a kind and reasonable master, so I shall give you the choice. Shall I mark you with the flat of my hand so that all who see you know you are mine, or would you choose instead the links around your neck?"

Her blue eyes are wide, and her breathing is labored. "I..." she falters, and frowns before answering, her gaze meeting mine from beneath lowered lashes. "Your hand, my lord."

She has chosen well. She will be rewarded for her bravery. With a nod, I pull her over to my knee in such a way that she straddles me, her legs on either side of my leg, her naked sex flush against the warmth of my skin. Her tunic lifts and she is bared to me. I bring my hand down firmly, the sharp slap of my palm against her exposed bottom resounding in my chambers. She gasps. The force of the blow pushes her sex against me. Her spanking will serve a two-fold purpose. Another hard swat follows the first, then another. I am careful to place her marks at the curve of her backside and lower, upon her thighs, the reddened hand prints rising on her pale skin. To reward her for her bravery, I dip one finger between her folds and stroke her. She moans, grinding against my knee. I smile. My woman will be pleasured this evening, but not until she is near begging for release. I give her three more sharp swats before I lift her. She is panting, breathless with desire. Grasping the back of her neck, I bring her mouth to mine and claim it with a savage kiss.

Then I stand. It is time to go to the marketplace.

• • • • • • •

It is with great pride that I take my woman upon my arm and exit my chambers, placing both her little hands around my elbow, so that I can keep her close to me as we walk. The moment we've entered the hall, my servants fall into line, trained guards wielding their weapons, prepared to defend and protect, flanking either side. As my guards follow us with disciplined, regular strides, I instruct Carina.

"Today, you will witness the privileges afforded you as my woman," I say. "Anything you wish to purchase in the marketplace may be acquired. Simply say the word, and any of the wares will become yours."

"Anything?" she asks curiously.

I smile. "Yes, my Carina," I say. "There is no possession too costly for the woman who belongs to the Warrior King."

She is quiet for a moment. "I know little of the ways of your kingdom," she says. "But I do wonder why you do not simply call yourself king. Why is it that you are instead the Warrior King?"

I turn the corner of my hallway and feel the men who walk with us listening intently. They well know why I am Warrior King, and it is with pride they have taken their appointed positions by my side. It is the greatest honor.

"I have earned my rank in battle," I explain. "Under normal circumstances, I would await the crowning as king until my father passes to eternal life. As I stood as both prince and victor in many battles, my father granted me headship over Avalere. He did so willingly, as he is aged and prefers to advise me rather than assume full responsibility as king."

"Battle," she repeats. "How many victories did you have?"

I smile softly. She is innocent, like a youngling, and it is with pride that I teach her the ways of Avalere. "My victories were many, little one," I say. "I have held a sword in my hand since I could bear the weight. It is not the sheer number of victories that earned me the title of Warrior King. It is because never, in both battle and single combat, have I lost. As an undefeated warrior, when I came of age, it was a choice both noble and strategic to appoint me Warrior King." I am proud to tell her of my victories. They were hard-won. Around me, the heads of my men dip in homage.

She says nothing, but seems to be contemplating my words. I take a moment to read her. She is in awe, and I am grateful. It will aid her obedience to me if she finds me worthy of her respect. The scent of her arousal permeates all. I temper a smile. This will serve us both well.

"Now, my Carina, you will listen well as we approach the marketplace." I pull her so that we are in the shadow of an alcove. Though we do not truly have privacy, I wish her to mark my words. I bend down to her, so that I can see in her eyes, and lift her chin with a finger. "Yesterday, I punished you in front of all." She shifts, her eyes looking away from me, but I lift her chin and her eyes come back to mine. "Today, I marked you again. When we go among my people, those are wise will know that you are mine. But not everyone is wise."

She frowns, her brow furrowing. It is fetching, her look of consternation, and I cannot help myself. I bow my head and kiss her lovely forehead. I pull away and continue to explain. "Our men are fierce warriors, and some are savage."

She huffs out a breath, and for a minute, I do not understand why. I eye her curiously. What a strange reaction.

"Why do you respond in such a manner?" I ask.

She raises her brows. "Apologies… my lord," she says, tacking on the required words hastily. "It was unintentional. I just find it somewhat surprising that you consider your other men savage. Do you not consider yourself so?"

Her question amuses me. "I make no apologies for what I say or do," I say. "I do what I am called to in my position. And perhaps what is barbaric is relative, dependent on comparison to others." I then sober as I must press upon her the import of my words. "Little one, though we have laws in place, there are men here who would take you against your will, and repeatedly. There are some who would find you little more than a vessel for their baser needs. There are some who would not spank you with their hands, but whip you, and some, if they were in my position, would have you crawling on all fours by my side, chained, rather than holding my arm."

"You are barbaric," she whispers.

"We are a society that values strength and might. We foster power and individuality in each member of our population, and we respect authority only if it has been earned, not because dissent or disobedience has been bred out of us. We cannot discuss this further, as now I must meet with my commanding officers for our midday meal." I pause. "But, yes." I look at her soberly, ensuring she marks me well. "You are right to realize the peril on Avalere. It is *especially* dangerous for those who wish to question authority."

Her eyes reflect the fear I hope to evoke, before I take her hand and walk toward the exit. My little one has much to learn.

· · · · · · ·

As we exit my castle, the beaming rays of the sun welcome us. I enjoy the warmth, walking with pride with my woman upon my arm. It is not until dusk that the color of the sun will fade and become dimmer, purple rays touching us as we prepare for slumber. As I move among the Avalerians, now surrounded by my servants, I feel the weight of responsibility descend upon me. Though the requirement to chastise her last night took precedence, I can delay my interrogation of her no longer. My intelligence officers will be coming soon with fresh information that I must weigh along with her answers. I must learn why she was sent here so that I can take steps to protect the Avalerians. She will be honest with me, or suffer my displeasure.

Soon, I must take her to see the Wise One.

People are milling about, as it is the day in which the Avalerians will display their wares. Yesterday, the day of the festival, was merely a day of preparation. As we approach the tables, the vendors stand taller, and as we pass each table, they behave as they should, bowing their heads and bending on one knee in reverence. I nod appreciatively, allowing Carina time to take in all that surrounds us.

To the left is a table laden with vibrant spices, piled atop parchment in mountains of gold, purple, and crimson. Merchants scoop the precious spices with tiny golden spoons, weighed on a silver scale. Beside that table is another with bolts of multicolored fabric and yarn, woven from the very hand of the woman who now sells it. Beyond that, sizzling meats upon skewers roast, prepared to be sold for the midday meal. My little one watches everything with wide eyes, taking in the colors, the sounds, and smells. Her lips are parted, a look of wonder upon her pretty face. I smile, pleased that she appreciates the talents of my people. In other lands, handmade items are no longer valued, and it is with much effort we have revived the ancient arts. She walks with me quietly, as if transfixed by what she sees, but when we approach a table of jewelry, she stops.

On the table lie swaths of rich black velvet, laden with golden necklaces and earrings, artfully arranged—bracelets made of the priceless pink gold that is native to my planet, gleaming pearls fetched from the salty waters of our ocean and fixed atop bands of gold and silver, rubies that gleam like fire, and diamonds as bright as the stars in the sky. Carina lets go of my hand, and steps over to the jewels. The vendor is a young wisp of a woman with long blond hair that reaches to her waist. Her mouth is agape, her eyes wide as my woman eyes her wares. The young woman's eyes go to me, as if she's just realized I am standing there. She drops to one knee, her blond hair a golden curtain that flutters around her and settles like a halo as she lowers her head. "My lord," she greets with reverence. I nod, pleased at her show of respect.

"Rise, young one," I say to her. "My lady is here to peruse your wares, and it is my wish that you attend to her. Allow her anything she wishes from your table, and I will see you paid in full from our royal purses."

The woman rises to her feet, nodding eagerly. "Yes, my lord," she says, turning to Carina. "My lady, may I assist you?"

Carina looks at her in surprise, then to me.

I smile with a nod. "Go, now, Carina," I say. "You pick something that you will like, and then I will."

The vendor looks to me with wide eyes. My choosing from her wares will be the highest honor.

Carina does not move, still staring at me. "Carina," I say, my voice dropping a bit as I encourage her to hurry.

"I do not know what to choose," she says. I look to the vendor and nod, encouraging her to assist Carina. She nods vigorously.

"Given your coloring, my lady, I would recommend diamonds in your ears, perhaps a slim bit of silver at your neck."

"Not the neck," I say. The woman's eyes widen and

Carina looks at me in surprise. I gesture for Carina to continue looking as I explain my purpose to the vendor. "The jewelry about her neck will be mine to choose." Carina frowns a bit, but I do not explain. She will see when the time is right.

I allow the women a few minutes to discuss and sample various items, but my patience is waning. Finally, the vendor looks to me with a small smile and turns to my woman. "Your lord grows impatient," she says. "Let us choose." She adorns Carina's wrist with a silver bracelet, and sends Carina to the end of the table to choose the gems that will be embedded in the gleaming silver.

I lift a silver necklace. "The clasp upon this necklace. Is it fashioned to be removed?"

The blond woman nods. "It is, my lord."

I frown, eyeing it. "So, then, are you able to fashion it so that it *cannot* be removed?"

She smiles. "Certainly, my lord."

"Do so. I shall return at the end of the week to retrieve it, and pay you handsomely. Will you have it ready by then?"

She nods vigorously. Carina, who has been at the other end of the table apart from us and has not heard our conversation, eyes me thoughtfully. I beckon for her, and when she comes I take her by the hand. I escort my Carina from the marketplace, but as we exit, Idan, my chief adviser and head of my military *Hisrach*, advances eagerly.

"My lord," he says. "You are needed in counsel promptly. The *Hisrach* wishes to speak to you."

I shake my head. "Idan, you are capable of handling whatever decision must be made before our meeting shortly," I say, but to my shock, Idan contradicts me.

"No, my lord," he says. "It is imperative you come."

I scowl at his impertinence. No one contradicts me. How dare he speak to me thus? I take a step toward him, but he holds up his hands. "My lord—I did not wish to say in a public place, but—" He pauses, and leans in closer to me, his voice dropping to a whisper. "We have news of your sister. The men have assembled at the dome."

My sister? I freeze. My heart thunders in my chest, and I am filled with both rage and sadness. The last news that was brought to my ears, devastation to both my father and me, was that my younger sister, merely nineteen years old and princess of Avalere, was killed at the hands of the Freanoss inhabitants. Idan is right. I must hear the briefing as soon as possible.

Women are prohibited from attending counsel, but as Warrior King I could change the rules if I chose. However, I know not why Carina is here, and I do not trust her. I look quickly about me. To whom can I entrust her? It is not simply that I fear she will escape, though that is a possibility. I also fear for her safety. Though word travels rapidly, it is still possible there are those who do not know that Carina belongs to me. She does not yet bear my silver about her neck. Barely twelve hours have transpired since I've claimed her, and I have yet to make her mine in full. Though my claim upon her as king is law, ignorance may put her in harm's way.

Idan eyes Carina. "You may leave her with me," he says. I wish for him to be with me when I hear news of my sister, but there is none other I trust with such an important task.

I nod to Idan, as I turn to Carina. I take her by the hand and pull her close to me, so that her body is pressed up against mine. I wrap my fingers around her neck, making sure her eyes are fixed upon mine. "You are to obey Idan as if his commands were issued from my mouth, Carina. Do you understand me?"

She swallows, but nods. "Yes," she says in a little voice, quickly amending, "Yes, my lord."

I nod, releasing her. Though Idan is the one by my side in battle, the man who can be both fearless and brutal when necessary, I feel unsettled leaving Carina. I tell myself it is because I do not trust her, but deep inside I wonder if it is something more. I must seek the news of my sister quickly, so that I can come back to Carina. I leave her with a parting kiss upon her forehead, determined that our separation be only brief. She looks saddened, her wide eyes watching me as I take my leave. I must return quickly. Already, I wish not to be separated.

CHAPTER SEVEN

Carina

I watch as my savage master takes his leave. I do not realize until I've taken an involuntary step toward him, my hand outstretched, that I do not wish for him to leave. Embarrassed by my reaction, I quickly tuck my hand up against my chest, as if to protect myself. What is this witchcraft? The king's aide has seen all. I give him a sidelong glance, trying quickly to assess his prowess. I must still find my communication device if I'm to be delivered from this place, and can only do so if I am to elude this man.

The king's aide—*Idan*, he called him—is tall, though not quite as towering as his master. He has dark auburn hair that hangs low, tied at his neck, and a thick auburn beard. His chest is bare like his lord's, strong and muscular, deeply tanned. The familiar black tribal markings also mar his neck, shoulders, and arms. He wears the same leather about his waist, the sword belt laden with two weapons, their handles gleaming in the light of the sun. He looks prepared for battle, though we are but standing in the marketplace. He gestures for me to follow him.

"Have you eaten?" he asks.

"Yes," I say.

He frowns. "When?" he asks. It seems he's as demanding as his master. I am not sure how often these people eat, but it seems far more often than I'm accustomed.

"This morning," I respond. But as we walk around the bend by the marketplace, I see he is leading me to a place with long wooden tables and stools flanking a long bar. My heart quickens, for just beyond the tables, I can see the arena we visited last night, where the king punished me. If I can but get to that place, I will be able to find my way to the forest, where my communication device lays hidden. If I can only reach the Freanossians, I can alert them to what has happened, and request backup. I've learned nothing of the Avalerians' plans, though. I must discover their purpose.

I have paused too long. The man comes to my side, and to my shock, his hands go about my shoulders, pulling me closer to him and walking rapidly.

"Come with me," he said. "Though you are marked by my lord, he has entrusted you to my care. You must stay close to me and do as I say." His voice softens a bit. "I cannot let a hair on your head be harmed, my lady. What are you called?"

I begin to give him my identity, "R—" but pause. No. I have been given a name. I clear my throat. It is the first time I have uttered my name aloud. "Carina," I say. The word feels pleasant to my tongue, and I feel a bit shy saying it.

"Very good, Carina," Idan says. We have now reached the long table. "Sit upon a stool, and I will fetch you something to drink." He pulls a stool out for me and I sit, while he lifts a hand, gesturing for the young woman at the counter to come to him.

She approaches our table and bows when she approaches Idan. "What may I get you, my lord?"

Idan waves a hand. "Glenderberry juice for my lady," he says. "Nothing for me."

She scurries away. I take a moment to observe my

surroundings. There is an older, wizened man at the counter, drinking a small tumbler of amber liquid. To the right, there is a round table with a young man and a woman, talking and laughing quietly to themselves. Behind us, I see a young woman rise, and the man she is with accompanies her, as she walks to two doorways. She holds a finger up to him, and he politely turns away as she enters one door. I then realize she is perhaps visiting the Avalerian facilities. Though they are likely primitive, this very well may serve my purpose, if all men of Avalere refrain from entering the area dedicated to women. I will observe the others, and see if this might be my chance.

It is odd for me to see people about like this. We do not partake in such activities on Freanoss: milling about, jovial laughter, various couples of men and women bowing their heads and speaking to one another intimately.

When the girl brings me my drink, I thank her and look to Idan. He nods, as if giving me permission to drink. He smiles. "I am not your lord, Carina, so you may eat and drink at your leisure with me."

I feel a faint flush of the cheeks. The ways of the Avalerians are still quite foreign to me. I lift the glass. The juice is a deep red, fragrant, and when I sip, I note it is both sweet and tart. I see another woman walk toward the door, and yet another man refrain from following her. This is exactly what I need.

I enjoy the juice. Like everything else I've tasted here, it is delicious, and I find myself quite refreshed. But my time is short, and I must hurry if my plans are to fall into place.

"I need to... relieve myself," I say, intentionally trying to sound embarrassed. My voice shakes a bit, and I hope he assumes I am merely shy, not nervous about attempting an escape.

Idan frowns, his arms crossed on his large chest. His jaw clenches, as his eyes flit around. He raises a finger to the woman who fetched my drink. She scurries to our table. My heart is thundering in my chest. Will my plan work?

"Please show us the way to the facilities," he says.

"Certainly, my lord," she says, gesturing for me to follow her. I feel Idan close at my heels, as we walk. For a moment, I fear that the 'facilities' will be as barbaric as the rest of this land, or that Idan will behave unlike the other men and follow me inside. She leads me to a small doorway and gestures for me to go inside. It looks to be a very simple, but fortunately clean latrine. I nod my head to Idan, and can tell from his stature and the stern nod of his head that I am indeed correct—he is not following me. I duck into the door quickly. Outside the door, I hear Idan talking to someone. A minute later, I peek through the doorway and see Idan gesturing to the man, whose face is red, angry, his voice raising as his hands fist by his side. This will be my chance. I quickly duck out the door and shut it behind me. Idan has not moved, his voice rising as he responds to the man's challenge. No one is watching me. This is my chance.

I move quickly past the tables and chairs and out by the open doorway, keeping my head down and my steps quick, but not so rapid that I will draw suspicion. A minute later, I have escaped. No one is around me now as I pick up speed and trot to the arena of the night before. It looks different in the light of day, smaller than I remember it. I quickly skirt behind a large stone wall so that I am not as visible as I was before. The wall allows me to observe while still providing me cover. There in the distance, I see the large stone dais and chairs upon which the warriors sat. But my stomach drops as I look.

I need to get past the dais to the woods beyond. But right between where I am and where I must go, is the dome-shaped building where the king was headed. I fear my path will bring me closer to the savage himself. I groan. If I am captured, I will be punished.

I have no choice. When my savage master returns, I do not know when such an opportunity again will arise.

Ducking low, to avoid being seen, I begin my quick mission to the dais, past the dome that leads to the men who are at counsel. My feet move swiftly, but I feel exposed in the bright light of the sun. The heat warms my skin, perspiration dripping between my breasts and down my neck. My mouth is dry, my stomach twisting in nerves and anticipation. I am but a few paces away from the dais. I feel as if my cover is insufficient, and I am on display for all to see. As I approach, I hear the deep, commanding, very familiar voice. To my left is an entrance, and my suspicions are confirmed as I near. This is where the men have convened. I stifle another groan.

"This news changes everything," the king says. Unable to stop myself, I sneak up to the doorway, listening to his words. "If what the messenger says is true, then we must hasten to Freanoss at the first opportunity. It is clear now their accusations of theft against us were merely meant to distract us from their real purpose." I grow cold. A distraction? So the Avalerians are *not* stealing the resources from Freanoss? My eyes close. If what he says is true, then my mission has been in vain. He lies. The barbarian lies.

"At my command, I wish the Legion of Warriors of the First Rite be prepared for battle," he says. "I have much to ready before we go. It is my wish to convene at our scheduled time to meet, but the agenda will be quite changed." I hear a scraping of chairs, voices rising, and I realize with a sudden drop of my stomach that they are preparing to end their meeting. I turn from where I crouch. I must flee.

Speed is now more important than ever. My feet quicken to a run. I have trained well, and can run swiftly, my feet flying, chest rising as I gasp for air. A few more paces, and I will reach just beyond the dais. It is thankfully vacant. Without another thought, I quickly move to the large stone wall. Just a few dozen paces beyond the wall I will come to a clearing, and it is within this clearing my device has been hidden. I step quickly behind it, and when I do, I freeze. There are four large, bearded men huddled around one another, conversing. Their heads snap up when they see me.

Each is thin and wiry, with the same long hair as the soldiers, but they are without the tribal markings about the neck and arms. The one in the center grins at me, but the smile makes my stomach clench. He begins to walk toward me.

"What have we here?" he says, licking his lips. "A fair maiden unaccompanied?" I see that behind him, the other men have several pouches spilled on the ground between them, a pile of golden coins reflecting the rays of the sun. Though the men look friendly enough, my instincts tell me otherwise. The man's eyes darken as he frowns at me. "A maiden caught unawares," he says. His words are slurred, his eyes unfocused. "She's seen our faces and our purses," he murmurs. I am beginning to backtrack now. I need to get away, but if I go back to where I came from, I will be visible to anyone who is within sight of the dais. I hear shouts behind me, and footsteps approaching. My stomach twists. I am trapped. Before me are men who would do me harm and behind me, certain capture.

He takes another step toward me. "And here we have a helpless maid," he drawls.

I freeze, waiting for him to draw closer. "A helpless maid who will fight you to the death," I hiss, hoping my threat will at least delay his advance while I can plan my move. Behind me, the voices grow louder, advancing.

The man's eyes narrow to mere slits. "You'd challenge me, woman?" he asks.

"I challenge the lot of you," I taunt. The others now approach. I will soon be taken, as even with my fiercest struggle I cannot conquer four grown men. But I will try.

He reaches close enough to me to grab me, and his hand lashes out, snatching at my hair. I deftly block him, my left forearm halting him, as with my right, I drive my fist to his stomach. He groans, doubled over, as his partner reaches me. I kick out my foot and connect with his stomach, but the third has now grabbed me, his arms around my chest. I kick back, and his arms rise, going to my neck but I bite down as hard as I can, tasting blood as he howls in rage and pain.

"She's marked!" shouts the fourth. "Hands off! She wears the king's blue and is *marked*!"

The man holding me releases me and I spin, landing another well-placed kick. With a howl of rage, he charges toward me with a vicious backhand blow. My head snaps back. My vision is blurred, my ears ringing, as I fall to the ground. Strong hands grab me, and I fight with all I can, until a stern voice makes me freeze.

"Do not resist, my lady."

I crane my neck to see the familiar auburn beard, hair, and stern eyes of Idan. He is holding me tight, dragging me backward, away from the brawl in front of us. When we are a few paces away, I can now see the scene in front of me.

"You stay by me and do not fight," Idan growls. "You will answer for your flight, as will I. Do not make this worse for either of us than need be." Though my heart sinks, as I know my chance to escape is gone, I am riveted by the scene in front of me.

Half a dozen warriors have joined us, but in the very center is the king. He advances upon the man who attacked me. I have seen him angry, but I have never seen him as furious as he is now. His eyes are cloudy and dark, his cheeks aflame with anger. He charges the man who hit me, the full force of his fist hitting the man's jaw. I hear a snap, and the man howls, falling to the ground as the king grabs him by the hair, yanks him up, and knees his stomach. The man grunts, trying helplessly to defend himself but he cannot. The king lifts him to his feet and hits the man repeatedly. Blood spurts from his nose, and he cannot stand upright, but falls to the ground. The king grabs the back of his head, baring the man's neck, while at the same time I hear the ring of metal as he removes his sword from its sheath. He is going to murder him, slice his head from his neck without another thought.

"No, my lord!" I shout. The king's hand freezes, his sword raised to slash. He turns to face me. My stomach twists in fear. It is the face of a warrior that now stares back at me. Ruthless. Vicious. Prepared to kill.

"You have no say in this," he hisses. "This man laid hands on my woman, and the wages for such a crime is death."

"Please, my lord," I beg. It is not that my sympathies lie with these men, but rather than I cannot abide the thought of the king executing another in front of me. "Perhaps it is not the custom of your people, but execution after a trial is justice. This would be murder."

He is the king. He can do whatever it is he wishes, with no recourse. He stares at me, inhaling deep breaths through his nose, his narrowed eyes causing me to shake. He drops the head of the man, who falls to the ground limply. The king takes a step back and orders his men. "Take them to the arena and have them flogged, then imprisoned. We will investigate their actions, and they will answer in court for their infractions." He turns and speaks in quiet words to the men around him, giving orders.

Idan's grip on my arms is strong, and I wish to be released. "Let go of me," I hiss at him, but his grip merely tightens.

"You have disobeyed the king's orders as well as mine," Idan says. "I know not from where you come, but in this land, women are to obey the men above them. If you were *mine*, I would take you across my knee and whip you soundly, but the king will see to your discipline. Do not compound your punishment now."

I scowl at him and he merely lifts a heavy brow. "He's chosen a feisty one," he murmurs, with a shake of his head. I simply turn away. Perhaps I will find a means to escape just yet. Or perhaps I will be even longer at the mercy of the barbarian.

• • • • • • •

In short time, the robbers have been taken away in

shackles. I am still in the mighty grip of Idan, as the king sees to ordering his men about. Finally, I am left with only the king and Idan, the three of us standing in the clearing, Idan's grip immovable.

"You will come to me, now," the king says, his nostrils flared, eyes dark with fury. His lips are thinned, and he's still panting from the exertion of charging the men who attacked me, his chest gleaming with perspiration. "If you run now I will catch you," he growls. "I will strip you bare and whip you, taking you back through the marketplace striped and naked." He pauses. I know he means every word of what he says. "Release her, Idan."

Idan obeys. Though free from his grip, I am far from free.

On trembling legs, I approach the savage. He is scowling, his eyes mere slits as he grasps my arms firmly, pulling me to his chest. I crane my neck to look at him, and his eyes meet mine. Though he is furious, I also read something else. Could it be... disappointment? To my surprise, I am struck with a faint twinge of sorrow at having disobeyed him. I tell myself that it is merely exhaustion and the strangeness of my surroundings that have muddied my emotions. I owe him no allegiance. I must escape. I *will* escape.

"You have disobeyed me," he says severely, his voice a deep rumble I feel through my entire being. But then he looks at my cheek, where I was struck, and his eyes soften. He looks sorrowful, even, as he reaches and gently strokes my cheek with the back of his hand. "He struck you," he says, as his voice lowers to a rumble. To my shock, he bends down and his whiskery kiss flutters across my bruised skin. "Did he harm you in any other way?"

I shake my head dumbly, unable to understand the strange emotions welling in me at his unexpected tenderness. He pulls my head to his chest. His voice is still low but now tremulous as he speaks. "Would that I had killed him," he says. "I may yet."

I do not respond. I do not know what to say. This man is my captor, and yet he would seek vengeance for *me*.

He lifts his head and speaks sharply to Idan. "You and I will have words after our meeting this afternoon. After I've had time to decide on how you should be punished for your failure to keep her safe."

I look in surprise at Idan. He has fallen to one knee, his head bowed. "Yes, my lord. I offer my most sincere apologies," he says. "My life is forfeit for my failed duty."

His life? But the savage shakes his head. "Your life shall not be forfeit for having allowed the little brat to slip from your fingers," he says, "but you *will* answer for it. Go, prepare for our meeting. We will speak of this later."

Idan rises, and with a nod, takes his leave.

I am left alone with the savage. He grasps the back of my neck, tilting my face so that I may look into his eyes. "Why were you here?" he asks. "What is it that you were hoping to accomplish by sneaking to the dais?"

I cannot tell him. I avert my eyes and shake my head. "I merely needed some space and privacy."

A jerk of my hair startles me, as he pulls my head back to look at me. "An isolated cell would give you both space and privacy, if that is what you desire," he says. His voice lowers to a growl. "And you lie." His patience is now gone, the tenderness wiped from his features, as he grasps me by the arm and we take our leave. I am going to be punished. I know of no means to escape.

CHAPTER EIGHT

Aldric

I am shaking with fury, but I must temper my anger, maintain control. Idan has failed me and will answer for it. But the woman... she belongs to me, and yet she dares to defy. I regret having left her for a moment. I should have kept her closer to me, and not let her out of my sight. Though women are not allowed in the court of the *Hisrach*, I must not allow her such an opportunity again.

When I saw the man strike her, I was filled with the rage of a warrior in battle, prepared to slice the neck of the man who dared raise a hand to my woman. Her voice, the terror in her eyes, and her pleading for me to show mercy halted me from exacting fitting retribution for his crime. Now I wish I had not allowed myself to be swayed. My thirst for vengeance has not been sated. Though I will punish her, and my punishment will surely bring about pain, I would never raise a hand to her as he did. Only weak men would raise a fist to a woman. Even in a land where women are taught obedience, even as I am master over her, it is weakness to strike a woman in such a way. Though I will administer a firm punishment, I will not mar her or inflict more than a stinging backside that will remind her of her obedience to me in the days to come.

I can be a merciful man. But now is not the time for me to show mercy. Today, she *will* feel the sting of my lash.

As I march her through the marketplace, my men flank either side of us in military formation as they've been instructed to do. I am deaf to the noises and blind to the sights, intent only on ensuring I have taught my woman the lesson she must learn. She skips beside me, her little legs trotting to keep up with my long strides, and I lose patience at the length of time it is taking for me to get her alone in my chambers. Briefly pausing, I pull her in front of me, bend down, and lift her in my arms. She gasps, but now that she is safely secured, I can walk more quickly, unencumbered by her slower steps.

We enter the palace. My servants line the walkway, awaiting our approach. I turn to Lystava. As head of staff at my palace, she will command the others to do as I say. "See to it that we are left alone," I order. "I wish for no service until I call you." Turning to the rest of my servants, I raise my voice. "Away!"

They scatter from our presence, as I approach my chambers. I place Carina down on her feet, but quickly grasp her arm as we make our way to the door. We enter quickly, and I slam it behind me. Now that we are alone, my duties cleared for the time being, I think about what she's done. She deserves a whipping. She disobeyed me, disobeyed Idan. I know not why this woman is here, or what her errand in the forest was. Was she attempting to thwart my plans and eavesdropping on the *Hisrach*? Does she have spies here in my land who would join with her in arms against the Avalerians? She deserves to be whipped for her secrecy and lies, but as I think of what's just transpired, my hands shake with tempered fury.

Her actions could have gotten her *killed*, and it infuriates me that the realization somehow trumps her other infractions.

I point at the bed. "Remove your tunic and sit at the edge of the bed," I order.

She shakes her head. "No, my lord," she begins, as if somehow she has anything to say that will convince me not to punish her. She stands, her hands splayed out in front of her, a plea for mercy.

"No?" I ask in shock. The woman is *mad* to defy me.

"I-I merely tried to get away for a bit," she explains.

Does the woman think me an imbecile?

"What was your errand in the forest?" I ask her. "Your purpose? Carina, why have you *come* to Avalere?" I must know.

She shakes her head, as I advance upon her.

"You will be punished for your lies and secrecy. I will know why you are here, and what your purpose in the forest was."

"No errand," she says, and I know she lies. "I merely tried to have some time alone. I am sorry that I fell upon those men, but—"

"Sorry?" I ask, my anger rising along with my voice. "Do you think me an imbecile? You think I believe a woman from Freanoss infiltrates Avalere with a weapon for sport, with no harm intended to my people?" My temper flares as I step closer to her. "You are *sorry* that you put yourself—*my possession*—in harm's way?"

Her eyes flash at me, her arms crossed on her chest. "You do not own me!" she shouts.

I close the gap between us in one long stride, as she backs quickly away from me, the back of her legs hitting the bed and making her stumble into a sitting position.

I grasp her hair and pull, eliciting a cry from her. "That is where you are wrong, my Carina," I say. "And when I am through with you, there will be nary a doubt in your mind that every inch of you belongs to me."

She is staring at me wide-eyed and trembling, her fear apparent. It is well that she is afraid. She ought to be afraid of me. When I am done with her, she will fear me all the more. I have been too gentle, too merciful. Today, she will learn her lesson. I grasp her chin in my hands, leaning down to order in a harsh whisper, "Now *strip*."

Her hands shaking, she reaches for the edge of her tunic and lifts it up, slowly revealing her naked form beneath, the swell of her breasts rising and falling with each breath she takes. She lifts it over her head, her eyes closed as she finishes undressing. When the fabric is bunched above her head, I snatch it from her, flinging it away. It falls to the floor in a pool of vibrant blue. She now sits in front of me naked. Her eyes open and she stares.

"If you hadn't been seen passing our company, and I hadn't found you, what would have happened to you?"

She frowns, but does not answer. There is no need to continue discussion. I stand above her, my eyes focusing on hers, as I remove the two swords at my waist. I lay them on my table, then unfasten the leather sword belt. Her eyes travel to my waist. She swallows, as I hold the belt in my hand and draw closer. I could bind her hands before I punish her. I could require she lie face down on the bed. But it is far better for me to hold her upon my lap. When her punishment begins, she will want to escape. If she is over my lap, I can be sure she stays until I've delivered every last stripe.

As I approach the bed, she begins to shake her head from side to side, moving backward. I have had enough of her disobedience.

Quickly, I grab her arm and pull, sitting on the edge of the bed and dragging her bodily over one knee. I double my belt, making sure that the buckle is well hidden in my hand.

"No!" she shouts, her hand reaching back to stop me. I grab her hand and push it on her back, as her small form squirms, trying to get away, trying to fight me. She has no recourse. I will whip her soundly until I feel she's sufficiently punished. "You cannot do this!" she howls.

I ignore her protests, lift the belt, and snap it, delivering a hard lash to her naked backside. She screams, jerking away from me, an angry red stripe rising across her bottom. I lift the lash and deliver a second blow, this time lower, then another, the loud snap of the leather on naked skin mingling with her shouts and protests. I continue whipping her backside with steady, firm strokes of my belt. She is nowhere near sufficiently punished, as she is still fighting me, howling in protest. She has not seen the errors of her ways.

She will suffer, but she will see.

Finally, her hands stop flailing, and she seems less combative. I push her off my lap and onto the bed as I get to my feet behind her, my hand on the small of her back.

"Stay in position," I order, my instruction a harsh release. Now that I've gotten her to take her whipping, or at least to stop flailing her arms, I no longer have to subdue her as securely. I can administer a firmer punishment if I stand behind her. I release the doubled-over belt and allow the tail end to form a lash. I bring it back and swing it, the tail curving around her upturned bottom. Her feet come straight off the floor as she howls in pain, but I do not stop, building a steady rhythm as the lash falls again and again. Her naked skin is now striped thoroughly. She will feel this strapping for a good long time to come.

"Why did you leave?" I ask, underscoring my desire for her honesty with a cut of the belt. She flinches, but shakes her head. "What purpose was your errand?" Another hard lash as she remains silent. I growl. "Were you attempting to get to a portal? Spy on my people? *Escape?*"

She shakes her head. "No!" she wails.

My pulse quickens at her stubbornness. I must teach her what will happen if she disobeys. I must keep her safe.

I lean in close to her, my hand on her lower back. "Why am I punishing you?" I ask. I will not get to the bottom of her deception now, so instead I will focus on underscoring the need for her to obey me.

"I disobeyed you, my lord," she says, a near shout, desperate to stop her punishment.

I nod. "You did. My instructions were meant to keep you safe. You belong to me, and I will not allow you to endanger yourself again." I stand, rear back, and swing the belt hard once again, landing with a solid *thwap* against her naked bottom. She screams, coming up on her toes. I deliver another stripe, then another, before I lean in to her again. "And what could've happened to you if I hadn't come for you?"

She shakes her head. I am not sure if she is defying me, or she simply does not know the answer to my question. I bring my arm back even further, the belt connecting in the hardest swat I've delivered yet. I reach for her hair, yanking a fistful of it back. She gasps, her body braced in pain. I lean down and hiss in her ear, "I said what could've become of you? Answer me!"

She does not.

I will find her tongue with my belt. Growling, I step back and snap the belt on her backside three more times without pausing a beat. She screams in pain. I lean down a second time. "I asked you a question. What would have happened if I hadn't come for you?"

Still, she is silent. I stand, prepared to spank her again, my anger rising at her stubbornness, but as I raise my arm to strike, she yells, "I would have gotten hurt! I may have been violated!" A sob escapes her now as she fists the blanket beneath her hands, her eyes shut tight. "I might have escaped."

I feel my eyes narrow, as I fight the urge to sympathize. She belongs to me. The woman is *mine*. I will not cow to sympathy when I need to stay strong and discipline her for her willful disobedience. "You would have been hurt," I growl. "You *would* have been violated. You might have been murdered." I punctuate my words with a final cut of the lash. She gasps from the sting of it. "But you would *not* have gotten away. You would *not* have escaped," I insist. "Because by the gods, you belong here. You were meant for me. We are fated to be together, and you are *mine*."

She quiets. I wonder at her stillness. I must maintain my sternness before I minister to her. "Will you obey me, Carina?"

Her shoulders slump, her body stills, as she whispers into the blanket, "Yes, my lord."

I exhale. She has taken her whipping. Now I must complete my job.

• • • • • • •

I drop my belt and go to her, gathering her in my arms, prepared for her to push me away, but she does not. I have never seen my little one cry, but she weeps now, tears flowing freely. I carry her to the head of my bed, where I lie down and position her over my chest, her head over my heart. I run my hand through her hair, while hushing her. "Shhh, little one," I say. "It is over, my Carina."

But she cries on. I hold her in silence until her tears slow. I am not sorry I punished her. If given the choice to repeat my actions, I would do the very same. It is *imperative* she obey me.

I am sorry to see her weep, though. It is time she be consoled.

She is curled up on my bare chest, while I run my hand down her head and over her back, slowly stroking my hand over her punished bottom. She flinches a bit, but as I massage firmly, she relaxes. "Hush, my Carina," I say. "You must *not* disobey me." I suspect she weeps now for what she has lost, her home and her people, perhaps despair at not being able to complete whatever mission she intended. I cannot be angry with her now. She hurts. "I do not know much about your planet, but what little I do know has taught me thus: I do not wish for you to return. It is my firm belief that though it is your native land, it is best that you are with me now."

She does not respond.

"And since you are mine, you will obey me."

I hold her until she stills, her tears finally slowing. She does not tell me what is in her heart, but I can feel it, sense it. I know she is mourning the loss of her home planet, but there is more. I am not sure yet what it is, but she clings to me upon my chest, an almost desperate holding on. I bend down and kiss her damp forehead, her naked form and her submission to me causing a deep stirring within me, my manhood hardening beneath her. I long to claim her, but I will be patient.

I run my hand slowly through her soft, dark tresses, from her crown to her neck, and when my hand reaches her neck, I gently but firmly grasp. "Will you obey me, Carina?" I ask. "Are you going to do as you are told?"

She nods her head slowly. "Yes, my lord," she whispers. After a moment of silence, she asks, "What will happen to those men?"

I frown. It is an honest question, but it angers me to be reminded of their filthy hands on her. Vengeance still flares within me. It is only out of deference to her wishes that they do not lie now, heaped in shallow graves.

"They will hang," I state. "They laid hands on the king's woman. They stole what did not belong to them."

"It is a harsh penalty," she says. Her reaction puzzles me.

"You think it harsh, little one? You come from a land that ends the life of humans past their prime, and infants who bear marks of imperfection. And you think it harsh that in this land, that those who choose to defy the law are accordingly punished? We are no more savage than those on Freanoss. The only difference is that here, people have the choice. Those men chose poorly."

She lifts her tearstained face to mine. "You speak lies," she whispers.

She is brave to accuse me of such when I have just striped her soundly for disobedience. I am well within my rights to punish her again for such an accusation, but I will not. Her words need further probing. I am surprised for a moment that she accuses me of lying. Is she not aware of the ways of her people?

"I do not," I say to her. "I wish to find what your thoughts are on the ways of your people. And you will tell me why you have come here. But I must meet with the *Hisrach* shortly, and news I have received today makes the meeting imperative."

Her eyes look troubled and her lip trembles. "You must leave me?" she asks. The minute the words leave her mouth, she casts her eyes down. She seems as if she regrets speaking so frankly, but it is clear my little one does not wish for us to be separated.

I kiss her forehead again, this time threading my fingers through her hair and resting them on her neck as I do so. "Would you prefer I not meet with my men?" I ask.

She is quiet and does not respond, a little finger tracing along the dark, curly hair on my chest. "It is strange, how you have hair on your chest," she says.

I stifle a chuckle. It is endearing how she's changed the subject, but she must learn to answer me when I ask her a question.

"Carina," I warn. Her eyes widen as she looks up at my tone. I tug a lock of hair.

"Yes?" she whispers.

"Answer the question. Do you wish me to stay with you?"

She closes her eyes briefly, biting her lip. She does not speak, but nods.

Though I wish to have her near, and also wish to be present at the counsel, it occurs to me that much of what I need to learn I've already learned at this morning's gathering. I have an option that may work in our favor.

"If you wish me to stay, then it will be so," I say softly, bringing the hand that lay on my chest to my lips, and kissing her fingers. "I will give the orders necessary so that I may be informed, but I shall stay with you. Yes," I say, sure now that my decision is the right one. "I shall stay with you."

She pushes herself up from my chest, her eyes bright from crying and her cheeks flushed. My desire for her grows with every second that passes with her skin against mine, with her complete and utter submission to me, dependent on me to take care of her. I pull her closer, crushing her mouth in a heated kiss. I hold her neck in my hand as my mouth explores hers, the sweet, vulnerable softness of her lips pressed against mine. I feel her naked body pushing against me, her hips grinding as my hands finds her breasts. I groan from the perfect feel of her satiny skin, her nipples pebbling with each stroke of my thumbs. Her desire is mounting as I kiss her. With every touch, I elicit little mews and gasps from her pretty mouth.

I push up, gently moving her so that she is now on the bed and I am over her, she pinned beneath me. I brace myself with one hand as the other cups her breast. I take my mouth from hers with a moan of regret as my lips travel down her naked skin, past the flushed skin just under her neck. My tongue laps at her collarbone. Her hips rise as my mouth travels lower still to her nipple. I flick out my tongue, taking her nipple in my mouth, sucking. Her head drops back, her mouth open as she writhes.

"Ohhhh," she sighs, as I continue to tease her breasts with my tongue, but move one hand between her legs. Her hips push together, effectively barring me from touching her.

I lift my hand and spank her thigh, a sharp swat. "You will not prevent me from touching what is mine," I growl, pushing my hand between her legs again, spreading her thighs apart.

"My... my lord..." she stammers, her thighs still closed together. She is stubborn, tenacious, willful. I thrill at the challenge to tame her.

"Open your legs," I growl. "You do as I say or I shall take you across my knee a second time. Do not try me, Carina."

Her eyes closed, biting her lip, she slowly spreads her

legs apart. I inhale deeply, intoxicated by the scent of her. It is not merely fear I smell but all of her—the sweetness, the sultriness, the arousal.

I slowly stroke my finger along her inner thigh, the back of my fingertip just grazing the warm, soft skin there. She pants, her hands holding onto the breadth of my shoulders.

"Why do you resist?" I ask her, my mouth just beside her ear. "Do you not wish for me to pleasure you?"

Her breath is labored, her body tensed beneath me. "If you... I..." she begins haltingly. "I am not... prepared for coupling," she says. "I am terrified of your size and strength. I have never experienced anything like this before."

Her honesty pleases me. She will be rewarded for being so frank.

I kiss her warm temple, brushing the hair from her face.

"Sweet girl," I murmur. "I am not preparing to claim you. Not now. Not yet." My length presses against her as I talk to her. "Though it is not for lack of desire for you. I have punished you, and it is my pleasure to now minister to you."

She eyes me curiously. "Minister to me?"

I nod, bracing myself above her so that our eyes meet. "It is the way of Avalere. As your master, it is my duty to train you in obedience. But after I've punished you, it is my duty to minister to your needs. To tend to your body. Comfort your mind. Help you heal in all ways from the punishment you have received."

She shakes her head. "The ways of Avalere are strange."

Her comment amuses me and I chuckle. "I could say the same about the ways of *your* people, little one," I say. "Now will you allow me to minister to you, or shall I be forced to take more drastic measures?" I let her imagination form what drastic measures I will take. I have my methods.

Her knees fall open. She is watching me warily, but she licks her lips. My eyes focus on hers as my finger traces a pattern from her navel to her thigh.

"Relax, Carina," I say, as I move my finger to the apex

of her thighs, to the sweet spot I will pleasure, but not until I am ready. I trace my finger just over her mound, the warmth of my touch ever so gently teasing her. I move my mouth to her breasts again and flick my tongue to her nipple with slow, lazy strokes, as my finger traces along her sex, barely touching her, moving so softly, she lifts her hips to meet my hand.

I take her nipple wholly in my mouth as I move my fingers between her delicious folds. She gasps, her fingers threading through my hair and holding tightly, her hips jerking from the touch. I release her breast. "I said relax, little one," I order. She nods. She is trying.

I slowly stroke upward through her folds until I find her sweet spot. I circle, watching for visible signs of her pleasure. Her eyes are shut, her hands still grasping me as she grinds her sex against my hand. "Very good," I croon. "What a very good girl. Allow me to pleasure you, now." I stroke over and over, each brush of my finger against her causing her to writhe beneath me.

"Ohhh," she moans. "Please."

It is both my duty and reward to pleasure her.

I bring my mouth to hers and kiss her as I continue the deliberate strokes of my hand, gradually increasing the tempo of my movements. I kiss her, her soft mouth upon mine while I stroke her. She moans in my mouth, tearing her mouth away as she reaches the pinnacle of her pleasure. She gasps, writhing, a cry of ecstasy escaping, as she rides the waves of pleasure. I continue to stroke her until her breathing slows. Gently, I take my hand away from her womanhood. I kiss her head, lifting her so that she is tucked against my side. She curls up beside me, grasping me with her arms about my waist. She seems shy now, turning away from me. I realize that she is not used to such bold frankness.

"You are beautiful," I say. "And you will do as you are told. Will you not?"

She nods. "Yes, my lord."

I kiss her forehead again. "I am glad, my Carina. For though it is my duty to pleasure you, it is my duty to instruct you. Obey me, Carina, and there will be no need for me to punish you again."

She nods. She will disobey me again. And I will punish her again, this I know. She is too willful and I too exacting for it to be otherwise. But for now, I will focus on making sure she is taken care of.

CHAPTER NINE

Carina

    I lie in the arms of the king. He is strong, his arms folded around my frame. I can feel his latent power and strength beneath me, above me, surrounding me, as my heartbeat slowly begins to settle. I have never felt anything so exquisite in my life as I have just now, as he brought me to ecstasy. I want him to hold me forever. The thought of his warm embrace leaving me has me near tears. I must be held, must be comforted, must be reassured that everything is going to be fine.
    Because I'm not fine. I've experienced a painful punishment unlike anything I've ever experienced before. My backside aches from the lashes of his belt. Though he was angry, he was in control the entire time. This was not an act of brutality I've experienced, but rather retribution for my disobedience. I knew when I made my choice what he expected of me, and I chose to take the risk of being caught and punished, but I was unprepared for how the punishment would make me feel. I didn't know my fears would surface, my worries about never returning to my homeland of Freanoss. Nor did I know that I would weep.

Crying is discouraged on Freanoss, as emotion is a sign of weakness. We are taught to train ourselves to suppress such emotion. But there are no reasons for tears on Freanoss, in such a regulated environment. Here, it is quite different. Fear, anger, longing, and now… ecstasy.

I am also angry. If what the king says about my people is true, then I am furious I have never known such brutality existed on my home planet. Have the Freanossian accusations against Avalere been false? Where, then, does that leave *me*?

You come from a land that ends the life of humans past their prime, and infants who bear marks of imperfection.

He is mistaken. He must be. It is not possible such things happen, and I have no knowledge. But as I lay in his arms, I remember. Though my work on Freanoss kept me removed from the elderly and the innocent, I have not forgotten things that I have seen. And now I wonder, as I am no longer cloaked in the darkness of ignorance, how much of what he has said is true.

After all, I was told on Freanoss that coupling was a base and vile act, and until now, I have never experienced the exquisite pleasure the king has brought to me. I squirm at the memory. I was so vulnerable, laid so bare before him that now I wish to hide myself from him. I now bury my face on his warm chest, his arms encircling me, the dark hair on his chest prickling my cheek. How could I have allowed him to touch me like that? But as I squirm from the memory, I wonder. How could I have not?

I feel his warm mouth come to my forehead and kiss me again. My mind is teeming with unanswered questions, but as he holds me, a strange sensation overcomes me. There is an emptiness, a sort of gnawing in my belly. I hear a strange growl come from my own body. I start, unsure of what I've just felt.

"Relax, little one," he says. "You are merely unaccustomed to feeling hunger. Come now, sit up and I will fetch us food."

I shake my head from side to side. I wish to stay right where I am.

He sighs. "Carina," he chides, his voice in a deep warning tone. "When I give you an instruction, I expect immediate obedience. If I ask you to get up, you do not shake your head at me. Defy me again, and even now, you will find yourself stretched across my lap for punishment. I am loath to punish you again, but if you continue to defy me, I shall."

I certainly do not wish to receive another punishment. Reluctantly, I pull myself away from him. When he is no longer holding me, his arms no longer surrounding me, I feel a desperate sort of longing. I feel a lump rise in my throat. I look away from him. I dislike how my body is behaving unexpectedly. He has seen all.

He reaches a hand out to stroke my cheek. "It is as it should be then," he says softly, almost as if to myself. "My little one even now clings to me."

My eyes fill as I look to him, my vision suddenly blurred. I frown, unsettled by the uncontrollable desire to weep yet again. "What do you mean?" I whisper.

He tucks a damp piece of hair behind my ear. His dark eyes, so fierce and stern just moments before, now look upon me tenderly. "I told you once that we were fated," he said. "You are my mate. I have claimed you as my own. And as we grow together, it will become more difficult to be separated." He smiles. "You will see."

I frown, looking away. I dislike the idea of being somehow dependent on him. I long for the independence I was taught to embrace. Humans should not be dependent on the other. Choosing one over another means that we are not equals, not the same.

His eyes twinkle as he lifts the bell to ring it, his stern lips twitching. He thinks it amusing that I like the bell so much, but there is something magical about it. The sound resonates in the small room, and minutes later, I hear a knock at the door. I gasp, crossing my arms on my chest. I have just realized that I am still naked.

He lifts me as if I weighed no more than a feather, holds me over one shoulder, pulling back the blanket. He then lays me back down and brings the covers up over my shoulder. I hiss as the cool blanket brushes against my punished bottom. He frowns, but quickly turns away and raises his voice.

"Come in," he says, his deep, booming voice resonating in the chamber. To my surprise, I feel a pulse of desire deep down in my belly. There is something about his stern demeanor and his deep voice that causes my nipples to harden beneath the blanket. I squeeze my thighs together. Is there magic in this man? Am I enchanted? But no, I know such things do not exist. I have been taught they are the mere fabrications of little minds.

But how else can I explain the enigmatic pull of this man on me?

Lystava enters, bowing before her king, and places a silver tray on the table. Her eyes flick toward me, still covered beneath the blankets on the bed, and quickly, she looks away, scurrying out of the room. When the door shuts, he addresses me.

"Come here, Carina."

"I'm not clothed, my lord," I protest.

He merely turns to me, scowling, and lifts a heavy brow. I quickly toss off the blankets and come to him. He points to where my tunic lies. "If you are more comfortable, you may wear that. For now. It is best you are to be dressed when I call Idan to me," he says.

I cross the room and lift the tunic, slipping it over my head. It falls, free of wrinkles, and I feel an odd mixture of emotions. I should embrace being able to conceal my nudity, yet with my body now covered, I feel as if my attraction toward the king is muted.

He gestures for me to take a seat, so I obey, hissing as my bottom hits the chair. He purses his lips, frowning. He is not sorry.

He hands me a glass of something hot, steam coming from the top of the cup.

"Easy, Carina," he says. "It will burn you if you drink too quickly."

I nod, taking a tentative sip. It is warm but bitter, and I dislike it. He chuckles, and I look at him in surprise.

His eyes are crinkling as his deep laughter resonates in the room. "You don't like the tea?" he asks. "It is meant to bring nourishment and good health. You should drink it."

I look at him, trying to see if he is testing me. Must I drink it though I dislike it? But he shakes his head, taking the cup from me, handing me a piece of bread with something golden smeared on it. "Eat," he orders. I take a small bite as he rings the bell again. The response is immediate, and I wonder if his servants flank the door outside, prepared to do his bidding.

"Lystava, fetch Idan for me," he orders. She hastens to obey as he eats a large slice of bread and eyes me. I do enjoy this, and he nods appreciatively as I eat, first the bread, then berries and cheese. I am beginning to be familiar with some of the food of this land, and I even look forward to the meals. "Feeling better, little one?" he asks. I nod. I do.

A knock comes at the door, and the king tells our visitor to enter. Idan enters, a leather strap crossing his bare chest and ending with a holster at his hip. He looks prepared for battle. The king eyes him, frowning, his eyes darkening. He is harboring anger toward his friend for what happened earlier today. Idan falls to one knee. "My lord."

"Rise." The king's tone is crisp. A shiver goes through my body. Though he can be gentle, his latent power and authority are fearsome. I know it, and Idan does as well, as he fairly trembles before the king. I am holding my breath.

"Your failure to obey me today might have been costly," he said. "It was by mere chance we were able to save both my people and my woman from danger."

Idan swallows, nodding. "I am sorry, my lord—" but the king cuts him off with a flick of his hand. Idan silences.

"Sorrow does not change the circumstances. Today, you will take upon your shoulders the duty bestowed on me. You will attend the counsel, report to me your findings, and do your duty by deciding the outcome of any disparities. It is a long, arduous task ahead of you, and will take you until dusk settles this evening to do what you must. You will write the details of the meeting for me and have them delivered within an hour of close of counsel. Do you understand what I am asking of you?"

Idan nods. "Yes, my lord."

The king waves his hand. "Then *go*."

With a bow, Idan takes his leave as the king turns to me. "He will perform my duties today," he says. His eyes are gleaming as he lifts a goblet to his mouth and drinks deeply. "We will be undisturbed for the remainder of the afternoon."

I nod my head slowly, curious what the afternoon will bring.

• • • • • • •

It is now midafternoon, I surmise. We have eaten our food, and now the king rises. "It is time you see the lay of our castle," he says. I wonder at his choice of words.

Our?

He stands me in front of him and runs his fingers through my hair, as if to tidy it, then spins me around, looking over my dress. "Very good," he murmurs to himself. I am not sure what it is he approves of, but if he is momentarily appeased, it is fine by me. He draws me close to him and kisses my forehead. I wonder if this is the custom in his planet. He has done this now several times to me, and it never fails to make me feel quiet and pleased.

"Do you need to freshen up?" he asks me.

I have no idea what he means, and shake my head, bewildered.

His eyes crinkle around the edges as he smiles. "I am

going to parade you through the caste so you know your whereabouts. Do you feel comfortable as you are?"

I still do not know what he means, so I merely nod dumbly.

His lips twitch upward. "Before the next feast, I will see to it that Lystava prepares you properly. You will then see what I mean."

He extends his arm, and I finally realize it is his wish that I hold onto him. I reach tentatively for his large, muscular arm and when my fingers meet his skin, he draws my hand close to his chest, as if holding my grip to him. He opens the door to the room, and we exit into the hallway. As earlier, when we enter the hallway, as we pass servants, they stand tall and at attention, though none flank our sides as if to guard us this time, as he leads me.

"The dining hall," he says, extending his arm to where a long, gleaming mahogany table stands in the middle of a large room, lined on either side by chairs.

"What do you do there?" I ask.

He chuckles, deep and low, as he speaks to me. "I forget how strange your ways are," he says. "That you do not know what transpires in a dining hall. It is where we feast, little one. I often take my meals there, but it is my preference that while you acclimate yourself to living here, I will allow you to eat with me in my chambers. I frequently take my meals alone when I am busy with my duties. But soon, you shall dine with me in the hall as well. You will see, eventually, that the dining hall has a place where we receive guests as well." We continue, and he gestures to a room that is adjacent to the large hall. "There, they cook the food." His eyes twinkle with humor. "This is called the kitchen." I feel my jaw drop open. It is remarkable to me that they have an entire *room* dedicated to the mere use of feeding themselves and an entire room dedicated to the preparation of food.

"Why do you do this?" I ask him. "Why do you not choose the simpler methods of Freanoss?"

He is quiet for a minute as he eyes me. "Simpler is not

always best, Carina." But he offers nothing else as we walk through the hall.

He points out various paintings and sculptures as we move onward. Some are odd to me, yet some stir something within me that I am wholly unfamiliar with. I feel both sad and happy, a strange mixture of emotions I cannot quite decipher. I wish to stay longer, but he wishes for us to continue. Beyond the kitchen there is a pantry and larder, and as we move past the large hall and smaller rooms, we come upon a comfortable-looking room with elegant furnishings. The walls are flanked with old-fashioned books. I eye them, marveling. I have never seen so many books in my life. Simpler, digital methods of reading are encouraged on Freanoss. I hope I am given some time to peruse this room, but as I find myself wishing, I banish the thought. I cannot allow myself to be enamored with the ways of Avalere. It is far more important that I remain detached and aloof, so I can find what I need to, but even as I begin to think of leaving Avalere and returning to Freanoss with the information I need, my heart twists. Do I really want to leave Avalere?

We move on, and he shows me a room that he refers to as his cabinet, a place where his men will convene later. We have now made a nearly complete circle, arriving back at where we began. I see the door to his chambers, and as we draw near, I see a few more small rooms. There is a golden door to one room near the entrance to his chambers. "That is your room," he says. "Traditionally, you would retire in that room. It is my wish that you do not," he says. "You may use that room to ready yourself for gatherings, but you will reside in my chambers."

My heartbeat begins to quicken as we near his chambers. We have spent some time exploring the inside of his home, and the sky just outside the oval-shaped window in the long hallway shows that the sun is beginning to set. "You will rest a bit, as I await news from Idan. And after I have spoken with Idan," he pauses, drawing closer to me, as he places his hand upon my neck and his mouth close to my ear, "you and I will get to know each other a bit more."

I have somehow forgotten how to breathe. I may be ignorant of the ways of his land, but my intuition tells me that what he has planned for me may be something unlike what I have experienced before. He wishes for me to be in his chambers, and he has freed his obligations for the evening. I intuitively know that the time is drawing near where he will wish to couple. Although I feared his type of intimacy before, and I cannot say I do not fear it still, the very thought of his hands on me has my breasts swelling, heat simmering in my belly. I am at a loss for words. I simply nod, and follow him to his chambers.

CHAPTER TEN

Aldric

I see that my little one's eyes grow big as I mention the plans I have for her. I am deliberately cryptic in my word choice. She is afraid. Though I wish for her to fear me inasmuch as it will make her more likely to obey me, I realize that I simply wish for her to fear punishment. I do not wish for her to actually fear *me*. There are men who enjoy taking what is theirs at their leisure, and in my youth, there were times when I did take what was due me without much thought for the woman beneath me. It is different with my little one. She is my mate, my chosen one, and though I will demand her utmost obedience, I wish for her devotion. There is no pleasure in the immediate capture. No. First, there must be chase.

"Come, Carina," I tell her.

She follows me, though her eyes are still flitting about the palace. I imagine there is much for her to observe, and she may have questions yet.

"Fetch me the bell," I instruct.

She obeys, lifting the bell gingerly, as if afraid that if she moves too quickly it will break. I smile, nodding to her, and she hands it to me. I give it a sharp ring. Her eyes widen, her breath catching as the sound echoes and Lystava appears as if by magic.

"Please take Carina to be bathed," I instruct. "It is my wish she present herself to me in one hour, robed and prepared. Do you understand my instructions?" Lystava knows all that my duties require, and will take care of my little one with attention to every detail.

Her diminutive frame bows, her head inclined. "Certainly, my lord," she says, opening her hand so that Carina can follow her. It is only because the room where she will bathe is connected to my chambers that I have allowed her leave to depart from me after what she's done earlier today. I nod, and Carina and Lystava cross my room, Lystava showing Carina how to access the connected room through a door in my chambers. They leave, the door shutting behind them. Next, I summon Arman, my most trusted servant. He arrives in short time, as the *Hisrach* has begun to convene in counsel. His dark hair is drawn back with a tie, his short beard trimmed. His stern eyes are ready to hear and obey. He inclines his head, and I accept him with a nod.

"Arman, I wish to speak to the Wise One," I say. Arman's eyes grow wide. Though he knows better than to defy me, I can see him hesitating at my command.

"The Wise One, my lord? You do know he has not left his home in several decades?"

I frown. "Of course I know," I say. "But if it is my wish as king to have him brought to me, then I expect he will be brought to me." I speak impatiently, as it is my strong desire to have the man brought to me *now*. I have questions that only he can answer.

Arman frowns. "Certainly, my lord, and if you do truly wish that he be brought here, then I will make the necessary arrangements. But I—"

"I do wish it so!" I snap. My temper is rising. I want to know what it is that troubles my little one. I have many questions about her that she herself cannot answer, since she can only frame what she knows according to what she has experienced. I also wish to know why it is I feel the enigmatic pull to her, my mate, though she is a woman of *Freanoss*.

"My lord," Arman begins, lifting a placating hand to me. "I am merely saying—"

But he is interrupted by a small knock on the door from within my chambers. Lystava is ready with my Carina.

"Come in," I say, and the door opens. Lystava first emerges, followed shortly by my Carina. Silence descends upon us, and I do not realize at first that I am holding my breath. Is this my little one, or an angel from the heavens? Her skin has been washed fresh, gleaming ivory in the low light of my room. Her hair is still damp, the midnight curls pinned in ringlets about her heart-shaped face. Her dusk-colored eyes look to me almost pleadingly. These are not the defiant, angry eyes of the woman I have taken over my knee. These are the eyes of my lady prepared to please me, and she is seeking my approval. The curves of her luscious form shimmer beneath a simple tunic of silver, her bare feet noiseless as she approaches me.

When she is within arm's reach, her head bows, her eyes cast down, and her knee dips in reverence. Lystava has instructed her to approach me properly. I warm at the sight, my sudden desire for her so strong I wish to banish my servants from my chambers, lay her upon my bed, and take her. I swallow, a futile attempt to quench my thirst for her.

"My lord," Arman says. "If I bring the Wise One to you, it may be a threat to his health."

"I need to speak to him," I insist, my eyes on Carina, reaching my hand out to cup her cheek, running my thumb along her cheekbone. Her eyes flicker over mine and she bites her lip.

"Perhaps you will go to him," Arman insists, but his words are nearly drowned out by the rush of blood in my ears.

I nod to him. I am heady with her fragrance, an intoxicating yet subtle smell, sweet yet seductive, the scent curling its lacy tendrils around me. I will tell him anything now to get him to go away. "I will go to him," I murmur to Arman, though my eyes are fixed solely on my little one. My hand reaches to her slim waist, drawing her closer to me. "Tomorrow. Go to the counsel and see that no one disturbs us for the remainder of the evening. I will see Idan at the first light of dawn. Give him those instructions."

I am dimly aware of both Arman and Lystava taking their leave. The room is darkened.

"Are we alone?" I ask her softly. She nods her head. She is still afraid, but there is far more at play now than fear.

"Though your lovely garment protected your modesty for the moment," I murmur, "it is my wish for you now to be bare to me."

Her immediate obedience thrills me, as her hands reach for the hem of the garment, lifting it over her head. I hear a low growl in the quiet room and it takes a minute before I realize that it is my own instinctive response.

I have had many women. I could, even now, have legions of women to do with as I pleased.

But there is only one I desire.

When she is bare, I reach my hand to the small of her back, drawing her close to me. I dip my mouth to her navel, planting a delicate kiss at the sweet skin at her waist. I feel her anticipation begin to rise, her breaths becoming shallow, her body slightly trembling at my touch. I draw her on my lap so that she is facing me, her legs wrapped around my waist, her arms encircling my neck. I take her mouth as my hand travels to her neck, her lips parting, welcoming my kiss. The gentle kiss slowly intensifies as my hunger for her grows, my lips bruising hers, my tongue plundering her mouth. When the moan deep within her resonates through my own body, the length of my hardness below her bottom presses. I want her. All of her.

I rise, taking her to the bed, and gently place her down,

her arms still upon me.

"Release me, Carina," I order.

She blinks and hesitates. I smack her thigh, not harshly but firmly enough that she understands she must obey. With a little mew, she complies.

I bend down, my mouth close to her ear. "Little one," I say in a low growl. "Your warning time is complete. You are now going to be trained to obey me so thoroughly you will fear the mere thought of disobeying. There will be no more warnings, Carina, no more allowances for your failure to obey immediately. When I instruct you, you will do as I say."

This will not be easy for her. She will be punished, and often, while I train her. But she will be rewarded when she obeys.

I take her wrists and lift them so that her arms are stretched out. I place them firmly on the bed, pressing them down with just enough force to covey my command. For now, I will aid her obedience with verbal instructions. Eventually, she will be expected to understand and obey without my having to tell her what to do.

"Do not move your wrists," I say. "You will maintain whatever position I require of you unless I give you leave." I look into her wide blue eyes, full of anticipation, fear, and arousal. "If you disobey, I will punish you."

She swallows.

Hovering over her, I lower my mouth to her forehead first in a gentle kiss, slowly bringing my mouth down to her ear. I flick out my tongue. She squirms, but stays in position while I drag my tongue in a circle around her inner ear. Lowering my mouth, I take her lobe between my teeth and nip. Her hands fly out, grasping my head. Within seconds, I have her bent over the bed as I punish her, two sharp swats to her backside for her disobedience.

She gasps. "I am sorry, my lord!" she says. Good. Her words halt my hand, raised to strike a third time. I toss her back down on the bed, taking her wrists far less gently this time as I pin then down.

"Move your hands again and I shall cuff them," I say.

"Yes, my lord," she murmurs, her hips writhing. I return to her ear, kissing and nipping and torturing her with my tongue. I move to her jaw, planting fluttering kisses along the edge and down her neck. When I come to the tender skin there, just above her collarbone, I flick out my tongue and lick before sinking my teeth in the soft flesh. She gasps, her hips jerking, but her hands stay in position. She will be rewarded for her obedience.

"Good girl," I growl, "such a very good girl." I move my mouth down her chest, my mouth alternatively licking and biting and kissing. I long to consume her, to take her in, all of her, and as I hover above her, my own instinctive desire begins to flow. I can feel it now, the energy between us, the warmth and light of her longing to entwine with me, but circling still, cautious. Though I am the one in power over her, she is the one who will open the gateway to more. I can and will demand her obedience. She well knows she faces my discipline and displeasure if she fails to obey. But there is more than power and control at play. I desire far more for us.

It takes all my strength to hold myself above her as I continue to make my way lower still, to her sweet, bare mound. She is shaking her head but her hands stay where I put them.

"What are you doing?" she whispers.

"Shhhh."

My tongue flicks out to the tender skin of her thigh, so delicious and enchanting.

"Open."

She has two choices: disobey and incur discipline, or obey and I will take her to ecstasy. I give her seconds to comply, and just as I'm prepared to flip her over and administer my discipline for her disobedience, she obeys. Her knees bend, lifting, her legs spreading wider. She is welcoming me. With a wicked grin, I move to between her legs, allowing my thick whiskers to graze her thighs. She likes this, moaning as she writhes beneath me.

"You may move your hands as you wish," I whisper, just as my tongue flicks between her legs, starting low, drawing up slowly, her folds the most delicious thing I have ever tasted. I growl in approval as her hands fly to my hair, gripping, anchoring herself onto me. I move my hands beneath her bottom. Cradling her entire backside in my two hands, I lift her mouth to me as an offering, an unblemished gift. Circling her sensitive nub with my tongue, I hear her moan, her fingers holding onto me as I tease her again, and again, squeezing her punished bottom, pulling her to me.

She writhes, holding onto me, and I can tell by the way she feels that her arousal is reaching peak. I release her, lifting my head up, enjoying her groan at the loss of my mouth on her sex.

"Please, my lord," she begs, panting.

"Not yet."

Near frenzied with desire, she pounds the bed with her fists and growls at me. "Yes, *now*," she says. I shake my head, both hands reaching for her breasts, I grasp her nipples and pinch, harder than I would to pleasure her. This is punishment.

She howls in pain, swatting at my hands to move them away, but I only grip harder, shocking her as I dip my mouth to her waist and bite. Her screams echo in the chamber as I lift my mouth, the teeth marks stark against her pale white skin. Her nipples still in my hands, I twist again. "Care to contradict me again, Carina?"

Her voice is thick with emotion, her eyes damp as she shakes her head from side to side. "No, my lord," she moans. I release her breasts.

"Good girl," I praise, even though her obedience was wrung from her with pain. I move back lower, to her mound, and begin the assault with my tongue, bringing her just to the cusp of climax before I once again release her. This time, she does not beg for more. Her eyes are shut tight. I can see her pulse under the thin white skin of her neck, throbbing. Her arousal is so heady I am drunk with it, the scent and flavor of her permeating my senses. She is delicious, the finest of delicacies.

"Spread your knees," I order. "Wider."

She obeys as I remove my own clothing, her eyes taking in the wide breadth of my chest. I am a warrior, my body strong and muscled, honed to perfection with years of training, darkened by the sun. When my clothes are fully removed, her eyes go to my cock, hard and ready for her, and she looks both excited and nervous. I lower my body over hers, holding my weight on my forearms as my mouth finds hers. I kiss her, slowly, savoring the taste of her, the way her breath mingles with mine. My hips move gently, as I hold her close. I take my cock and swipe it along her slit. She gasps as I flick the head of my cock over her sensitive parts, faster, more insistent, bringing her back to the cusp of climax before I remove my touch. Her eyes close and a small sob escapes.

"What is it, my little one?" I ask softly. "Why so sad?"

"You know, my lord," she replies. "You know that I obey your command and that you will not bring me what I want unless you desire so."

I kiss her cheek and whisper in her ear.

"You learn well, little one. Now tell me. Tell your lord what it is you desire."

"Pleasure," she breathes.

I take my cock again and slowly drag through her slit, and now I feel it, her welcoming me as her legs part.

"My lord," she whispers, her hands now freed from my commands coming around to encircle my neck. We are on the cusp, the very edge. She is no longer circling me in fear but now welcoming. "Come inside me." She swallows before she takes a deep breath. "Please, my lord," she whispers. "I trust you."

My chest expands with pride as my mouth meets hers in a brief kiss. "I cherish your trust."

I nudge my cock between her thighs, to her pussy.

"Relax, little one," I croon. "You will take me fully now. It will hurt, but I will make it feel better."

She tenses. I will talk her through this. "Trust me, Carina," I say. "It will hurt more if you tense. There, now," as I feel the tension loosen, "there, sweetness." Slowly, I enter her, her warm, tight pussy hugging my cock. I groan from the immense pleasure I feel, her virginity a gift as well, one that I will cherish. I lift my hips and thrust gently but firmly. She gasps. She is wet enough it will help, but it does hurt her until I slowly build a steady rhythm and build her pleasure. Her head falls to the side and she moans, her hips rising to mine, begging me for more as I keep up the steady tempo of pleasure. She is ready for me. I feel her desire mounting, but I can wait for her. I *must* wait for her. In this, our first act of coupling, her soul welcoming mine for the very first time, we will reach ecstasy together.

"My lord," she moans, her eyes closed. "I am afraid. It feels... so nice," she whispers. "I am going to lose control."

"You've already lost control, Carina," I whisper. "You have given it to me. Allow your body now to surrender as well." I pause, allowing her to digest my words before I issue my command. "Now. Climax, my little one."

She moans as my own climax reaches a crescendo, her moans getting louder while the pleasure consumes her. As she climaxes my own desire pinnacles and I spill inside her, my heart racing, veins throbbing, my cock pumping into her in exquisite ecstasy. Her pleasure is intense, her body lifting straight off the bed as I hold her and we milk every drop of pleasure from each other's bodies before collapsing on the bed.

"Oh, my lord," she whispers. Is she crying? Are those tears I see upon the cheeks of my little one? I reach my thumb to her face and gently wipe them, bringing my thumb to my mouth and licking. I will take what is hers wholly. I own her.

"Shh," I whisper, falling to my side and drawing her upon my chest. "Hush, sweetness."

She clings to me as I withdraw. I release her, as I must get a cloth for her.

"No, no, please, my lord," she begs, reaching her hands to me.

"Just a few moments, Carina," I say. "I must clean you." My voice drops. "Now be a good girl and stay there. I shall return almost immediately."

She nods. I move as quickly as I can, retrieving the cloth and joining her back on the bed. The moment I am reclined next to her, she pounces, her arms grasping me almost painfully as her legs wrap around me like vines.

I chuckle. My little one has responded as she should, then. She does not wish to be separated. I gently pry her off me and open her legs, drawing the cloth over her and cleaning her.

"Thank you," she whispers, and I am not sure to what she refers.

I nod. "It is my pleasure," I say to her. I mean every word, all of it, her obedience, our lovemaking, caring for her, and even training her. I will allow her to bask in the afterglow. The days ahead will be a trial to her. She must enjoy what she can for now.

• • • • • • •

I wonder if my little one will sleep well, given that she's experienced both exquisite pleasure and pain in one day. Her mind is likely racing with confusion and fears. It is my hope that now she has begun to trust me a bit more, I will be able to find her more willing to state her purpose. I will train her to obey me, but not break her with interrogation. My men have pressed me for more information. I assured them after my meeting with Isidor that we will meet to discuss whatever Freanossian plans I am able to obtain from her. It is my hope that if she is trained to obey, and she trusts me, she will be less likely to withhold vital information. For now, I must encourage Carina to continue to feel safe with me.

"Are you tired, Carina?" I ask her. Her eyes are already closed, her breath shallower.

"Yes, my lord," she whispers.

"Hungry?"

She shakes her head. "No, my lord."

I lift the blanket and tuck it around her, eager to comfort her, but I know she needs more from me. If I am to train her to obey, she must learn to denounce her own desires and follow mine.

"Carina," I say, my voice harder than it was just a moment ago.

"Mmm?"

"I wish for you to rise and fetch me your tunic," I say.

Her eyes open and she frowns a bit. She does not wish to leave the comfort and warmth of my bed, but it is her ability to leave such comforts that will strengthen her. "My lord?" she asks in confusion.

I am not pleased with her delay. My voice deepens and I frown. "I said rise and fetch me your tunic. *Now*, Carina."

She looks hurt, angry even, but she obeys nonetheless. She retrieves the silky tunic from earlier and hands it to me, looking like a child who is ready to stomp her foot in anger. If she does, I am prepared to discipline her. I have not become who I am by allowing disobedience. She takes a step toward the bed, and I shake my head.

"Not yet," I say. "Go into the hall and seek Lystava. Ask her to bring a pitcher of water."

Her frown deepens, and she reaches for the tunic. I lift my hand so that the tunic is out of her reach, wagging a finger. "Oh, no. I did not give you permission to wear this."

Her eyes widen and her mouth forms a perfect O. "My lord!" she protests. "I am to go, dressed in nothing?"

I simply nod once and gesture for her to go, reaching over and giving her bottom a sharp swat to get her going.

She turns back to me, still frowning. "And if I say no? You will punish me?"

I purse my lips at her, maintaining my stern position. "Certainly."

Her feet drag as she approaches the door, her head hung low. She goes as far as placing her hand on the doorknob before I raise my voice. "Stop! That is enough. Come back to me, now."

She turns back to me in confusion, looking first to the door and then back to me. I beckon for her to approach me. Dragging her feet, she approaches me, her brow furrowed. "My lord? I did not disobey you. Are you going to punish me?"

I shake my head. "Why would I punish you if you have not disobeyed me?" I ask.

She shakes her head.

When she reaches me, I draw her close to me and tuck a strand of hair behind her ear. "I am teaching you to obey me, Carina. I will not betray your modesty."

She nods, as understanding dawns on her. "You wish to taunt me, then?" she asks. "To tease me?"

"No, Carina," I say, shaking my head. "I wish to train you. Now join me in bed."

She does. I draw her onto my chest. "The time is coming," I explain to her. "The time when you will have to obey me whether you like it or not, whether your heart tells you otherwise, and your mind contradicts me. You must obey me."

She nods into my chest, still looking confused and a bit angry. She will learn.

"Sleep now, Carina. Tomorrow there is much to be done."

As she falls asleep, I listen to her breathing. I feel the darkness settling in around me. My instincts tell me she is troubled as she sleeps. I am not sure what it is that troubles her, but I will make it my mission to find out.

CHAPTER ELEVEN

Carina

He has woken before me the next day. I wake, but after briefly glancing to notice the indentation on the pillow next to me, I shut my eyes quickly, allowing them to remain shut for the time being. It is the only privacy I have in this place, when my eyes are closed, my thoughts unable to be read by others.

I assess my situation. I am unfamiliar with any type of pain that lasts. On Freanoss, pain is extinguished immediately, with either medication or electric nerve stimulation. Now, it seems my entire body is uncomfortable. My head throbs, my backside and upper thighs sting from the lashes of his belt, and between my legs, I feel a dull but welcome sort of ache. My muscles are sore as well. I wish for my head to stop throbbing, but as I focus on the other pain I am experiencing, I feel an unfamiliar thumping of my heart. I remember how his eyes watched me when his hands went to his waist to remove his leather belt. The feel of his hand on my lower back, holding me in position while he whipped me. It stung—oh, how it stung! I do not wish to be whipped again. But then why do I clench my thighs together at the memory, my breath shallower? And the ache between my legs. It hurts, but I'm also confused. I have been taught on Freanoss that coupling is vile, and my experience with the king was hardly vile. It was... *exquisite*. I lost control completely, moaning with pleasure, my head thrown back in ecstasy as every nerve in my body seemed to zing in response to his ways.

Despite all of that, a part of me longs for the ways of Freanoss once again. I *feel* too much here on Avalere. It is disconcerting. I dislike the loss of control I have here... the loss of control in all ways. I think back on the night before when he ordered me to leave the room unclothed, how I felt I had little choice—humiliate myself or face his certain punishment. And when he called me back to him—why? To prove that he could? Anger rises even now as I lie in bed.

"Time to rise, little one," I hear from the foot of the bed, the king's deep voice startling me. He chuckles. "I am sorry to scare you," he said. "But we have little time to stay here. Much has to happen today, and lying abed will not ready our cause."

I open my eyes, but quickly shut them again, wincing. The brightness in the room hurts my head. I hear him come to my side, and feel the bed sinking under his weight. His large, warm hand descends on my head, a bit of the pain lifting with the pressure of his palm.

"Are you in pain?" he asks.

I nod. "Yes, my lord."

"Tell me. Where does it hurt?"

My stomach churns from the effort it takes to speak through the pain. "My head," I whisper. "My head aches. There is throbbing in my temples and pressure."

"Is that all?"

I shake my head. "My... well, between my legs aches as well. And my..." I pause, tucking my head in embarrassment, before I continue. "Where you whipped me. My thighs and backside burn as well."

He smoothes his hand over my head. "I will relieve you

from your headache." His hand travels to my bottom and squeezes. "I will let you feel the ache of your punishment, as a reminder to obey me." His fingers travel over my hip and I gasp as he moves his hand firmly between my legs, spreading them apart, dipping his fingers between my folds, already slick and ready for him. "And when time allows later, I will ease the pain between your legs."

I nod, embarrassed yet thankful. At this point I will merely trust what he says. I need relief from the pain. He stands and I feel the sudden loss, but keep my eyes shut. I hear the musical twinkling of the bell, and the knock on the door. Murmured voices, and moments later, he approaches me.

"Sit up, Carina," he instructs. Though it is hard to move, I obey, trying to shift my weight to the side to avoid my backside hitting the sheets, but that is impossible. I give up, wincing as the cool sheets hit my punished skin. He does not react. He does not regret punishing me.

On the tray in his hand, he has a dark cup with steam rising from it. "Drink your tea, now," he says. "I've placed your remedy in it. It is bitter but will quickly bring you comfort."

I do not like their tea, and frown as he hands me the cup. I do wish for relief from the pain, however. I eye the cup warily, lifting it to my nose and sniffing. It smells bitter and strong. Though there is only a small amount in the cup, I do not wish to drink it.

"Is there nothing else I can take?" I ask.

His lips purse, crossing his arms across his chest as he eyes me, though his eyes twinkle.

"Nothing else," he says. "And you have precisely one minute to finish that entire cup before I take you across my lap and renew that sting you feel in your backside."

I huff out a breath. Savage!

He uncrosses his arms, coming to me, and I quickly lift the cup and take a hasty sip. It is hot but not scalding, so I am able to drink it. It doesn't taste pleasant, but it's acceptable. I frown, handing him the cup.

"Happy?" I snap, before I realize what I am saying. He has me in his arms, and I cringe. I've spoken hastily, and may now incur punishment. But he merely sits against the pillows and lays me across his chest so that my cheek is flush against the curly hair and his bare skin.

"I am happy you obeyed, yes, Carina," he says. "But your tone of voice needs improvement." He draws his hand through my hair, entwining the locks in his large fingers before he gives a little tug. It hurts my already sore head. "So let's try that again."

"Yes, my lord!" I say, eager to avoid punishment.

He nods, accepting my answer. "Very good, little one. How is the pain in your head now?"

I close my eyes and assess. It is gone. The pain has completely subsided.

"Better," I say.

He nods, as his hand travels down my back to my backside and he squeezes. The sting is renewed. I gasp, squirming, as he moves further down the bed and spins me so that I am over him and he beneath me. "Move this way," he orders, positioning me so that my head is near his legs and my lower body above him. "Your sweetness over my mouth."

Does he mean? *No!* He cannot!

"My lord!" I gasp.

"Do it," he orders, moving my hips roughly, lining me up so that his mouth is now under my sex, already pulsing with need. My hands grasp his large hips as he opens his legs. He is ready for me. "Relax," he says. "Close your eyes for a moment."

I obey, still straddling his face, my own cheek resting against the small hairs along his strong, muscular thighs. I feel his hands reach for my nipples and squeeze, the very moment his tongue strokes along my folds. I gasp from the sensation, as he swirls my sensitive nub with his warm, sensual tongue. My hips buck from the feeling. I gasp as he pinches my nipples again, then kneads my breasts, his tongue moving persistently, my pleasure mounting as he licks lazily then sucks, laps then sucks, again and again.

"My lord," I gasp, at the verge of losing control, my cheek against his thigh, my hands grasping his legs, panting as he strokes and sucks, his hands moving in time to my nipples as his tongue brings me right to the cusp of ecstasy.

"Come, little one," he whispers, the momentary loss of his mouth while he speaks unbearable. "Now," he breathes, one final stroke of his tongue all I need.

My eyes squeeze tight, my pleasure bursts within me, waves of ecstasy pulsing through me. My hips jerk from the intensity, but he holds my aching backside to keep me from escaping, his tongue torturing me as I continue to climax, hard. Finally, I collapse on him. His hands reach for me, pulling me over his chest as he runs a hand through my hair, caressing.

"Good girl," he croons. "I will pleasure you with my tongue until the ache heals, and then I will take you again."

I squirm, feeling thankful, sated, and exposed all at once. He continues, as if we've just had a cup of tea together, or gone for a leisurely stroll. "Now you will prepare for the day. Dress. I will fetch Lystava to arrange your hair and clothing. We have a visit to pay someone, and I must meet with my counsel. There is much you and I need to learn about one another that will be aided by one who knows more than us both."

I look at him in surprise. "Do we?" I ask.

He nods. "Yes," he says. "I will know what your purpose here is. Are they coming for you?"

I blink at the unexpected question, unwilling to state my purpose. Until now, he hasn't pressed me hard for information.

"My lord?"

He frowns as he gets to his feet, lifting me to mine and bringing me over to get dressed. He stands me in front of the bed as he goes to the wardrobe and fetches another blue tunic, this one a darker shade than the one I wore the day before. "To make sure you are safe," he says. "Are they coming for you? Must I prepare for an attack on my people, a rescue mission of sorts?"

"No, my lord," I whisper. That is not the way of the Freanossians. I have never known them to come for anyone.

The stab of loss hits me between the chest. Though I've gone my entire life without the aid of human companionship, I wonder now if it would be different for me if I *did* have someone to come fetch me. Someone who cared if I was hurt, or lost, or imprisoned.

"No father? No brothers? No military to defend your honor?"

I shake my head as he slips the tunic on me. "The military defends the planet, not my honor."

He frowns, and speaks low, as if to himself. "A strange land indeed," he murmurs. "So strange. We must hasten to the Wise One while there is still time."

I wonder at his words. The tunic now covering my body, I feel the gnawing at my stomach, reminding me it is time to eat. I am learning.

He is distracted as he calls for food, his fingers stroking his beard as he paces the room. A moment later, the man he called Arman knocks and enters.

"My lord?"

The king looks at him, his brow furrowed. "I must hasten to the Wise One this morning. I met with Idan last night and heard the briefing, but we shall convene again today at noon. See that all meet here, at the \cabinet."

Arman bows his head, acknowledging the king's order, and takes his leave, at the same time Lystava brings a tray of food. The king doesn't even speak to her, merely gestures hastily for her to leave the food. I give her a small smile, nodding my thanks, as she rests the food on the table.

When the door shuts, I reach for the pretty, round purple fruit, prepared to take a bite, but a low growl stops me. I look up, surprised to find him glaring at me.

"You have permission to eat?" he asks. I look away in embarrassment. It seems that I am becoming familiar here, and have forgotten that he expects me to wait for him. I drop the food and hang my head.

"No, my lord," I whisper.

He pulls out a chair from the table and sits, his large frame foreboding as he scowls at me. His knees spread apart, his hands flat on his thighs, his eyes never leaving mine.

"Come here," he orders.

Tentatively, I stand, dragging my feet as I walk to him. Am I to be punished? He said yesterday he will no longer warn me, but advance my training. He points wordlessly to the table and says one word. "Hands."

Swallowing, I obediently place my hands on the table, my back to him now. He places one hand on my lower back. I am shaking with nerves. Without another word, he delivers three sharp stings in rapid succession, hard enough that I gasp out loud. My cheeks flush with embarrassment as he puts his hand to my waist and spins me around to face him. He chucks a large finger under my chin, his dark eyes boring into mine, his whiskers appearing even heavier and darker than the day before, the dark slashes of the markings on his skin underscoring his inherent danger and power.

"You will obey me," he says. "You will wait until I eat before you do."

I nod. "Yes, my lord," I whisper, not trusting my voice.

He does not release my chin. "The next time you eat before I do, I will have you fetch your hairbrush, and spank you with the flat. Am I clear?"

Lystava placed the solid, varnished brush on my vanity when she bathed me the day before. I do not wish to have him spank me with it. I nod quickly. "Yes, my lord."

He nods briefly, then pulls me down upon his knee, ignoring my wince when my backside hits his leg. He plucks a grape.

"Open," he growls.

This is not the laidback meal of before, but rather hasty. I open my mouth as he feeds me, then he hands me a cup of the white liquid I had before.

"Drink."

Automatically, I obey, finding this has become easier as I enjoy the delicious food, a sweet bread speckled with soft, dark fruits and spread with warmed butter. I drink from the cup, and the creamy, delicious liquid complements the tang of various fruits. After a time, he simply hands me the food, allowing me to feed myself, after he seems satisfied that I will obey him.

When we have both eaten our fill, he leaves the food upon the plate, the blankets on the bed askew, and stands, pushing me to my feet. "I must get ready to leave. I need a few minutes of preparation." He points to the corner of the room, a stark, empty place. "You will stand there while I get ready, and while you do, you will think about your obedience to me today. Focus on submitting yourself to my will."

Confused, I move to obey, walking to the corner of the room before turning to look at him in bewilderment. "Like this, my lord?" He's never instructed me to stand here before, and I am confused by the request.

He smiles, his eyes lighter when there are little crinkles around the edges. He walks to me, places his hands gently on my hips, and spins me around, so that I am facing the wall.

"Like this," he says into my ear. The warmth and nearness of him makes my nipples harden. He rakes his hands down my arms and grasps my hands, entwining them behind my back. "Clasp your hands behind your back," he whispers. "Think about how you will obey me. How you will defer to my authority, and do as I ask. Think about how I will reward your obedience by bringing you pleasure." His hands travel to my backside, kneading the tender skin. "Think about how your backside belongs to me, and how I will punish you if you disobey me."

Need pulses between my legs as his tongue rakes across my collarbone. "So delicious," he murmurs. "I could eat you." His teeth sink into the tender spot at my neck. I gasp, but keep my hands clasped as he's told me to. "Another mark for you," he says. "Another mark to show that you are mine." He growls, the sensual pain of his mouth and teeth causing the ache between my legs to throb, though he's pleasured me just a short time ago. It seems every time he brings me to ecstasy, my need for him grows. I gasp as he thrusts a finger under my tunic and pumps between my legs briefly, before drawing his finger out, trailing across my backside, and then slapping my bottom, hard.

"Stay there," he orders.

I stifle a cry as he pulls away from me, his voice, his warmth, and his presence somehow the only things keeping me upright. When he's gone, I stand with a greater effort. I have been told I must think about my submission to him. And truthfully, as I stare at the blank wall in front of me, with the certain knowledge that if I leave my position I face punishment, I find it a bit easier to think about obeying him. I find myself thinking about how I will wait demurely to be fed, and come to him when he calls, listening for his voice and hastening to obey. I will wear what he puts on me, and walk with him in the marketplace. If he desires my body, I will submit myself—I freeze, mid-thought. *What am I doing?*

I am not here to submit to this savage. I am here to save my planet. I am not going to sink to the barbaric ways of his people! I have been trained already, to listen to him, drawn to the enigmatic pull of his power.

But no. I will *not* stand here and think about my submission to him.

I will stand here and think of my purpose here on Freanoss. When we move to the forest, I must find my possessions. I must prove to myself he lies, and that my purpose in coming here was not in vain.

The walk through the marketplace is different this time, though the strings of guards flanking either side of us has not altered, their measured footsteps in time with ours. Today, there are no vendors in the marketplace.

"Why is the marketplace empty today?" I ask him. He doesn't look at me, merely holds my hand, his eyes still fixed ahead, as he answers me.

"Market days are only a few days a week," he says. "Today is not a sale day."

"Oh," I say, wondering then where he is taking me. I remember for a moment that I am to obey him, the stark corner of the wall coming to my mind's eye as I trot to keep up with him. It is better to follow him and not ask questions. Past the marketplace we go, and now we have arrived at where he convened with his men yesterday. Just beyond this place is where I met the robbers. Where he found me.

We move past the pavilion, heading further into the area in the woods than we did yesterday. My heartbeat quickens. My communication device is nearby, just a dozen or so paces from where we are now. I recognize the area and can even see the 'X' mark from where I am. He leads me on, to a darker area in the woods, and now he is telling his followers to leave us be, shooing them away. I look at him in surprise. Why is it that he has taken me to the woods, and now wishes for us to be alone? But he is merely making them step several yards beyond us. He doesn't wish for us to be completely alone. It is then I realize there is a dark, hidden hovel in the woods. It is camouflaged, with dark leaves and wooden planks for the door, walls, and roof. Vines entwine the doorway and walls but it is the only adornment. Beside the leaves and such, the little abode is nearly completely hidden. I am entranced.

"Carina," the king says, drawing me closer to him. "Remember your obedience to me," he says, warning in his voice.

I nod.

"It is my wish you do not speak unless I give you leave."

I am still confused, as he approaches the door and knocks sharply. At first, there is no answer. He frowns. I hide a smile. He is not used to having to wait for anyone, or anything. He knocks a second time, harder, and this time I hear a rustling within.

I hear a growl and thumping and bumping on the other side of the door. To my surprise, the king raises his hand to knock a third time, this time undisguised anger on his countenance, but the little doorway is dragged open, creaking and groaning, as if it hasn't been opened in decades.

In front of us stands an elderly man, wizened with age, his hair white as snow, eyes tiny and shrewd behind a pair of metal spectacles. He looks up with curiosity at the king, and then me, and it takes him a moment before his eyes widen in surprise. He dips his head. "My lord," he greets, then turns to me. "My lady." He steps back, gesturing for us to come in. I follow the king.

The moment we cross his threshold, the little man attempts to bend on one knee, but the king sees his effort and immediately stops him. "Do not bow to me," he says. "You are pardoned from such expectations. My time is short and our visit must be hasty, but there are many things I wish to discuss with you."

"Certainly, my lord," the man says, going ahead of us to a small room, with a sofa and chairs, and a roaring fire in the fireplace. If the king's home is old-fashioned, this little hovel is positively ancient. I hear thin notes of music coming from some place, though I'm not sure from where. There are odd bits of papers here and there, and books, *so* many books, piled far and wide, on shelves, sideways and diagonally, stacked as high as the ceiling in teetering heaps. The man makes his way over to where an iron stove sits, a kettle spewing steam, and shuts off the heat. "Can I fetch you something to eat?" he asks. His voice is husky and warbles. I wonder at the man's age. The elderly do not exist on Freanoss, and until the king mentioned to me how my planet does away with the aged, I have never given this much thought.

"No, no," the king says impatiently, taking a seat on the sofa and tugging my hand so that I sit down hard next to him. "I have much to discuss with you. We have no need of food."

The man nods, gingerly sitting in a wooden rocking chair across from us. "Before we begin, may I ask why you have a woman of Freanoss with you?"

The king's eyes widen in surprise. "How do you know she is from Freanoss? I have not given leave for anyone to divulge her home."

The man waves an impatient hand dismissively. "It is one of the gifts," he says. "I am able to tell the planet or origin of anyone by the smell, look, and feel of them." His eyes come to me. They soften, as he takes me in, from the top of my head to my feet. Neither the king nor I speak as the older man observes me. "He has marked you," he says with a nod, and then his eyes widen. "You went into the circle, woman?"

His tone is curious. I swallow, looking to the king, who nods, giving me permission to speak. "I did," I said. "I did not know... what it was."

"Mmm," he says softly. "And you now know the errors of your ways?"

I look at him, shaking my head. I do not know to what he refers. He leans back in his chair and address me with the patience of a teacher with a student. "You now know that you belong to our king as his possession, with no recourse to Freanoss outside of battle? The king has informed you of your obedience to him, of that I am sure."

I look away from him, twisting my hands in my lap. I dislike how much he knows about me without me having to tell him anything.

"Answer him, Carina," the king instructs, his voice deep

and stern.

I look up at the king, who raises his brows and waves a finger toward the man. But when I turn to the man, he is looking at us both quizzically.

"Carina?" he asks. "You have named her? The people of Freanoss have no distinction."

I look from one to the other. The king nods. "I have."

Understanding dawns on him. "And so it has begun," he says softly. "She clings to you?"

As if in on cue, I instinctively move closer to the king, who places a warm, possessive hand on my neck and squeezes gently. "It has begun," he says.

"I see," the man says. "You may call me Isidor," he says to me. He then turns back to the king.

"In here, I am Aldric," the king says.

"And what is it I can do for you, my lord?" Isidor asks. For some reason, the 'lord' seems more a casual reference and less a show of respect. This man, filled with greater knowledge and wisdom than Aldric, pays homage to his lord, yet it is of a different caliber than the others.

"I have questions of the ways of her people," he says. "What it is I can expect, now that she is my possession. The best means to teach her obedience to me."

The man smiles to himself. "You have at least surmised that the ways of Freanoss are far different than those of Avalere. Freanoss garnered the scientific minds and progressive influences at the council of the New Dawn, and its people advanced technologically at a far more rapid pace. You know when Avalere was founded at the New Dawn, that the ancients were the ones to populate Avalere. We did away with most scientific advances and returned to a simpler time, keeping only such measures that would keep the Avalerians healthy. As the years have progressed, so, too, have the differences between the two countries." His eyes twinkle. "Tell me, my lord, what your Carina thinks about your insistence on teaching her obedience?"

Aldric frowns. "She has resisted, though she is learning

it is best she obey me."

Isidor smiles again. "Certainly. As far as your teaching methods, and the means to teach her obedience, I advise you do whatever you think is best. You are, after all, the king. She will, like most members of the human species, respond well to both punishment and rewards, though over time, as your bond strengthens, she will desire to obey you more of her own will."

Aldric nods, and I squirm. I dislike that they are talking about me as if I am not there.

I wish to ask a question, and remember a moment before I speak that I must have permission. I pat the king's knee, and he nods his approval.

"What has begun?" I ask. "I do not understand."

Isidor takes his eyes from Aldric and looks to me.

"Your bonding," he says. "It is the ancient way. Your people have *your* methods of progressing." He shrugs. "We have ours. Mates are chosen, and once chosen, bonding is what keeps you connected, together."

Is this why my body yearns to be close to Aldric, even as I resist his control, his power and the enigmatic pull?

"What if I don't want to be... *bonded*?" I ask, a note of petulance in my voice, for I am torn. Aldric has done exquisite, unfathomable things to my body. I feel alive more so than I ever have. And yet... he punishes me. I am his property, to do with as he wills. And I want to return to my home planet, where everything is familiar.

Isidor places his fingertips together. I feel the king stiffen next to me, moving closer, as if he's prepared to grab me if I go to run away.

"Don't wish to be bonded?" Isidor asks quietly, his eyes growing serious, his mouth turning down at the edges. "My girl, you forfeited your rights when you stepped foot in the ring. As the king's mate, you may not reverse the bond that now embraces you both." He turns to Aldric. "Under what grounds did she become yours? Did you choose her from the circle?"

"I did," Aldric explains. "However, she brought a weapon into our presence, and I saved her from execution. I took it as my duty to punish her."

I look from Aldric to Isidor, who nods.

Isidor addresses me. "You brought a weapon to Avalere. You arrived here against the treaty put forth by our people. You broke the agreement, and as such are subject to the laws of Avalere. You belong to the king. Resisting bonding will be to your detriment, and once the process has begun there is no reversing it." He pauses. "There is a concept on Avalere you are unfamiliar with on Freanoss." He nods, as if to himself. "There are many, actually, but an overarching belief in one's *prana vitae*—your life force—means that you have an aura about you. Aldric has no doubt observed your *prana vitae* in depth." He looks to the king. "No?"

Aldric nods. "Certainly. It is the way of the warrior to observe all, and it was *all* of her, not just her stunning beauty, spirit, and courage that drew me to her to begin with."

He states all this as if it were fact. He's not trying to flatter me. He believes what he says, and though I feel myself blush from the praise, I also feel quite vulnerable as the two of them continue to discuss me.

"Though," Aldric continues, "I must know of her purpose for coming before we continue."

I freeze. "Why do you ask this?"

Aldric frowns. "It was my wish that as you and I grew closer together, you would want to tell the truth of your own accord. But you haven't, and now that we are in the presence of Isidor, it will be far more difficult for you to tell a falsehood."

My eyes widen. Aldric has been cunning.

"What does this mean?" I whisper.

Isidor speaks first. "It means that while you are in the presence of both me, an ancient of Avalere, and your king, to whom you are bonded, it will be near impossible for you to *lie*."

My heart beats rapidly, my palms sweaty. I open my mouth, but I can do nothing but speak the truth, even as I fear the reaction to my transparency. I wish to close my mouth, but my voice carries clearly in the small room. "I came to spy," I say, my eyes closing as the words utter from my mouth unbidden. "I was sent to find what methods the Avalerians will use against Freanoss while you rob us of our resources. Freanoss is rich in natural resources needed by the Avalerians, and we have been robbed. It is my duty to inform the Freanossians so we can thwart your efforts."

Aldric nodded. "It is no more than I expected," he says with a shrug toward Isidor, then, turning to me, "but Carina, you must understand you've been lied to. We are not stealing from Freanoss. The Freanossians have taken my sister as hostage, as *they* wish to pilfer the gems of my people. The accusations against *us* were meant to distract us from their real purpose. We have intelligence of this attempt, and the evidence is overwhelming."

"No," I whisper, but it seems that along with my inability to lie comes the ability to decipher the truth. I know in my heart what he says now is true. I've been used. I did not serve a real purpose. I should not be here.

"And now," Isidor says to Aldric. "You wish to know of her past?"

I suddenly feel very exposed and petulant. It doesn't seem right that they are talking as if I'm not there. It's unsettling. And I'm beginning to understand now that I am bound to Avalere, to Aldric, even more than I imagined.

"You could've asked me," I mumbled, feeling angry at how this all has transpired. Aldric reaches his hand to my leg and squeezes, a warning gesture to remind me to behave.

"And you could've stayed on Freanoss," Isidor says with a frown. "Your people should've warned you of our ways. But because they did not, you now suffer for your ignorance." He pauses, eyeing me thoughtfully, his voice softening when he speaks. "But is it really punishment, Carina?"

I think of the zing of Aldric's leather on my naked skin, his teeth nipping at my waist, the tugs of my hair, and time I have spent over his knee. I think of the ways he has brought me to ecstasy, feeding me, clothing me, and soothing me. I think of how he would have killed to protect me.

I do not respond. Isidor turns back to Aldric.

"The regulatory pills taken by the Freanossians suppress appetites. *All* forms of hunger. This, I surmise, you have noted."

Aldric nods, and I blush.

"There are some minor physical differences you will note, over time, but those can be easily remedied." Over time? My stomach clenches as I contemplate my future. I sit up stiffly, pulling away from Aldric. Isidor eyes me thoughtfully.

"Think before you act, young one," he says. "Perhaps barbaric ways are not to your liking." He shrugs, and his eyes wander before coming back to mine. "Or perhaps they *are*."

I get to my feet. I have had enough of this.

But I stand for mere seconds before Aldric pulls my hand and pulls me straight down onto his lap. He wraps his arms around me and holds tight, holding me upon his knee. I feel his mouth at my ear as he whispers, "One more move. One more disobedient act, and I take you across my knee right here, with an audience." He sits back up. I feel the struggle go out of me, as they continue to discuss Freanoss. It is fascinating, the history of my people, and even more fascinating to hear that this ancient man knows things I, a resident of Freanoss, never knew. It seems hours later when finally, Aldric indicates it is time for us to leave. He rises and bows to Isidor.

"I thank you for your time," he says. "Perhaps I may return at a later date?"

Isidor returns the bow. "Always, my lord. You are always welcome in my home." He turns to me and inclines his head. "As are you."

I follow Aldric to the exit. I will keep in mind that I am welcome. I wonder if his offer still stands if ever I wish to hide.

CHAPTER TWELVE

Aldric

I wish I could give Carina freedom to wander while I am at counsel, but yesterday she escaped my most trusted servant. Though she has been honest with me in the presence of Isidor, she has confessed to being a Freanossian spy. If she were not mated to me, the punishment would be execution. Today, she must stay with me.

"We have counsel and I must be briefed this morning," I say. "You must stay by my side." I aim to enjoy our walk back to the castle. It is here that I can introduce her to the gardens of Avalere.

She frowns and pulls her hand away from mine. What is this resistance? I look at her curiously for her a moment, not responding. She seems conflicted and her coldness to me raises my ire. "Come here, Carina," I say, tugging her hand impatiently as my men flank our sides and we walk back toward the castle. She pulls away for a moment, but then seems to change her mind, as a mere second later, she draws near to me. Her eyes soften and her mouth parts. I am baffled by her sudden change.

"My king," she whispers, as she comes so close I have

now gathered her in my arms, the top of her head just below my chin, my arms encircling her small frame. She places both hands flat on my chest and whispers in my ear. "It is magical in this forest. May I not have just a moment alone with you? Without your servants watching?"

She is fetching, this one. I am happy to give her just a moment alone.

"Away," I say to my servants. "Give us one moment, please."

They scatter for a moment. I turn back to my Carina, my hand on the back of her neck as I lean in to her. Her mouth parts, and I lean in to kiss her, pleased at her desire for me. But as my mouth meets hers, I feel a sudden sharp pain as her knee connects between my legs, shooting pain radiating as I shout out loud. I reach for her, intent on pulling her to me, but she has already slipped out of my fingers and is running, fast, in the opposite direction of the hovel, back to where we first met.

I see red, the heat of my fury momentarily slowing me as I growl and race after her. She will be punished. But first, she must be caught.

Nimbly, she races beneath tree branches, ducking low-lying limbs, and turns a corner in the forest. I turn to face her, encumbered by my larger frame, but when I turn, she is now vanished. She has completely disappeared. What witchcraft is this?

"Carina!" I shout, fury making my voice louder and hoarser than it normally is, my voice shaking in anger.

I call my servants back to me and set them searching, and for a time, it is no use. She is nowhere to be found. I will not leave this area until it is scoured, and my woman is returned to me. She will pay dearly for her attempt to escape. We search for several minutes, when several yards ahead of me, I see her, the telltale flash of dark hair on white skin, behind the greens of the forest. She is reaching down for something, desperately lifting leaves and throwing them in the air as she looks. I approach silently, the tread of the warrior now soft as I do not wish to betray my presence. So intent is she on finding what it is she is looking for, that she does not see me in the shadows. I continue my pursuit, leaving my servants behind, until she is a few paces away from me. But still, I watch, as she flips leaves and looks, muttering to herself under her breath, looking over her shoulder but not at where I stand. I shake my head.

"What is it you seek, Carina?" I ask, my voice carrying through the stillness to her. She gasps, her hand coming to her mouth as her eyes meet mine. She knows she was wrong to trick me, to strike me, and to run. She knows she is caught.

She knows I must punish her.

Her lips purse and her eyes shutter, the light I have seen in them no longer visible. She is a cornered animal, prepared to pounce and claw if necessary. I talk in a low, stern voice as I walk toward her.

"Is there a portal, sweetness?" I ask conversationally. "Hidden, yet accessed by a touch of a button?" Her eyes flit from side to side. "Or perhaps you dropped something of importance to you? A token of Freanoss?" I am now within arm's reach of her. She is crouching like a tiger, prepared to pounce.

But I am stronger. And I am her master.

"Or perhaps," I continue, "you are looking for your communication device?"

Her eyes widen and fill, pools of blue both sad and desperate. Her lower lip begins to tremble as I now reach her, drawing her close to me in a grip so tight she cannot escape.

"How did you know?" she whispers.

I take one hand and brush a piece of hair off her dampened forehead. "The day you were attacked," I say. "I knew you came in the forest for good reason. There are few methods of travel between our two countries. I knew there was either a portal, or something you had hidden. We have our methods. We found your hidden things. They have been locked away, and you shall not access them without my permission."

Her eyes cast down. "Yes, my lord," she says, but I do not trust her submission. Not after she betrayed me. Not after she ran.

"I expected better from you," I chide, anger causing my words to be low, reproachful. "I could have chosen much harder methods to train you than I have, and yet you resist my gentler methods."

She gapes at me. "*Gentle?*"

I merely take her hand. It is time to bring her home.

It is time she is punished.

I do not wish to draw attention to us as we make our way back to the palace. We speak conversationally. I tell her of the day ahead, what we will do. "You will work on handiwork with Lystava while I speak to Arman, and we make our decisions. When I am finished for the day," I say nonchalantly, "I will punish you."

A small moan escapes her. I look to her, and she's gone pale. I scowl. I wish for her to be nervous in anticipation of her punishment. After even Isidor has explained to her that she is mine, she has the nerve to trick me, hurt me, and try to escape? Oh, no. She will answer for this.

At the palace, I send the guards on their way and beckon for Lystava to join us. She walks, trotting to keep up with our quick paces.

"Lystava, my men will join us a few minutes, and I wish for Carina to be occupied, near me, when we meet."

Lystava's eyes widen. Women do not accompany us to counsel, but my command trumps tradition.

"If you wish it so, my lord," she murmurs.

I turn quickly. "It *is* my wish," I order. "Now find something with which she can occupy herself."

Lystava scurries away, as I take Carina to our room. I take some bread and cheese from a servant, and instruct Carina to sit down, placing the platter on the table. To my surprise, she reaches for a slice of bread, but when she sees my eyes burning into hers, she quickly takes her hand back and eyes me, wide-eyed.

"Good," I say. "You are learning. Had you eaten that before I'd given you leave, I'd have taken you across my knee without another word." I take a large bite of bread, chew, and swallow, before I gesture for her to do the same. She does, hungrily eating the bread I've given her. I dislike the feeling between us, her disobedience and my duty to punish her hanging in the air between us.

After we've eaten, Lystava joins us, a skein of ivory yarn and needles in one hand, and several books in the other. I nod.

"Very good. Now go to the antechamber and get her situated." I turn to Carina. "Come here," I say, gesturing.

She comes to me, dragging her feet. "My lord?"

I am so angry with her that her submissive words stoke the fires of my temper. I merely raise a brow. She looks down, as if afraid to speak. I do not feel badly for her. I am so angry with her, she is lucky she is not over my knee now. I do not trust myself to punish her when I am so furious.

I look at her, barely tempering the anger I feel. "You will sit by Lystava. You will not leave your chair. You will not speak to my men. You will not interrupt me during our meeting. Do you understand?"

"Yes, my lord," she says miserably. She dislikes my displeasure. It is well that she does.

"Go, then," I say, waving my hand for her to follow Lystava.

Would that I did not have to meet with my men. I dislike the discord between us as much as she. I am eager to punish her and be rid of the breach.

• • • • • • •

Arman sits at my left, and Idan at my right. Several more men from my ranks are with me, as we discuss our plans. I begin our meeting, keeping an eye on Carina in the other room. She is holding the fabric in her hands awkwardly. If I wasn't so angry with her, I'd find her fetching, her pretty mouth frowning as she looks at the cloth in her hand. I've no doubt that on Freanoss such activities are completely obsolete. Here, we value handmade goods. Lystava sits patiently, instructing my Carina.

"My lord?" I look back to Idan, startled. I have completely missed what he has said.

"I'm sorry. Please say that again, Idan," I say.

Idan nods and continues. "My lord, we have news of the inhabitants of Freanoss. Are you sure that you wish for your Carina be privy to this?"

My ire rises as I narrow my eyes at him. "Is Carina in the other room?" I ask.

He shakes his head, confused. "Well, certainly, my lord," he says. "Did you not know that she—"

I slam my hand on the table, and the men still. "Do you think I am unaware of her presence?"

Idan shakes his head.

"Then how dare you question my judgment? She is here because I will her to be. What harm will come of her hearing the news of Freanoss?"

Idan clears his throat. "The news of our plans, should she be able to communicate with those on Freanoss, could compromise security, my lord," he begins.

I silence him with a slash of my hand. "It is of no consequence," I insist. "She is not communicating to them." In my peripheral vision, she freezes.

Idan nods. "Yes, my lord. I am sorry, my lord."

I nod, as we continue.

Arman speaks next. "My lord, yesterday you were informed that your sister was discovered as a Freanossian hostage, held captive and not harmed, as we'd been led to believe."

I nod again.

"She has been brought to a distant planet and hidden, but she is to be returned to Freanoss in one week's time."

I nod. "We are to move at first light, after we've assembled our troops," I say. "I will have myself ready to lead."

Arman shakes his head. "No, my lord. The counsel has discussed this, and we are of the unanimous opinion that you must stay here. It is our belief that Freanoss is luring you to their planet so they can kill you, thereby leaving Avalere without a king. They wanted us to discover your sister's presence so that you would act. Instead, the counsel believes it is best you send a decoy ahead of you."

I stand, my anger raging within me. They held counsel behind my back? They seek to overthrow me?

"How dare you!" I am enraged at this news. In the anteroom, I see Carina drop the fabric, her hands coming to her mouth. Lystava reaches her hand out to soothe her, before I continue. "How could you do such a thing? I am not to be held at home when my sister is at the hands of those people!"

"My lord," Idan says, rising to his feet. "Please. We wanted to be prepared to present to you the strongest plan possible. We believe that a decoy is best, because they will suspect it is you while you still reign here on Avalere. Please. Sit down, my lord."

I sit, glaring, as Arman speaks to me. "Please, my lord. Allow me to be your decoy. You can trust the *Hisrach* to do their duty."

I look sharply at him. He is as dark as me, nearly as tall, with black hair that reaches longer than mine, plaited in the back. I'm too angry to dwell on this for the moment. Arman continues. "There is no need to decide at this moment. If we plan this correctly, my lord, all will be well. We will be able to retrieve your sister, keep you safe, and restore peace between Avalere and Freanoss."

"Peace?" I thunder, slamming my fist on the table yet again. "We will have peace when I've exacted vengeance on Freanoss." My sister did not deserve to be treated like a pawn. She has barely reached womanhood, and has yet to experience the joys of companionship with another. She deserves this, and so much more.

I see Carina sit up straighter in the other room as Arman responds to my insistence. "Certainly, my lord."

I take a deep breath, keeping my temper in check as I consider my options. "Did you bring to me further news of my Carina, and the Freanossians' concern of her whereabouts?" Though I am well within even interplanetary rights to keep her as mine, it would not be unheard of for her people to come and fetch her. "Have they sent anyone to come and get her? Should we be prepared?"

Idan and Arman look at each other. Idan's eyes quickly look to where Carina is. "No, my lord," Arman says finally, dropping his voice. "We do have news. The only concern was..." he pauses, "her communication device. It seems it is of great value."

I look to Carina. She has frozen, her hand now on a small book. The book falls to her lap. I wish now I hadn't been so arrogant as to insist they speak in front of me. Although I am angry with her... although I will punish her this evening... I do not wish for her to know of how little she is valued on Freanoss, so little that their greater concern is for the device she took with her. I sigh and try to look to her, but her eyes are cast down.

"Is that all?" I ask.

Idan's voice lowers and he speaks to me in a tone low enough that she cannot hear. "She is not free to return to Freanoss even if she wanted to, my lord. By law, she now belongs to you, and even if you were to forfeit ownership of her, she is considered defiled by her people."

I am filled with a different kind of fury toward the Freanossians. They do not wish to contest my ownership of her. Of my Carina?

No one is coming for her.

I run a hand over my face and sigh.

The room has darkened, the sun low on the horizon now. I lift my voice so that she may hear me. "Carina. Come here." My voice carries, stern and deep, through the great room and into the antechamber. She stands and begins to come to me, her head hung low. She hands her work to Lystava, who tucks it into a basket. Lystava follows behind her.

"My lord, are you prepared for your evening meal?" Lystava asks.

I shake my head. "We will have the evening meal in my chambers tonight," I instruct. "I wish to be left alone with Carina, but will summon you when I wish for us to take our meal."

Lystava bows low and takes her leave. Carina now stands in front of me. I rise, and take her hand, bringing it to my lips. My anger from earlier has now vanished. Though I still must punish her—she needs to be punished for what she's done—I am no longer angry. I feel badly for my little one, who has no one to come for her. But she must still learn obedience.

"It is time you come with me," I say. "We have something we need to address."

She hangs her head low, her eyes on the floor, as she shifts her weight nervously and nods. "Yes, my lord," she whispers.

I sigh. "Let us go to my chamber."

I walk with her slowly, holding her warm hand in mine. "What did you do while we held counsel?" I ask.

"I did something called *stitching*..." she says haltingly, as if she doesn't know the right word. I nod, encouraging her to continue, but she doesn't.

"And what did you think?"

She shrugs. "It seems useless, when we have machines to do such things."

It is a fair assessment. I nod. "Did you read?"

She shrugged. "A little."

My little one has much on her mind.

"Very well, Carina," I say, as we now approach my room. "Go wait for me in your chamber. I will call you to me when

I am ready." I thread my hands through her hair, drawing her head toward mine, and I give her a kiss upon her forehead. "We will move on with what needs to be done."

"Yes, my lord," she says, her voice a mere whisper.

I hate that I must still see to her punishment.

CHAPTER THIRTEEN

Carina

I wait for him in my room, my thoughts churning, choking me, a lump in my throat and my eyes stinging with tears. I nearly put myself against the corner to stare at the wall, as he's had me do earlier, to calm my churning mind, but decide instead to lie face down on my bed as I await the king.

The Freanossians care little for me. This I understand. If I were in their position, I would do the very same. Other human beings are not worth disrupting the normal course of events to fetch. And as Isidor explained to me, I have broken the laws my people failed to tell me were laws on Avalere. My servitude to the king is of their doing. Why would they come and fetch me?

And yet the king... Aldric... pounded the table in fury at the mere suggestion that he not fetch his sister.

I only have a vague idea of what a sister even is. I do know she is somehow related to him, as the Avalerians still have ancient familial connections. I know that that they shared the same parents.

I was shocked at his insistence on saving her.

If someone took *me* from him… would he be as insistent on fetching me?

And now, I am to be punished, as soon as he is ready for me. He doesn't seem as furious as he earlier was, and at least for this I am grateful. As I await my punishment, I wonder how it will be. Will he take me across his knee and use his hand? Or have me lie across the bed for his belt, as he did before? Oddly, I feel arousal stirring within me again. Though I am not eager for my punishment at all, I cannot help but feel aroused by the vision of him standing, his belt in hand, or the memory of being restrained while over his knee. I feel the pulse between my legs, dampness at the apex of my thighs, a throbbing low in my belly.

"Carina." His deep voice carries to my room. I stand, trembling. He is going to punish me. I still remember the licks of the sharp leather he used on me earlier, and I fear the worst, another whipping with his belt. Or perhaps he will use something else, something even more fierce than the leather?

He is staring at me sternly, his dark eyes serious. "You have disobeyed me, Carina," he says. There is a thread of regret in his voice. "Come to me."

The punishment for my deliberate disobedience will be firm, of that I have no doubt. When I shuffle to him, he reaches for me, drawing me between his legs. He lifts one large finger and places it under my chin, holding my eyes with his. "I told you that I would spank you if you disobeyed me. And you've chosen disobedience. The rules I've given you were for your own protection and wellbeing. Your disobedience put you in danger. And for that reason, I must punish you."

Surprisingly, my throat gets tight and my nose stings. Do I feel remorse for having disobeyed him? How could it be that I care about his displeasure? And even there is something about his firm but gentle declaration that has turned my insides around, my knees shaking, weak.

He releases me but only so he can take me by the waist

and position me over his knee.

"I was prepared to whip you," he says. "If it were but one hour ago, I would have. You tricked me. You hit me. And then you tried to escape." He pauses, his hand on my bare skin as he raises my tunic. "But I've changed my mind. Instead, I will punish you with my hand." His warm palm smooths my skin.

I am mortified. Oh, the shame! I wriggle on his lap, but a firm hand on my lower back holds me in place.

"You must be punished bare," he insists. "I want you to feel every stroke of your correction. My Carina, whether you wish to admit it or not, you are bonded to me." His voice lowers as he speaks to me. "You know that deep down inside, you do not wish to displease me."

Lifting his hand, he brings it down with a resounding *smack*! He pauses, a few beats between each spank. "Deliberate disobedience cannot be allowed," he explains, before he gives me another sharp swat. It burns, the sound of his palm striking my bare bottom sharp to my ears. But between strokes, he is caressing, his large, masterful hand roaming my stinging bottom before he continues. How can it be that through all of this, I am aroused? I feel the pulsing between my legs, my nipples hardening as they chafe against his knees. My thoughts churn as he spanks me, each slap of his palm painful yet somehow welcome. After three more swats, he pauses, and I realize I do not wish him to stop. I *need* to feel more. I am still tense upon his lap, holding onto his leg as he lifts his hand yet again.

"I have primed you," he says. "Now that you are warmed and ready, you can take more." His hand rests on the curve of my bottom. "And now you will."

The next slap of his hand on me takes my breath away. It is hard, vicious, biting. Before I recover, he gives me three more searing swats. I cry out, and without conscious thought, try to pull away from him, twisting my torso to stop the onslaught, but he is ready. His hand anchors my waist, bringing me back over his lap, and his leg traps mine. My hands flail out in front of me helplessly, but it is no use. He has me trapped, unable to escape, at his utter mercy. The sound of his palm smacking my skin mingles with my own cries. I close my eyes, the pain of his spanking me my most pressing thought. I must escape the pain.

"Noooo," I wail. "My lord, I am sorry." Could it be that moments before I wanted him to punish me? Now, all I can think of is getting away.

"You will obey me, Carina," he growls, applying swat after swat, my thighs burning, my bottom on fire, every inch of my exposed skin in agony. "And though you are sorry now, you will be sorrier when I am finished."

I cannot escape the pain. Fighting him has only gotten me restrained further. I have no choice now but to accept my correction.

"Ow, *ow, ohhhh*," I moan as his hand claps down mercilessly. My hands are fisted in front of me now, my eyes shut tight as tears stream down my cheeks. He pauses. Is he finished? Somehow, I know he is not. I feel his palm on my skin, his large hand seemingly covering the entire surface of my exposed bottom.

"There is no home for you now but with me," he says, the warmth of his hand roaming my punished skin. "Freanoss is no longer home, Carina. Your home is here. And as such, you will be taught to obey."

At the punishing feel of his palm, my emotions are released. They are not coming for me. No one is coming for me. I am exiled, and he knows it. Why has he reminded me of my most painful reality? Does he wish to hurt me with more than a spanking?

A painful cry echoes in the room, and I realize with a shock that it is my own. Freanossians do not cry like this.

What has he done to me?

I do not flinch as he spanks me again, one swat after another landing on my sore bottom. I do not fight him. I accept the punishment, my pain for not being worthy of my home, forever exiled to a foreign land, victim to whatever whims the savage desires. His *property*. I accept each biting slap of his palm against me as I weep, my tears falling and splashing on the floor in front of me, the pain driving every last tear from me. I do not even realize when he stops punishing me. I feel nothing but the tears that are rent from me as I cover my face with my hands, lying helplessly over his lap. I should not have tried to run from him. He is the only one, this savage warrior, who has ever cared for me, in whatever capacity he is capable. To where would I run now? If I somehow had even managed to get back to Freanoss, what would there be for me? Has my identity been wiped from their record? I am nothing but a useless number to them. All these thoughts and more have me weeping, the wretched sound of my complete loss of control the only sound in the chambers.

"Come here now," he says. I have never heard his voice so soft. Never has the strong feel of his hands on me been so welcome as he lifts me, turning me over on his lap and cradling me like a child. I bury my face on his chest as his arms encircle me, holding me so tightly it hurts. He rises with me, kissing the top of my head as he brings me to his bed, lying down with me still cradled in his arms. "Do not hold back, Carina. It is natural to weep as you do. Allow the tears to cleanse you."

I do not know what he means, but I have no power to stop my tears now even if I wanted to. They are rent from me, and it takes some time before finally, the tears abate and I am simply lying quietly on his lap as he holds me. He does nothing but hold me.

It is all that I need. It is like a cocoon, being held like this, against his bare chest, his heartbeat under my cheek. I am enveloped in his scent, surrounded by his strength. He has taken from me the burden of anything but feeling.

When my tears finally cease, I hear nothing but our breath, mine ragged and his slowed. I feel exhausted. My eyes are swollen, my head throbbing. I close my eyes to drown out the pain, but it does not stop.

"Do you cry because I punished you?" he whispers.

I nod. It is that, and so much more, but yes, I do cry because I was punished.

"Are there more reasons for your tears, little one?" he asks softly.

"Yes, my lord," I whisper, my voice a mere whisper. "So much more." But how can I put it into words?

Fortunately, he does not wish for me to do so and his voice is so tender as he speaks in low, soothing tones. "Home is a place where one is safe, Carina, where one is welcome and loved. Was Freanoss such a place for you?"

He knows it was not. But still, I must answer. In my punished, subdued state I can do nothing but answer truthfully. "No, my lord."

His arms tighten. "It is as I thought, then," he says to himself. "We will speak no more of this for now. For now, it is my duty to minister to you."

CHAPTER FOURTEEN

Carina

He releases me onto the bed, and to my surprise, I resist. I cannot have him apart from me. I feel as if he's dropped me, though he still lies beside me. I reach back for him, not yet ready for him to stop holding me. I am afraid of even lying here without him now.

"Ah," he says, nodding to himself. "You are not ready."

I shake my head. I am not. I must cling to him.

"This will be interesting, going about my duties with a half-naked woman clinging to me," he murmurs to himself. It takes a minute for me to realize he's teasing me. I lift my head from his chest and look at him curiously as he continues. "They may question why I'm holding you on my lap at counsel." It seems as if he's considering his choices. "And I may need a larger horse or at least a saddle if I'm to have you on my back or in my arms the whole time I ride..."

"My lord!" I protest, and despite trying to stay serious, I cannot help but laugh. "You cannot be serious!"

"Meals can be taken together," he says, then he perks up, his eyes twinkling. "And *bathing* together... yes, I quite like the sound of that."

"Aldric!" I say, and my hand comes to my mouth, covering it. I have called his name. In the Wise One's presence, he allowed his name to be spoken, but I've never been given such leave.

"I'm sorry, my lord," I say, wishing to take the words back, but he merely shakes his head. "Never in the presence of others," he chides. "You shall address me as master or lord. But within the intimacy of my chambers, you may call me by name. You are my Carina."

"Yes, my lord," I murmur. I do not know what it is that has transpired between us, but the pain in my chest is beginning to lessen. He leans down, his mouth meeting mine, a tender kiss I lean into. A soft sigh escapes me as his hand wraps around my neck and draws me closer. He lays me on the bed, but I do not protest the release as he is now above me, seemingly entirely covering me, his kisses insistent, his hands at the edge of my tunic. He takes his mouth off mine only briefly enough to remove my tunic altogether. His eyes rove over my body, heated, possessive, his chest heaving as he holds himself back. He leans down and kisses me again, his hardened length against my thighs as his mouth roams mine, then he is planting kisses over my cheek, down to my neck, past my collarbone. My hips rise at the feel of his tongue on my neck. He does not order me to be still, but rather holds my wrists by my sides, firmly pushed into the bed beneath me as he makes his way down from my neck to my breasts. Still holding my wrists, he takes one nipple fully into his mouth and sucks, the exquisite pleasure-pain causing me to moan out loud, my head thrown back.

"Aldric," I say, as his mouth travels further, to my bare mound at the apex of my thighs. It seems he's encouraged by hearing his name spoken.

His tongue flicks out. I cry out from the intensity. He releases my wrists, and my hands fly to his hair, the dark length of it falling around me as I anchor myself to him. He sucks my nub into his mouth and I cry out loud before he flicks his tongue against me. He knows exactly how to bring me pleasure, stroking firmly with quick flicks of his tongue. It seems my pulse has gone between my legs now, my sex throbbing, aching with each thrust of his tongue. He cradles my sore bottom between his hands as he lifts my sex to him, hungrily lapping at me. To my dismay, he removes his mouth from me just seconds before I've reached climax.

"Ask me," he growls, his eyes burning dark and heated as he meets my gaze. "You ask me for permission before you give in to your pleasure. If you do before I give you leave, I will punish you."

Oh, the sweet torture.

"Please, my lord!" I beg, my hands gripping his hair so tightly I fear I will hurt him, but he does not flinch.

He shakes his head and returns to the sweet, delicious torture. I am going to lose control, and what will happen if I do without his permission?

"My lord," I moan, "*pleeease.*"

His bearded mouth grins wickedly as his tongue strokes my nub, his eyes glittering. He smiles so rarely, that the unabashed way he does so now undoes me. He nods his head. It is all I need. The next stroke of his tongue has me toppling over the edge, riding the waves of ecstasy as he pleasures me. I writhe beneath him. My eyes shut tight, I am dizzy with pleasure and it goes on for what seems like forever. He finally takes his mouth off mine and straddles me, removing his clothes quickly, the soft pile tumbling to the floor as he releases them. He is hard for me, his length full and intimidating. He leans down to me and nudges my legs apart with his knees. I open for him as wide as I can. I do not fear him. I yearn to feel him in me.

Slowly, he enters me. "Shhh, my little one," he says. "Does it hurt?"

I am full, stretching for him, but I shake my head. "It is a pain I can bear, my lord," I whisper. He is hesitant, filling me but not moving any further. I place my hands on his broad shoulders, pleading. "Please, Aldric. I want to feel you."

His eyes warm at that, and he lowers his body to mine, the heat of him like a blanket of warmth as he holds me, driving his cock into me. It hurts, but I welcome it, part of me welcomes being this for him, being his with which he will seek his pleasure. He wants me. He needs me, not the way I need him, but he needs me. He growls in my ear, his breath catching, spasms of pleasure shooting through me with every thrust of his hips, before he climaxes, a deep sound that rakes across my chest and through my core. Both of us sated, he rolls to his side and holds me. I still do not wish to be separated. I need him with me.

He holds me close, until my breathing slows. I no longer care about the Freanoss rules about physical contact and mating. I am saddened and alone, but I feel more with this man than I ever have. I realize in wonder that I once though he'd enchanted me, but the true spell has been broken. All these years... *my whole life*, I have been asleep, and he has awakened me.

"Stay with me," he instructs. I am not sure exactly what he is asking of me. Stay with him now? Or stay with him... forever? Never to return to my people, my planet?

I do not respond. I merely grasp him tighter, closing my eyes, willing sleep. I cannot think of this. Not now. For now, I must rest. He holds me close to him until slumber takes me.

CHAPTER FIFTEEN

Aldric

The next day when Carina rises, she is quiet. There has been much for my little one to process. I was gentler with her last night than I should have been. Her infractions were worthy of a thrashing I should have given her. Though I didn't show her total mercy, and did punish her, I fear I was lenient. If I am too gentle with her, she may feel too free to disobey me, and such actions will threaten her safety. She must learn her place. She *must* learn to obey me if I am to keep her safe. She has had the evening with which to nurse her wounds.

Carina returns from her room where she has freshened up, and eyes me sitting by my desk.

"Good morning, Carina," I say. "Come here, please."

She comes to my shyly, her eyes cast down. I wonder what she is thinking as she approaches me. When she is in front of me as I sit at my desk, I gesture for her to turn around. "Lift your tunic, please."

Flushing slightly, she lifts her tunic. She is only slightly reddened from the spanking I gave her last night.

"Bend over the desk, please."

She obeys, eyeing me curiously, her tunic lifted above her bottom, her legs splayed out. I shove my hand between her thighs, running my fingers along the inside edge of the soft, sweet skin there. She gasps, trembling slightly, and I can smell her scent, her arousal in the air between us. If I were to touch between her legs, I would find her wet for me.

"This is mine," I say, my hand moving between her legs. "All mine." When I reach the lips of her sex, I pause. She is no longer smooth as she once was. She gasps as my fingers rake across her mound. "Tsk, tsk, Carina. I like you smooth and ready for me."

"My lord," she hisses. "I am… what have you done to me?"

I chuckle. "It is not of my doing, Carina," I say. "As Isidor explained, your body is beginning to respond the way it should without the manipulation from Freanoss. You were sedated, and your body muted against natural inclinations."

She stiffens. I slide my hand over her bottom and lower, dipping my finger to her sex. My finger easily glides in and out, as I stroke her. She is already primed with arousal.

"Tell me, Carina. Before you met me, did you know anything of sexual pleasure?"

She shakes her head. I continue pumping my finger inside her.

"Freanoss didn't allow for this," I murmur. "Your body has been hidden from its true purpose, confined to chastity and sterility. It will be my pleasure and duty to denude you," I say, moving closer to her. I open my mouth, my teeth sinking into the soft skin at her lower back. She gasps, but as she straightens, my hand comes down with a sharp crack that makes her yelp. I take her hands and push them forcefully on my desk. My tongue flicks back to her skin, tasting her, the sweet, salty, seductive taste of her enchanting as I drag my tongue down her back. I kiss her reddened skin, my fingers pumping in her core. Her eyes close and she moans. I stroke her, gradually bringing her closer to orgasm, but just as her chest begins to heave on the desk, I remove my fingers.

"My lord," she groans, her voice garbled.

"You will not be allowed pleasure now," I say, as I pull away from her. My voice is hardened, my tone corrective as I address her. I must teach her. "Today, I will not pleasure you unless you please me. Now, you will lie there while I prepare for the day. Do not move. Do not speak." I stand, and walk to where my sword belt hangs. I take it from the peg, the sound of the metal buckle clinking as I walk back to where she lies. I double it over and slash it against my hand, the sound of the leather striking my palm like a gunshot. She jumps, but maintains her position. I straddle her from behind and lean over her, my entire body flush against hers, my legs on either side of hers as I envelop her, my mouth coming to her ear. I place the folded belt in front of her. "If you disobey me, I will punish you." My hardened cock against her backside throbs. I press up against her, and she pushes back against me.

"Be quiet, Carina. Think of your obedience to me. Prepare yourself to submit." I grasp the rim of her ear with my teeth and nip lightly, then flick my tongue against the place where I nipped. She shivers. "You taste delectable," I whisper. "I mean to eat my fill of you. But first... you must obey." I reach my hand to her hair, wrap my fingers around it, and pull, lifting her head while I whisper in her ear, "Will you obey me, sweetness?"

Her eyes are closed, her breathing labored. She swallows, trying to nod but it's difficult while I am holding her like this.

"Yes, my lord," she pants. "I will obey."

I release her hair, smoothing my hand along the dark, satiny tresses. "Very good," I say, rising. "Do not move or speak until I give you leave, except to respond to my commands. Do you heed me, Carina?"

She nods once.

I rise and fetch the bell, giving it a sharp shake of my hand. Carina's eyes fly open. She does not wish to be seen like this, splayed upon my desk, her body on full display.

I go to the door, prepared to answer it. When I hear a familiar knock, I speak loudly. "Bring us breakfast," I order, my eyes on Carina, as my servants hasten to obey. She sighs, relieved that I have not opened the door. I go to her wardrobe and remove the sky-blue tunic I wish for her to wear today, placing it on the edge of my bed as I go to her.

"Come here," I say sharply. She rises, turns, and walks to me, her eyes focused on mine. I like that sometimes she casts her eyes down, but sometimes she challenges me like this. It is her fire, her conviction, the will of iron that draws me to her. I will train her, but I will not break her.

"Our food will arrive momentarily," I explain to her, as I remove her tunic and replace it with the clean one. "Come with me." I take her by the hand and lead her to the other side of the room, apart from the entryway door, to a corner hidden away from the entrance. I point to the corner. "Kneel," I instruct. "Clasp your hands behind your back and focus your eyes on the wall in front of you. Do not move. You must maintain that position until I call you. Do you understand?"

She eyes the corner tentatively and frowns, but nods. I lead her, pointing to where she is to kneel. She obeys. I can feel her will resisting mine, the thread of iron in her backbone as she faces the wall. She has not disobeyed or contradicted. She has done as I ask. I kneel behind her, my arms holding her so that I can cup both her breasts in my hands. I knead them gently, playing with her hardened nipples. She closes her eyes and little *mews* of pleasure escape her lips before a knock comes at the door. I lean over to her ear, my breath a low whisper. "*Stay.*"

I rise and go fetch the silver tray from Lystava, who inclines her head. "Shall I return to help ready your lady?" she asks.

I shake my head. "Not today," I say. She nods and takes

her leave.

I take my time bringing the food to the table, eyeing Carina. She has obeyed me, still kneeling obediently. "Good girl," I praise. "You may come here now, please."

She rises and comes to me, eyeing the tray of food. Will she remember that she does not eat unless I give her leave? I pull out a chair for her to sit, and she folds herself into it gracefully. I lean down and kiss the top of her head, compelled to do so by her utter beauty, her obedience so attractive to me.

"Good girl," I say. "Keep your hands in your lap." She obeys, but the look about her is not compliance. She is frowning.

I have a few choices with how I am to respond to her. I could put her back in the corner until she has rid herself of her temper. I could punish her, but I'd prefer to refrain from disciplining her unless I have good reason to do so. Or, I could find out what it is that has her so out of sorts.

I take a bite of the slices of ripe peach on the platter, before I nod to her, allowing her to take her own food. She scowls deeper and reluctantly takes a piece of cheese.

"Talk to me, Carina," I order, sipping my cup of scalding hot tea.

"About what?" she says, her lips pursed tightly as she scowls at the cheese in her hand, but does not eat it.

I place my mug down and push my chair away. "Come here. Now."

Her eyes widen, as she's just realized I am not pleased with her behavior. I can see the apprehension in them. Has she earned discipline? What will I require of her next? I wait patiently until she comes to me. She rises and slowly drags her feet to me. I stand her between my legs and take her hands.

"Why the ill temper?" I ask.

She blinks, apparently surprised by the question.

"My lord?"

"You are frowning. You are obeying me by the mere

letter, and your heart is uneasy. Why? Are you troubled by what you've discovered about Freanoss?"

She looks puzzled for a moment. I do not speak, allowing her the space to formulate her thoughts. "I am," she says honestly. "But I do not wish to be ignorant. I would rather know the truth and accept it, than be misled."

I nod. I like that about her. "Go on. There is more."

Her lips are so tight they are nearly white. "My *body*. It infuriates me. Despite what I try to will it to do, it *will* respond to your commands and barbaric mannerisms. I hate it. I cannot kneel in the corner without my pulse throbbing between my legs, and I do not enjoy the loss of control. I don't like how it growls for food. I don't like that it is beginning to grow *hair*." She makes a grimace, pausing, her voice lowering as her eyes look down as well. "And I... hate that you've brought me to the edge of ecstasy and just *left* me there. It's frustrating."

I barely stifle a chuckle. Perhaps denying her pleasure is more effective discipline than I initially thought.

"Is that right?" I ask, releasing her hands and lifting my fingers to her nipples, already pebbled and hardened beneath the light blue fabric of her tunic. She gasps, her eyes closing, her head rolling back as I fondle her breasts. "You dislike how your body responds, do you?" I say, my voice dropping as I draw her onto my lap, pulling her against my crotch, then lifting her legs so she straddles me, facing me. "You don't like how your body betrays you?" I now whisper, lifting the edge of her tunic as my mouth goes to her breast, my tongue biting her nipple as I glide my thumb along her sex.

"My lord," she says, her voice a near sob as her hands encircle me. I flick my tongue against her nipple and pump my finger inside her, spreading her juices along her nub, the tempo of my strokes increasing as I feel her body tensing, prepared to orgasm, so ready for the release.

"Do not," I whisper in her ear. "Not until I give you leave." I pause, my hand steadying on her sex, holding her right on the cusp. "You will obey me, and when you do, I will reward you. Do you wish to be rewarded, Carina?" I ask.

She nods. "Yes," she moans, wriggling her hips against my hand. "*Please.*"

I take my hands off her and stand her in front of me. "Then you do as you're told. Behave yourself, and I will reward you." I nod to her chair. "And you know what happens if you misbehave." She stares at me, agape, as if she cannot believe I have left her on the cusp of ecstasy yet again. I am unrepentant. Training her to obey me will be ultimately for her own good.

"Go," I order sternly, pointing to her chair. She purses her lips and frowns, sitting forcefully upon the seat. She is acting like a petulant child, and crosses her arms on her chest. I raise an eyebrow but she looks away from me, picks up her cheese, and takes a large, angry bite. She lifts her drink and glares at me as she sips.

I barely stifle a chuckle. My instinct was quite correct. I let her off too easily last night, and this morning, she is practically begging me to discipline her. Perhaps she needs to feel my correction more often than I surmised.

I take a sip of my tea and watch her. I understand it's difficult for her to adjust to the ways of Avalere. I doubt that she dislikes it here. She has only just arrived. What she is not familiar with is the complete loss of control. On Freanoss, all she knew was control—her body, her mind, and her environment were all regimented, denying her the very real human experiences she was created for. Here, it is the exact opposite.

I hear a knock on the door. She looks at me sharply as I rise. "Sit and eat," I order. "No more of the cheese without the fruit. It is too rich to be eaten in large quantities, and it will make you sick." I raise a stern brow to her as I go to the door. When I open the door, it is Arman. I step into the hallway, leaving Carina for a moment while I speak to him.

His dark brow is drawn, his eyes troubled. "My lord, we

have received further communication from Freanoss. Though they've given up complete interest in your woman, they are moving to complicate things. They have no access to your castle, but have means of communication in various public places."

I nod, encouraging him to continue. He clears his throat, and averts his eyes before speaking. I frown.

"It might be best for me to appear in public with your Carina... dressed as you, made to look like you, so the communication devices detect me as the king, if our decoy plan is to take root."

He wants to escort my woman? My eyes haze with fury, but before I can respond, he holds up a hand.

"My lord, please," he begs. "Please listen to reason."

We discuss things a bit more, then I give him leave to go. When I return to my chamber, my mind is focused on what Arman has told me, and it takes me a minute to realize what I see. Carina, completely contrary to my orders, has finished the food on the platter. But more—she now lies in the bed, curled up on her side, her eyes closed tightly as her hand works between her legs. Anger clouds my vision. How *dare* she? She has deliberately disobeyed not one, but two direct commands from me.

"Is that how it is to be, then?" I ask, my voice deadly calm as I hold my temper in check. She needs a good whipping for what she's done. That she would defy me so boldly indicates that my suspicion is right. I *have* been far too lenient on her. I regret having been so.

When she hears my voice, she freezes, but only for a moment as her eyes focus on mine. She stares into my eyes willfully, unrepentant for what she's done. Slowly, she drags her fingertip along her slit, her breath beginning to come in shallow gasps. She is on the brink of orgasm, prepared to bring herself over the edge. I feel my cock harden, painfully thick, as I watch her pleasure herself. It is the darkest, most erotic thing I have ever seen. I wish to take my own cock in my hand and pump myself to ecstasy while watching her please herself. I can already imagine her groan of pleasure, the flush of her cheeks as she writhes on the bed. But no. I have a duty to perform.

"*Stop.*" My voice is loud and harsh. Her hand freezes between her legs, her eyes still willfully trained on mine. I cross the room to her and lift her up from the bed. She must be punished.

I place her to standing on the floor in front of me. "What did I tell you would happen if you disobeyed me?" I ask, chucking a finger under her chin, not harshly, but enough that she quickly raises her eyes to mine.

She frowns. "You'd punish me."

I nodded. "Did you eat food I asked you not to?" Her eyes wander, but I bring them back to me with a tug of her chin.

"Yes!" she says defiantly, her eyes boring into mine.

My instincts were right. She *needs* to be disciplined. Perhaps she is craving my discipline. I know not her reasoning, but there is one thing I know beyond doubt. Today, I will not slacken from my duty. Today, I am not finished with her until she is submitted to me in all possible ways.

• • • • • • •

She stands in front of me, her chin lifted defiantly, as my hands go to my waist, and I unfasten my leather sword belt. For a moment, panic flickers in her eyes as she looks down, then back up, widened eyes betraying a shadow of fear. She thinks I am going to strap her, but no. Not now. I have another purpose.

I take her wrists in one of my hands, grasping them together as I fasten my belt snugly. When she realizes what I am doing, she glares at me and stomps her foot, her eyes flashing. She can rant and rave if she wishes. It is time she learns who is her master.

I take her by the hair, and pull firmly, not enough to hurt

but just enough to get her attention. "You will answer for your defiance, my Carina," I say, my anger barely tempered as I speak.

There is much simmering beneath her surface. Her waters run deep, her emotions high, and it troubles me to see her like this. I have been mistaken thinking leniency and gentleness would help her make peace with her circumstances. She needs more from me.

I turn her around, pushing her down on the bed so her bound hands are stretched out in front of her. She tenses immediately, expecting perhaps that I will begin punishing her like this. I am simply placing her there so that it is harder for her to escape as I go to her room, seeking the tool I need. I glance around her chamber until I see it, a stream of sunlight hitting the wooden handle of her hand-crafted brush, making it gleam. Perfect. I lift it, and walk quickly back to Carina, who is still splayed out on the bed. Good. I am not sure where she would go, but I do not wish to fight her further than I need to.

I stride quickly back to the room, and her head lifts, her eyes flitting to the solid wooden hairbrush in my hand. I grab the back of my chair and sit, my knees apart. I lay the brush across my lap. "Come here," I say in a low growl.

She turns her head to the side and glares at me, but does not move. Frowning, I rise, brush in hand, and walk quickly to her, placing my hand on her lower back. Without warning, I lift the brush and bring it down in one solid whack across her backside. She screams, not expecting the fire of pain for her disobedience.

"What was that?" she says breathlessly, turning to look at me. "What did you do to me?"

I apply the brush a second time, a hard smack that reddens her beautiful skin. "I said come to me," I repeat, going back to my seat and sitting. "Now *come*."

She rises, frowning, and turns to me. Her cheeks are red, her lips pursed, as she drags her feet. I watch her as she approaches. I have a duty to perform, and I must not let anything—not my temper, nor my arousal, nor my desire to make her happy—get in the way of what needs to be done. When she is only a foot away from me, I point to the floor. "*Kneel.*"

Her lips twist in a grimace, her eyes heated pools of fury as she eyes me. I give her no choice; grabbing the end of the leather belt, I tug and she stumbles toward me, falling straight into my arms. I lower her to the floor in a kneeling position. "Good girl," I say with mock praise. Now that she is kneeling, her hands in my lap by default—not choice—I place my hand under her chin and grip firmly. "Look in my eyes, Carina," I order. She tries to pull her chin away, but I hold firm. Utterly defiant, she squeezes her eyes shut, her lips pursed in fury. I release her chin, grasp her hair, and pull. Her eyes open in surprise.

"*Look at me.*"

I gaze in her eyes, now damp with tears. There is fear in her look, but more, so much more—hurt, anger, and a dark, deep arousal.

I nod. I have seen what I need to. I lift her up from kneeling, pull her to the side, then drag her across my lap, quickly yanking up her tunic and baring her. "You have defied me, and you will answer for defiance every time," I say, the flat part of the brush flush against her naked skin as I talk to her. She now realizes what she is going to face, and begins to squirm on my lap as I speak to her. I anchor her firmly with my hand around her waist. "It is my duty to see to your pleasure. My duty to see to your needs." I lift the brush and bring it down with a solid *whack* against her bare skin. "My duty to see to your training." She screams from the pain, but I ignore her, administering three more solid smacks, one after the other. The bite of the brush is keen, and she fights me, but she cannot escape. I easily trap her legs with mine as I continue to spank her, pausing several seconds before each biting snap of the brush.

Whack! She howls and twists, but I hold fast. She will feel the sting of this punishment for days to come, and given her level of defiance, I will likely be sure to renew the sting regularly.

"You will obey me, Carina," I say, with another hard whack. She howls in protest. I wait for her to settle, raise my hand, and administer another firm swat, the solid flat of the brush smacking her bare skin. This time when I pause, I feel her tension begin to ease a bit. I smooth the varnished wood across her hot, reddened skin, as I speak to her. "Failure to obey me will always be met with punishment," I say, the brush gliding over her punished bottom. I lift the brush and bring it down again, snapping it against her. I hear a soft sob escape. I'm getting through to her. I'm breaking down her defenses and she is beginning to accept her punishment.

I turn the brush so that the handle is now between her legs, slowly prying her legs apart. "Open," I growl.

She obeys. Her honey is glistening on her folds and on the sides of her legs. Though I've no doubt she does indeed experience pain when I spank her like this—my discipline is meant to deter her defiant behavior, after all—she has been aroused. Slowly, I dip the cylindrical handle of the brush, varnished and smooth, between her folds.

"Ohhhh, oh no, please, my lord, you can't mean to—ohhh!"

Her embarrassment and protests wane as I pump the handle in her wet pussy, easily sliding it in and out. I remove it, tracing her juices across her inner thighs.

Her hands fly to her face and she covers her eyes. "My lord!" she hisses. "Do not!"

Without another thought, I raise the brush and bring it slapping down again on her backside. She jerks, squirming from the pain with a howl of protest. "My lord!"

Whack!

"Aldric!"

I pause, brush raised midway. "Yes, sweetness?"

"I-I—this is—I'm mortified!"

I frown. "Good. You ought to be," I say with another harsh snap of the brush on her backside. "Behavior as you've displayed today is befitting a naughty child, not the woman of the Warrior King." I give her three more hard, punishing swats, waiting for her protest to die down, and when it does, I push the handle between her thighs again and open them. She mews in protest, but a quick flip of the brush and smack against her thigh has her opening for me. I take the brush handle and stroke the dampness between her inner thighs, then slowly penetrate her core with the handle, pushing until it's fully inserted. She squirms. She was already aroused, near release, and I've no doubt she's even more aroused than ever. I remove the handle just a bit, so that I'm barely at her entrance, before plunging it in again and twisting. I can feel her tension, feel her walls pulsing around the handle as I thrust it in and out. Her breath is shallow, her hands splayed out in front of her as she wiggles and squirms.

"My lord," she pants. I pause, the brush frozen halfway in but no longer moving. She moans in agony, and I feel my hardened cock jerk underneath the warmth of her belly.

"Yes, my love?"

She doesn't speak for a minute, frozen in place. "Please, my lord." Her plea a mere whisper now.

I insert the handle so slowly as I speak to her. "Please what, my little one?"

"Pleeeease," she moans, louder now, as I move the handle within her. "Oh, *please.*"

I freeze, my voice hardening. "Please *what?*"

She squirms. "Let me have my release!" she moans. "This is torture! I can't bear this another minute! I'll die if you don't allow me release!"

I leave the tip of the handle on the damp edge of her folds. "Release, Carina? You wish me to pleasure you? A naughty, defiant girl like you?"

She moans. "I won't be naughty," she whispers. "I will obey you, just *please* allow me release. I can't bear this!"

I remove the handle and turn the brush around so that the flat is against her skin again. My voice is harsh and corrective as I lift the brush. "Pleasure, little one, is for good girls who know how to behave themselves." I crack the flat of the brush on her backside. She jerks from the pain of it, and I pause as I allow my words to sink in. "*Obedience* is rewarded," I say, with another slap of the brush on her cheeks. "*Defiance*, however, will be met with *consequences*." I puncture my words with another solid smack of the brush. "What is it you prefer, little one?" I ask, the brush poised, as I demonstrate her options. "*Punishment*," a sharp crack landing on the tender place where her thighs and bottom meet, "or *pleasure*?" I take the handle of the brush and insert it, pumping hard and fast as she gasps and writhes.

"Pleasure! Oh, for the love of all things good, *pleasure*, my lord!" she screams, her back arching as she reaches closer and closer to orgasm.

I still. "Then what is it you need to do?" I scold.

She is panting now, her voice thick with arousal and need, "Obey you. Obey you, my lord! I am sorry for defying you. I will not defy you! I will obey you." Her words tumble out, pleading for mercy, begging for release. I smile slowly, the warmth of her obedience to me spreading across my chest as my hardened cock presses into her soft, sweet belly.

"You will obey me, Carina?" I whisper, releasing her waist and grasping a fistful of her hair, lifting her head back as I bend my head down. "Will you do as I say?" She squirms on my lap, her eyes shut tight, her lip caught between her teeth, completely at my mercy. "Or shall I whip you harder? Is that what you need from me? A whipping from my belt?" She attempts to shake her head but it is difficult with the firm grasp I have her in. "Or will you obey me so that I may pleasure you?"

"P-pleasure," she stutters. "Please!"

I release her hair and push her so that she is on her knees in front of me. Her eyes widen as she takes me in. Her hair is wild about her face, her blue eyes gleaming with passion and desire. I smile at her. She is exactly where I want her, ready to do my will, begging to please me. I take the brush and slowly run it through the hair that frames her face. Her eyes widen as I draw it through the midnight tresses slowly.

"Perhaps it shall be as it is at mealtimes," I murmur, watching her heated eyes widen as I stroke her hair with the brush. "Perhaps I shall require my appetite be sated before yours. If I were to ask you to take me in your mouth, little one, would you?"

She nods, her voice husky as she replies. "Anything you wish, my lord," she says.

"Even if I have you suck me until I spill in your mouth?" I tease, narrowing my eyes on her.

She licks her lips. My cock twitches in response. Her eyes lower. "It would be my pleasure," she hisses.

With my left hand, I grasp her hair, tugging so that her chin lifts and her mouth drops open. "Even if I tie you to my bed and make you wait until the sun sets for your own release?"

Her eyes close briefly and she swallows, before opening her eyes and nodding to me. "Even then, my lord. I am yours. Yours to command. Yours to take at your leisure."

I release her hair and drop the brush, reaching for my trousers and removing my cock. "Your obedience pleases me. Open your mouth."

Her eyes wide, she obeys, and I do what I've longed to do. She takes my cock in her mouth, wrapping her pretty lips around me as I thrust so hard she braces herself, but she takes me fully, the feel of her warm mouth and tongue already bringing me to near orgasm. I close my eyes and allow her to pleasure me, leaning back with my knees spread open as she licks and sucks. "Good girl," I murmur, stroking her hair. "Such a good girl. You will see how well I treat good girls."

I enjoy her soft moans and sucks, watching as her heated eyes meet mine, no longer defiant but now split wide open, holding me in the fire of her gaze as her tongue does wicked, wanton things to me. I reach out a hand and stroke her hair as she sucks, smiling at her.

"Very good," I say. On her knees, pleasuring me with her mouth, she is now submitted to me.

"Will I need to punish you further, sweetness?" I ask her, fully prepared to continue her punishment should she choose to defy me. "Or have you decided to submit to me?"

Her mouth slowly releases my cock. "I will submit, my lord," she says, her voice low and sultry.

I cup her face in my hands, bending down so that she must look me fully in the eyes. "Then things are as they should be," I whisper. I reach my hands lower and lift her to standing, guiding her to the bed, my hands pulling her tunic off and fully baring her to me. "On your knees. Chest down. Arms straight out in front of you." I guide her into position as she obeys, falling to the bed prostrate. I spread her legs, and run my hand along her reddened backside, over the slightly raised marks I've given her. Her back arches. I draw my finger through her folds, as she moans. I remove my finger and give her bottom a swift slap. She moans again. She is perfect.

I come up behind her, grasping her hair in my hand, yanking her head back so I can whisper in her ear, "Since you are submitted to me, it is time for me to pleasure you, little one. Are you ready?"

Her eyes are shut tight, her chin in the air as I grasp her hair, her chest heaving with her mouth open. "My lord," she gasps. "Yes, my lord. *Please.*"

Without further delay, I slip the head of my cock inside her warm pussy, nudging her open before I slide in fully. She is so tight around me, the feel of her in this position even more satisfying. She groans as I thrust with firm, purposeful strokes, one of my hands braced on her hip while the other delivers a moderate but stinging swat. She yelps, unable to contain herself now as she writhes beneath me, her pleasure building.

"You will learn to submit to me, Carina," I growl in her ear, plunging so deep I am fully within her now. She has stopped breathing, gasping for air, her fingers desperately clawing at the blanket on the bed. "You will obey me, or suffer punishment." Another hard thrust and her head falls to the side as she pants, little mews of pleasure escaping her mouth. I am building, preparing to release, her supple body beneath me unbearably beautiful. "You are *mine*," I growl as I topple over the edge at the same time she does, her screams of pleasure mingling with my growls. Her hips writhe, her fingers kneading the blanket. I shut my eyes at the intensity, her moans amping up mine.

She shoves her bottom against my flank and I hold her fast, my hands gripped so tightly around her waist I see fingerprint-shaped marks. I give her another hard slap of my hand as she continues to climax, marking her, reminding her, training her that this pleasure is only hers if she obeys me. She screams, and I don't know if it's from pain or pleasure but both are welcome, the emotions I've wrung from her my reward. A sob escapes, and I realize she is crying, her cheeks damp with tears, panting, still lying face down in front of me with me still plunged in her depths. She cries, and she cries.

CHAPTER SIXTEEN

Carina

I am rent open.

I have never cried like this before. Crying is discouraged on Freanoss, and part of me wonders at first if the way my body has been conditioned and manipulated also suppressed feelings, because never, ever have I *felt* like this. I hardly recognize the woman I am now. He's taken me from aloof and detached to begging, the range of emotion I've experienced overwhelming, and when he finally granted me my release, it was exquisite. But there is more, so much more. He shifts up on the bed, and my fingers claw at him, grabbing him, needing him not to let me go.

"Hush, sweet one," he says, running his large, rough hand over my hair. I am enveloped by his enormous arms, his hands gripping me so tightly I fear he will leave bruises, yet somehow it isn't tight enough. I don't know what to say. I don't know how to explain what is going on with me. But somehow, I know that I don't need to. He isn't expecting me to.

He holds me until I am quiet, the only sound in the room my soft hiccups and his steady breathing.

"My girl," he says softly. "This is hard for you."

I merely nod, as he continues to stroke my hair, and the steady beat of his heartbeat beneath my cheek settles me.

"You are safe here, Carina." I nod again. His hand travels down the length of my back to my bottom, cupping the warmed, stinging skin there. He squeezes gently. "It is in your best interest to obey me, and not simply because I'll punish you if you don't. You know that now, don't you?"

Do I?

I do not respond.

"You will see," he says. "Come here." He puts his hands beneath my arms and lifts me so that my face is close to his, his eyes penetrating mine. His hand goes to the back of my head and he pulls me closer to him. I inhale and exhale, enjoying the feeling of intimacy as his lips meet mine. He pulls away, his eyes darkening as he looks at me. "Will you obey me today?" he asks, his voice taking on a stern edge. I swallow and nod. I will. I know I will. My desire to defy him has fled and I'm left only now with the unfamiliar desire to please him. His voice lowers as his mouth comes to my ear. "I wouldn't want to punish you again."

I squirm against him, curiously aroused by his words. It is unsettling to me, the power he has over me. "Yes, my lord," I murmur. He pulls my head down to his chest and kisses my forehead.

"Stay here," he says. "I will be right back."

I reach for him, feeling immediately bereft as he leaves me, but he returns moments later with a damp cloth. He lies on the bed and holds me against his chest, drawing the cloth between my legs to clean me, then drying me with a second soft, dry cloth. A moment later, he reaches for the bell that sits next to his bed. I hear the musical tinkle as he draws the blanket over my naked form. Minutes later, a knock comes at the door.

"Come in," he orders, his deep voice reverberating through my frame. I shiver. The door opens, and Lystava comes in.

"My lord?"

"Carina has had a difficult morning," he explains. "Please fetch me the *chamomilia*."

With a nod, she leaves, and I lay against Aldric's chest, my dampened cheek against the roughness of his hair there, when I hear a knock again. She comes in the room, hands him something, and leaves swiftly. He lifts me up and props me up on pillows.

"Drink," he orders, holding a steaming cup of liquid to my lips. I obey, taking a sip, the warmth flooding my senses. It is sweet and spicy. As soon as I sip, the stuffiness in my head clears, the pain throbbing between my temples mitigated. He takes the cup and places it beside him on the table. In his palm is a small golden tin. He twists off the top and dabs the tiniest bit of white cream on his finger, then reaches to my face, smoothing it along the undersides of my eyes. The pressure is relieved. I no longer feel swollen and out of sorts. I feel almost healed, but for the burn in my backside. As if reading my mind, he frowns. "The reminder of your spanking will stay," he says. "You must remember to obey me." He reaches for my neck and draws me close again, the feel of his whiskered mouth meeting my forehead in a kiss, making me shiver.

"Yes, my lord," I whisper.

He picks up the hairbrush again and gestures for me to come to him as he sits up on the bed, placing me between his strong thighs. He brushes my hair slowly. It feels so nice, the tension seeping out of my body. I feel his fingers through my hair, pulling and tugging a bit. I am curious what he is doing, and turn my head to look at him, but he gently pushes my head so that I am staring straight forward again. I feel my hair caught in a band of sorts, tied back from my face. He's fixed my hair. My rough, fierce, fearless warrior has fixed my hair for me.

"We must leave soon, sweetness," he says. "But you will not depart from me today."

His eyes grow stern and his lips thin. The man does not

have to simply threaten punishment or force me to obey. For some reason I cannot quite fathom, my desire to obey him is strong, the mere thought of defying him unpalatable. It surprises me, as not an hour before I wanted nothing but to push him, to see how far I could, to defy him. Now, I desire nothing but to please him.

I cannot think beyond the present moment. I simply nod. I will not disobey him. "No, my lord. I will stay by your side."

He raises a brow. "That was a question?"

I look down shyly, but he quickly tips my chin back up to him. His eyes are twinkling. The fierce warrior king is smiling? His lips are tipped up, his eyes merry. "You will see if you obey me that I can be quite nice when I am obeyed."

I nod. "Yes, my lord," I whisper, offering a small smile of my own. "It is that simple, is it? Just do whatever you say?"

He bends down to me, his mouth at my ear, the low whisper causing the hair on my arms to stand on end. "Yes, Carina. It is that hard, and that simple."

Drawing back, his eyes probe mine, and I know not what he seeks, but he seems to have found it when he nods quickly. "Come, Carina. I have much to do today, and you must accompany me." He positions me by his side and takes my hands, wrapping them around his muscled arm. I no longer walk with apprehension, but oddly, pride. I am his woman. I have no doubt that I belong to him, and despite the way I've been raised, despite my past and my inclinations, it is nice to be wanted by this man, to know that I am his to protect. The discarded member of Freanoss, the useless spy they have no use for, is no longer cast away. I do not feel as if I am his property. I feel I am his prize. The difference means everything.

"Where are we going?" I ask.

"To the marketplace," he replies. "When we arrive there, no matter what happens, you are to remember that it is for your own good, and for the good of the Avalere."

I look at him, feeling my brows pull together. What does this mean? "My lord?"

He frowns. "It is best you obey and not ask questions," he says, as the doors open to his palace and the hot, bright sun beats down upon us. I can tell from where I am already that the marketplace is open for business today. I can see the people milling about, the tables laden with wares, and hear the clatter of voices and coins just beyond where we are. I walk in silence by his side, trotting quickly to keep up with his long, purposeful strides. He leads me to the table I went my first day here, teeming with jewelry, the gleam of precious gems and metals twinkling in the sunlight that dips below the tarp that shades the vendors from the sun's blazes. The same woman is there, and as before, she kneels on one knee, her head reclined upon our entrance. I hear voices quiet near us. Though there seems to be a pretense of doing what is normal, there is an undercurrent of anticipation and awe. It is a bit unnerving, knowing I belong to the man who has this much power and sway.

Aldric nods to the woman, giving her leave to rise. "Have you completed the item I asked for you to make?" he asks.

She nods eagerly, rising and reaching under her table for a metal box. She inserts a key and unlocks it, retrieving a black pouch that looks soft and elegant. She hands it to Aldric, who inclines his head and thanks her. He places a large handful of coins in her hand.

Her eyes widen as she takes in what he's paid her, and she begins to shake her head. "Oh, my lord," she says. "I cannot take this much for one item. Surely it is four times the value of what I've made for you."

Aldric casts her objection aside with a toss of his hand. "Take it," he says. "It is worth that, and more."

She looks troubled, as if it is against principle to take such a large sum. "But my lord," she says. "I would feel as if I were robbing the royal purses if I—"

"Do you mean to contradict me, woman?" Aldric asks

with a frown.

The woman's eyes widen and her mouth falls open.

I clear my throat, getting the attention of both the vendor and Aldric. I look at the woman. "I… wouldn't recommend it," I say quietly.

The woman's eyes soften and she smiles at me, nodding as she takes the coins. She inclines her head. "Thank you, my lord."

He merely nods at her, as his gaze is focused on me. For the second time this morning, Aldric's eyes are twinkling.

He reaches for my elbow and leads me to a quiet area, but then we walk on. We reach an empty little area where the tables are bare, and we are alone save the servants ready to defend, an arm's reach away. The king takes the pouch and unfastens the drawstring, pouring the lovely necklace into his hand.

"When I place this upon your neck, you will not be able to remove it," he says. "I have had it fashioned in such a way so that it serves as a reminder to you, and anyone that meets you, that you belong to the king."

I look at it. The silver gleams like liquid moonlight, and in the very center is an oval-shaped blue gem… the king's blue.

"This is sapphire," he says. The necklace is sturdy yet edged with a decorative pattern. It is simply breathtaking. "If we had but time, I'd have brought you with me to our chambers and done this properly. But we do not," he explains, gesturing for me to come closer to him.

I obey. His large arms encircle me as his hands clasp the necklace at the back of my neck. Though it is warm out, the metal is cool when it touches the tender area of my neck. I am not sure how I feel about this. I cannot take this off? Does it follow that I am then… special to him?

I don't realize until I feel his breath on my neck that I am holding my own breath. I gasp when his lips come to the side of my neck, grazing the tender skin there. "So lovely," he murmurs. "So beautiful." His voice lowers. "All of you, mine. Tonight, when we are alone, I will show you the ways I treat that which belongs to me." His fingers on the back of my neck tighten to near painful, possessive.

He pulls back and his eyes are flaming. His jaw is clenched as if chiseled in stone, his lips pursed, and I feel his entire body tense.

My voice is a mere whisper as I reach my hand out to him. "What is it, my lord?"

He responds in a low growl that only I can hear. "You must now leave with one of my men," he says, eyes narrowed and furious. "I cannot here explain to you why this must be, but it is so. I expect your obedience, Carina. When we leave here, you will be escorted upon the arm of another man." His eyes close for a moment before he continues, and when he opens his eyes again, they are fiery, angry. "You will do as he says in my absence. He will not cross the line of his station and touch you in any way except to demonstrate publicly that *he* is *me*." His voice drops lower, and the words tumble from him as if forced. "If he does, I will slay him with my bare hands."

I have no doubt whatsoever that he speaks the truth. I hate the idea of going with another man. "Must I?" I whisper.

His fingers grasp my neck even tighter. "You *must*."

His eyes probe mine, and I know what it is he seeks. I swallow, already feeling bereft of him, before I reply. "I will do as you say," I whisper.

He gives one quick nod, then he places my hand on his elbow, removes his from my neck, and marches me toward another alcove where there are several waiting for us. A hush of voices, and many hands are upon me.

"My lord!" I cry out, suddenly fearful as if we've been ambushed.

It is another voice that comes to my ear as strong arms embrace me. "I am here," he says, but it is a different voice. It is not the voice of my king. Before I can respond, I am being marched out of the tent into broad daylight. I look in astonishment at the man next to me, recognizing him as Arman. I do not know what they have done, but Arman now bears a remarkable semblance to Aldric. His hair is drawn back the same way as Aldric's, his eyes are dark, and the markings about his arms are the same black tribal slashes. He wears the same breeches and the belt about his waist is similar. But he is slighter in frame. Though this man stands erect and moves purposefully, his arm upon mine firm and unwavering, he does not have the same presence, the same *authority* as my lord.

To my right, tucked away in the corner of the tent, something catches my eyes. I freeze. It is *him*. His eyes are upon me. With as much courage as I can muster, I give a barely perceptible nod and continue walking in as stately a manner as I can. I want to shove the man holding me and run to my king. I want to feel *his* hands upon my arm, not the touch of the imposter that is with me, but I must be courageous and do as he's asked me. For some reason that confuses me, we walk in a sort of semi-circle before we end up at the pavilion. It is as if he is trying to parade me around, to show me off, and I wonder at his methods. How very odd. Still, I hold onto him, and we walk in silence for some time. He takes me to the very edge of the pavilion, and at this point, he does something strange. He pulls me to him, so that I am facing him, and as I watch him with wide eyes he leans in. I realize a second too late that he is going to kiss me. I panic. This was not part of the plan. I *was* told to obey, but I was also told he would not put hands on me.

Before I can decide how to react, his lips are upon mine, and he is kissing me. It is a rather detached kiss. I feel the difference instinctively, as if this kiss is for mere show. Still, I cringe inwardly. I can almost hear the fury from my king. Did he know this was to transpire? As he pulls away, Arman whispers in my ear, "Very good. You've done very well, little one."

My stomach twists in apprehension. I am little one to *one* man only.

"Enough." I hear the hissed word, and I turn but it is not the one man I wish to see, but rather Idan.

He addresses Arman. "You have taken this far enough," he says. "You are not to take further liberties." I am confused, looking from one to the other. Idan is marching next to the other man, and he addresses me as his eyes are straight forward. "Carina, you followed your role well." I hope so. I am not so sure myself.

I wonder where I am being taken to, and realize that we are going back to the room where Aldric and his men convened.

"It is clear," Idan says to Arman. I look at them both, but Idan merely shakes his head, and we all enter the building. I realize a second before we enter, that suddenly the man escorting me is reluctant to enter. I look curiously at him, and his face has blanched.

"*Go*," Idan says. "Now. He awaits."

• • • • • • •

We enter the massive structure stabilized by columns, one large entryway room followed by what looks like a small, makeshift dining hall, and several bunkers. It appears this is a place to convene without interruption, and perhaps for extended lengths of time if necessary. When we enter the large hall, to my surprise Idan takes me by the arm and forcefully moves me away from the man escorting me. My escort blinks after us, his hands suddenly bereft, when I see a blurry form out of the corner of my eye. It is my king, dressed as he was before we left, but now looking more furious than I have ever seen him. With a roar, he leaps from his feet and tackles Arman, leveling him to the floor as he raises his fist and delivers a vicious punch that snaps the other man's head back.

"My lord!" I shout, my hand raised up in horror, trying to get his attention, but he does not respond, and Idan's strong arms come around me.

"Stay away, Carina," Idan orders. "The king is within his rights to execute Arman for what he's done. Perhaps he will spare him his life and merely administer a beating fitting his infraction."

I am so confused, and turn to Idan for more explanation, but there is no time to discuss anything. My attention is once again riveted to my king. His muscles bunch at his neck and shoulders as he lets loose another punch to the man's gut. Arman tries to defend himself, but is no match for the king, who lands one vicious blow after another.

When Aldric has bested Arman, he reaches for his waist and removes his sword from its sheath with the sickening sound of clinking metal. I know instinctively he is going to kill this man, slice his head from his neck, in front of everyone. Not a sound is made by the men looking on. They stand as if they are prepared to defend their king, poised like guards by the door. Someone must stop this!

"My lord!" I scream, attempting to pull myself away from Idan, but I cannot, as his grip is far too tight. Aldric pauses as he did before, sword at the ready, prepared to strike. I shake my head. "No, my lord. He did nothing deserving of this."

"You are wrong to interfere, Carina," Idan hisses as I struggle. "Do not speak to the king of this."

But I am riveted as the king's eyes are fixed on me, his chest heaving, the blood of the man he's beaten smeared upon his knuckles, his body covered in a glistening sheen. "Release her," he orders Idan.

Idan's grip immediately loosens as he obeys his king. I blink, looking around me as now the king's men's eyes are upon me.

"It would be merciful of me to cut his head from his neck," Aldric hisses. "Rather than look upon me with shame all the days of his life. He put his lips on *my woman*!" His voice raises at the end, a shout, as he gets to his feet. Arman does not move. The king takes a step toward me. "As for you," he says in a low growl, pointing at me with the tip of his sword. "When I am finished punishing the traitor who took liberties with my woman, I ought to bend you over my throne and punish you with the flat of my sword." He is prowling toward me, his heat a pulsating wall of fury. I wish to step back from him as he advances, but my ire is raised.

"*You* were the one who made me walk about on the arm of another man!" I shout, taking a step toward him as he stalks toward me. "*You* were the one who told me to obey him. *You* were the one who made me go with him!" I do not know how it is possible that the hush in the room grows even quieter as the king looks at me, his eyes widening in shock that I have the nerve to contradict him while his men look on. Though I have much to learn about obeying my king, I know I have crossed a line, broken a rule that was understood between us. This is a man to whom others revere on bended knee, and I've contradicted him and raised my voice to him.

"I did not wish to kiss him!" I continue, defending myself. It seems that now I've begun my tirade I cannot stop. "I hated being upon his arm and separated from you. *You* were the one who *made* me." My fury carries my words away from me as I continue. "By the gods, I want *no other man's* lips upon mine as long as I live!" I step closer to him and gesture furiously to his sword. "Beat me with the flat?" I ask incredulously. "For *obeying* you? You, my fierce warrior *lord*, are *incorrigible*!" I am now in front of him, pointing an irate finger at his chest. I jab his hardened, muscled chest as I glare at him. My pulse races in the silence. His hand wraps around my finger, freezing me mid-poke, and with one hard tug, he pulls me into him so my entire body is flush against his.

"You hush, woman," he says. "You have said enough. One more word, and I *will* bare you and punish you in front of them all."

I blink, suddenly coming to my senses. What have I done? But before I can speak another word, his mouth is crushing mine, so hard I feel my lips bruise, but it is what I need, as nothing but his fierce touch will soothe my raging temper and pounding heart. I am dimly aware of him re-sheathing his weapon before he lifts me, and I wrap my legs around his torso. I hear somewhere in the distance the whistles and murmurs around us as we kiss passionately, his embrace around me exactly what I need, the perfect response to my wild torrent of emotions.

He pulls away for a minute, one corner of his lips quirking up. "Incorrigible, is it?" he growls in my ear. "Let me be clear, my Carina," he says. "I have only desisted in punishing you because you stopped when I told you. You will answer for shouting at me in front of my men." His eyes are heated, fixed on mine.

"Will I?" I whisper. My heart is pounding, my thighs dampened, flush up against his enormous, heaving torso, and I can feel my arousal beginning to pool at the apex of my thighs.

"Leave us!" the king shouts. "All of you." He does not turn, though he addresses his men. "Find another decoy. Arman is hereby banished from our territory for one month's time, and will serve as worker in the mines of Kleedan."

He catches my eye and shakes his head. "Do not contradict me again, Carina," he orders.

I nod. His fingers grip my backside as he walks with me wrapped around his torso.

"Put me down, my lord," I urge, "so that I can walk."

His only answer is a good, hard swat to my backside. I do not speak again.

He walks while holding me, whispering in my ear. "It is our plan to invade Freanoss," he says, "where my sister is being held hostage. I've been advised to have a decoy go ahead of me because my advisers believe that the warriors of Freanoss intend on ending me when I arrive. I was willing to allow this to happen but now see that I cannot do so." We are now past the marketplace and nearing the entrance to the palace. "In one week's time, my sister will arrive on

Freanoss. I will go myself to meet those who hold her captive."

"Let me go to Freanoss with you, my lord," I urge.

He shakes his head emphatically. "Certainly not," he says.

I say not another word. I do not wish to return to Freanoss. I have been betrayed by my people. But I will be useful to my lord if I am with him to aid him when he goes to fight for his sister. I will find a way to go with him. He will be angry with me, but it will be worth it. I need to go with him. I will find a way.

CHAPTER SEVENTEEN

Aldric

I am dimly aware of the people around us as I take her back to my palace, my purpose clear: to claim the little vixen who disrespected me. To erase the memory of Arman's lips on hers from her memory by searing a new memory in its place. To bring her back into submission to me. My servants fall away as I take her with me, the buzz of the town at my heels and the whispers around fades into the background. I have not had my fill of her and *by the gods* she has not had her fill of me.

I remember the way her eyes flashed at me as my men looked on, defying me, meeting my gaze with hers, as her little hand poked at my chest in fury.

I want no other man's lips upon mine as long as I live.

By the gods I will see to it that she has her wish.

The rage that pulsed through my veins upon seeing him kiss her surges me forward to my chambers. I need issue no warning to my servants. They well know what my purpose is. She is lucky I do not rend the garment from her and take her here, in front of everyone, staking my claim once and for all as her lord and master. Her lips are upon mine as I kick the door open.

I slam the door to my chambers behind me so hard I hear it rattle on its hinges.

"You'll break it," she hisses, pulling away from our kiss just long enough to warn me.

I narrow my eyes at her. "It is not the door you should fear will break, Carina," I warn.

Her eyes widen, then flare. In two strides, I am at the bed, tossing her down. Her head falls back and her hair flails about her as she bounces a bit, then pushes herself up on the palms of her hands as I stalk back to the door and throw the deadbolt in place. As I turn back to her I remove my sword, the broad flat of it gleaming in the light through the window. Her eyes widen, and she scrambles back upon the bed.

"Freeze," I hiss, at the same time I reach the bed, grasp her ankle and pull. She squeals as I issue my command. "On your knees, chest down." My power surges through me, heat in my veins and in my cock springing to life as she obeys me, splayed out on the bed, submitted to me. Without another word, I bring back my sword and swing it, the flat hitting her squarely across her backside. It will not harm her, but is thin and supple, and suitable for chastising her without injury. She screams, but I know it's from something deeper, and primal, perhaps fear at the unknown implement. I have not struck her hard enough to warrant such a scream. The flat of my sword and my tempered swat brings about a good sting, but is hardly severe, nothing like the snap of a birch or even my supple leather belt. The beveled edge prevents me from harming her, as she will only feel the flat. As I lift my sword for a second stroke, her back arches, asking for me, begging me wordlessly for the measured pain.

Thwack! The metal connects with her skin. She moans as I deliver a third smack. Honey glistens between her thighs. Just between her legs, I flick the finger of my left hand, delving into the dampened folds.

"So wet," I growl. "Already, she is aroused."

She squeals as I flick my finger through her. "That's right, lovely," I whisper. "I've punished you for your disrespect, have I not?"

Again, her back arches, and I know what she needs. I drop my sword and raise my hand, bringing my palm flat against the curve of her ass with a resounding smack. She moans, as I let loose a second smack, her backside red now from the spanking I've given her earlier and the one I give now.

I reach down and fist her hair, lifting her head off the bed. She gasps as I bring my mouth to her ear and hiss, "Who do you belong to?"

"You, my lord!" she says with a strangled cry, but her cheeks are flushed and her eyes half-lidded so that I know she *needs* this from me.

"To whom do you submit?" I ask.

"You, my lord," she moans, writhing beneath me, tugging her head but helpless to my firm grasp. I release her hair and point to the bed, silently commanding her to stay in position as my fingers deftly unfasten my sword belt. I double it over, pressing one hand on the small of her back as I rear the belt back with my right hand.

"Will you *ever*," I hiss, spanking her with a hard cut of the belt, so that she jerks beneath me but then writhes, "*ever*," another hard smack that she welcomes with an arch of her back, pushing her backside against me as if saying *more*, "disrespect me in front of my men?"

"No, my lord!" she screams.

The red marks of my belt on her skin have me so hard it is painful. I drop my belt. I quickly strip off my trousers and join her on the bed, behind her, my cock ready for her already. With no preamble, I press my cock into her, a hard thrust that takes her breath away. I grab a fistful of her hair as I plunge into her.

"Whom do you obey?" I grind, pushing into her so hard the breath is driven out of her and she is gasping. I slap her thigh. "*Answer me.*"

"M-my lord!" she screams. "*You!*"

I grind into her, thrusting, her pussy tight around my rigid cock, thrusting so hard I feel my length fully within her, my flank against her warmed, reddened backside. She is arching, writhing, but pushing into me as if begging me silently to take her harder, firmer, with everything that I have.

"You will obey me," I say. I want her punished and claimed, so that every time she walks, she feels the mark of my hand on her throbbing backside and the aching memory of my cock in her pussy.

"Yesss," she wails, her hands fisted on the bed so tightly her knuckles are white. "*Yesss, my lord.*"

I am reaching climax at a rapid pace. I can feel her building beneath me, her pussy ready for me, milking me, but her slender form so fragile I could break her. The beast in me *wants* to savagely claim what is mine, but I temper my power, sated by each thrust of my cock in her pussy.

"No one touches you," I growl, with a tug of her gorgeous tresses.

"No one, my lord," she says, her voice thick with emotion.

"No one fucks you but me," I insist, with another hard thrust.

"No one, my lord," she says, a near sob.

"You are *mine*," I say with a growl so savage I barely recognize my own voice. I am on the cusp of climaxing. I release her hair and grasp her hips, plunging a final time into her until I come, dizzy with the pleasure of her beneath me, under me, her soft hair and warmed backside, my power over her a pulse of energy between us. I roar as I climax, my body tense and vibrating with the ecstasy, victor in my claiming of the woman beneath me.

To hell with Freanoss and their citizens and their thievery. Carina was *made* for me, and by the gods, our destinies are written in our hearts, minds, and bodies. She was fated to be with me since her conception, every lesson she's learned, every step along the way leading her to *me*.

She is crying quietly as I withdraw myself and fall on the bed next to her, picking her up and laying her across my chest.

"You did not climax, Carina," I say, panting, needing to know.

She shakes her head. "No, my lord." Her leg is hitched up on mine. She is so ready, but she will wait, her longing for me emphasizing my ownership of her.

I close my eyes, my breath coming in gasps. "Tonight," I whisper. "Tonight, I will once again make you bare to me," I whisper, my finger going to her mound that is now covered in soft little hairs. She squirms, trying to get me to touch her again, but I pull away. She mews softly. "Tonight," I say sternly. She relaxes onto my chest, her head nodding slowly.

"I didn't know he was going to kiss me," she whispers. Her words surprise me. I kiss her forehead and gently brush her hair back.

"It is for that reason I didn't punish you more severely," I say. "Your punishment was for disrespect in front of my men." I pause. "That will not happen again."

She lifts her head up and looks at me. "I cannot make promises such as that," she murmurs.

I raise a brow at her. "Then I can make no promises to not blister your backside."

She squirms. "So I'm to stand by and allow you to kill another man?"

I sober, lifting her chin so that her eyes are on me. "If I say so? *Yes*." She blinks, but I continue. "Carina, if I deem it necessary to take such drastic measures, you will not heed my purpose."

She swallows. "You almost killed the man who hit me," she whispers. "And you would've killed Arman for kissing me."

I nod. "You do not understand our code, little one," I say. "Both would have been deserving of such punishment."

She looks away, troubled by my answer, but I will not retract my statement.

"But Arman is your man," she says.

"And *you*," I say, with a kiss on her head once again, "are my *woman*."

She is quiet for a minute.

"Now rest, little one, for a bit. I will meet with my men this evening, and then tonight you and I have further plans."

"Yes, my lord," she murmurs, her eyes already closed in a brief rest. I leave her on the bed and summon Idan. It is a mere five minutes later when I am sitting at my table, the tray of food I've ordered at the ready, when Idan knocks on the door.

"Come in," I say. Carina is in bed, covered by a sheet, when Idan enters. For a moment, he looks briefly at her. Her modesty is covered, yet he averts his eyes. He likely knows she's been punished and submitted to me, and is now choosing to be a gentleman. Carina, to her credit, does not stir.

"Be quick with your briefing," I tell Idan. "I must feed Carina."

Idan nods. "Arman has been sent as you bid, to the mines of Kleedan."

"Very well," I say.

Idan clears his throat. "My lord, I feel I owe you an apology," he begins. He pauses when I skewer him with a look and a raised brow.

"Do you?" I ask, feeling my ire rise once again. I wish to be done with this foolery and on to Freanoss, where I must attend to business. What I desire most is waiting for me in my bed, having taken both my seed and punishment in stride. I wish to solve the difficulties before us so that I can return to her.

"Arman was under my watch, and it was on my watch that he took liberties with your woman."

I nod, and dismiss his guilt with a wave of my hand. "Be that as it may, Idan, Arman alone is responsible for his actions. He was to pretend to be my decoy, and took his liberties too far. I spared him his life but not his dignity, as was my duty to do so. Is there any further news?"

He shakes his head. "No, my lord."

"Then are we in full preparation to make ready our way to Freanoss?" I ask. I see Carina's head rise at the name of her planet.

Idan nods. "Yes, my lord," he says. "It seems the Freanossians are behaving as we predicted."

"Very well," I say. "Then we shall proceed as planned. You may go," I say, dismissing him.

Carina will not be left out of my sight for a minute, until such time that I must go to Freanoss. I wish to take care of her before I go, to leave her pining for me. I know the separation will be difficult for us both.

• • • • • • •

"Did you like your dinner, my sweet?" I murmur, wiping a crumb from her lip with the pad of my thumb. She is sitting upon my lap with a blanket strewn about her lovely shoulders, her eyes still bright from having been punished and bedded. She draws her tongue along her lip. My cock stirs within me. I am amazed at how she arouses me even after I've taken her twice in one day. She shifts upon my lap, with my cock stirring beneath her bottom.

"My lord," she murmurs. "It seems I've awakened you yet again."

Smiling, I nuzzle against the soft skin of her neck. "My love," I respond. "It seems you never let me sleep."

Darkness has descended upon Avalere. I have one final meeting with my men to be sure everything is assembled and prepared for our departure tomorrow. "I must leave you with fitting memories of our coupling so that you long for my return," I say teasingly, though I am utterly serious.

Her eyes cloud as she absentmindedly fingers the locked necklace about her neck.

"Take me with you," she says, taking me completely off guard. I am shocked at her request.

"Nay, little one," I say with a gentle shake of my head. "I would no sooner take you to Freanoss than I would to battle." She turns her head away from me. I pause, wondering for a moment, unsure as to her motives behind the question. Does she wish to be near me, or is it something deeper than that?

"Carina, do you wish to accompany me because you miss Freanoss?" Though our journey is hardly one for sport, I do wonder at her audacity.

She looks away, her lower lip a pout, and I tug a strand of her delicate dark hair to bring her eyes back to mine. "Carina?"

She casts her eyes down, still twisting the necklace about her neck. She lifts one shoulder in a shrug. "Partly," she says. "But only because it is familiar. I am not missed by those from Freanoss, therefore I do not miss them." She is insistent, even stubborn in her response.

I say nothing, merely running my hand through her long hair. "There is nothing that you miss?"

She pauses, swallowing, her eyes going half-lidded as my hand runs through her hair. I pull her against my chest, cradling her, my arms encircling her. It is my hope that our intimacy will make her feel free to speak what is in her heart to me. I have laid her bare, punished her, made love to her, and claimed her as my own. I wish for more than outward obedience and sexual submission. It is my desire that she open her mind and heart to me as well. "Not at all, little one? Tell me," I urge.

My heart clenches when I realize her cheeks are damp.

I turn her fully so that she is facing me, and see that what I've feared is indeed true. There are tears upon her cheeks. She swipes them away, and turns her face away angrily from me, as if to hide what it is that she cannot control.

"My sweet," I whisper, turning her back to me by tipping her chin, my hand stronger than the pull of her jaw, insistent as I make her meet my eyes. "Do not be ashamed for mourning the loss of your home. Though it is my firm conviction you are far better off here with me, I do not desire to stifle your natural instincts. Do you have family on Freanoss?" I ask. It is the first time I have questioned such a thing. I know vaguely that familial connections are not like ours here on Avalere. The children of Avalere are born to a father and mother, and raised under the watchful eyes of their mother until they come of age. Boys are taught hunting, archery, swordsmanship, and many are trained to be warriors. I have fond memories of playing at my mother's feet, her voice singing to me as she stirred a pot upon the stove or stoked the fire, my younger sister babbling in her cradle. My chest tightens with the memory. Though I never wish for my Carina to return to the sterile world of Freanoss, perhaps there is something or someone she longs to see.

She shakes her head. "I have no… parents or siblings, or even, as you call them *friends*, on Freanoss," she says. "We were discouraged from forming strong connections, and I know now that there was more at play than I was led to believe. I never desired such connections, as it seemed unnatural." She sighs. "Like everything else, it seems I was manipulated into denying the most basic of human needs. No, Aldric," she says softly. "There is no one."

Heat rises in my chest and I clench my fists. Do the imbeciles who dwell on her home planet not know her exquisite beauty? Her intellect, and strength, and charm? How could she not be adored and *revered*?

Still holding her chin, my voice low but steady, I must question her. "Then what is it that makes you cry, little one?"

She swallows, her eyes glistening with unshed tears. "They didn't come for me," she whispers. "I forfeited my freedom to come here to aid my people. They lied to me of their purpose and… no one *came for me*," she says, anger and sadness welling up in her eyes until her emotions spill down her cheeks, two glistening lines of tears.

I pull her head to my chest, my hand cradling the back of her neck as I whisper fiercely in her ear, "I will always come for you. Do you know that, little one? My Carina? Do you know that you are mine, my very special girl, who was named by me and is now mine above others all the days of my life? Do you know that no matter what happens I will always come for you? My sweet," I whisper, my own emotions clogging my throat as I hold her in a fierce embrace. "It is the way of the warrior. We are joined together, and as such you pledge your obedience and even now feel the pull within you to be near me, inseparable. As for my part, I pledge my protection and devotion. Carina," I say, laying a kiss upon her forehead before I continue. "I would lay down my life for you." I repeat, "I will *always* come for you."

She closes her eyes briefly. "Thank you," she whispers. "And I understand why you wish me to stay here and not accompany you to Freanoss."

But there is a distance in her eyes, and she does not look at me.

I pull her chin back to mine. "Carina," I say, warning.

She looks at me with wide eyes. "Yes?"

"You are *not going*. Do you understand me?"

She frowns. "Yes, I understand you."

I sigh. Foolish, headstrong woman. "Have the lessons I've given you at my hand taught you nothing? Woman, if you try to defy me in this, you will suffer my wrath." I will tie her up if I must. If she *dares* to defy me... Still, she says nothing.

"I said I understand you," she says with a lift of her chin. I narrow my eyes at her. I do not believe her.

"Have you learned to obey me?" I ask her, my voice a mere whisper.

She smiles and squirms upon my lap. "Certainly, my lord," she says. "Do you think I'd be sitting upon your lap if I hadn't?"

I chuckle, giving her a teasing swat. She wriggles on my knee, her thighs clenched together and her eyes half-lidded. I grasp her backside and squeeze. She moans.

"After I meet with my men," I whisper, nuzzling her ear and taking the lobe between my teeth with a gentle nip. She gasps, her hands encircling my neck. I continue. "The evening is ours. I shall summon Lystava to prepare you." I pull away and meet her eyes. "And *watch* you."

She grins, her eyes lighting up with the full smile. "Certainly, my lord," she says.

I eye her warily before I shake the bell at the table. Lystava comes to the door moments later.

"I must meet with my men," I explain. "Take Carina to her chambers and prepare her for an evening with me." I give Lystava a list of what I will need. Carina's eyes widen but I ignore her as I am intent on giving Lystava my instructions.

Lystava bows deeply as I stand Carina on her feet. "I will have men stationed at every door and window," I say. Carina frowns at me, but Lystava merely nods. I turn to Carina and give her a teasing swat. "You may pledge devotion to me, my sweet, but I am no fool."

On that, I take my leave.

CHAPTER EIGHTEEN

Carina

Lystava comes to me, her dark skin glowing in the light of the flickering candles. Her hair is twisted in an elegant knot at the back of her neck. Though she's attended me numerous times, we have not spoken much. I have assumed she is merely reserved, or that it is not her place to speak with the king's woman. But now, she is full of speech, as she lays a silvery blue tunic and silky undergarments on the small table in my dressing room. I have never seen such undergarments before.

She smiles at me when she catches me eying them. "Such things are typically frivolous, if you're the woman of a warrior who will demand his claim on you whenever he deems it necessary," she explains. "But there are times when a bit of dressing up is required." She shrugs. "My lord has plans for you this evening."

I feel an inexplicable twinge of irritation at her use of the word *my*, the irrational desire to shake her and explain that no, he is *my lord*. But the childish impulse passes, as she is my servant and certainly he *is* her lord. She takes a small glass vial from the shelf near the large claw-footed tub, and pours the silvery grains into the tub as the warm water flows. I inhale deeply. The scent is slightly floral without being overpowering.

"What is that?" I ask.

"A blend of crushed leaves from the mountaintops of Kleedan," she says. "They are known for their pungent fragrances. These are extracted and made into a bath salt." She pauses, leaning against the edge of the tub, and gracefully swirls her fingers through the warm water. "Come, my lady," she says softly, gesturing for me to undress and go into the tub.

I hesitate a moment. Though I trust her and know it is the way of Avalere that ladies-in-waiting attend to their mistresses, I am uncomfortable still with her seeing me naked.

She smiles a small, knowing smile, and averts her eyes. "I'll give you privacy, lovely," she says.

She is behaving differently tonight. She has always been a bit detached, but now, it is as if there has been a shift. I am not sure why.

I step into the large tub, the warm, fragrant water enveloping me. It is lightly tinged blue-green, and the lovely fragrance invades my senses. I inhale and exhale, my entire body relaxing. I could fall asleep here, like this, in the soothing recesses of this bath. She approaches behind me, gently tilting my head back, and warm water flows over my temples and the top of my head. I feel her pouring something into her hand, then her fingers are lathering my hair. I love the smell, another slightly floral scent.

Lystava attends me by discreetly handing me what I need until I am cleaned sufficiently, and well groomed. Though this is very different from the sterile manner of bathing I have learned on Freanoss, I enjoy it. My legs are clean-shaven, but she has gently discouraged me from shaving anywhere else.

She holds a luxuriously soft ivory-colored robe for me to step into. "Come now," she says. "The king will arrive soon, and when he does, it is best you are waiting for him."

She gestures for me to change into the blue tunic she's laid out for me, and takes her leave. "Here," she says, gesturing for me to get changed. "Tell me if there's anything you need from me."

And she is gone. I stare in wonder at the thin garment, as I step into my undergarments and tunic. My skin is soft to the touch, the fragrance near intoxicating. My hair still damp, I run my fingers through it, but find that it is already almost dry. I wonder if it's due to the warm air in the bathroom, or some other trick Lystava has managed. I look down at my cleanly shaven legs and wonder at what she said to about shaving only my legs. My cheeks flame with embarrassment. I am not used to having hair on my intimate parts. Why would she not allow me to shave there as well?

Will I ever get accustomed to the ways of Avalere?

Do I *want* to?

To my surprise, I see a small door has been left ajar behind the bathtub. I quietly walk over and realize that the door is an exit to the garden, perhaps to allow servants to tend to this room without having to go through the main rooms and disturb the king. There is a silver key still in the lock, but on the inside of the door, so no guard outside would see me take it. Without a second thought, I remove the key and hide it deep in the recesses of my tunic, then I walk into the king's chambers. There is a wine-colored rug that lines the hardwood floor between his bed and the desk. I kneel, lift the edge, and quickly slip the key beneath the carpet. Then I stand, straighten my shoulders, and prepare for the evening ahead.

Night has fallen. I feel like I have lived several lives just today. My body has been played and hummed with need, released and driven to both punishment and pleasure, and now he has further plans for me. What will the evening bring? I leave my bathing area, feeling magnificent in my soft tunic, gorgeous undergarments, my own scent invading my senses and leaving me lightheaded, almost dream-like. I find Lystava has left me with a few small things to eat, a large cut-glass pitcher filled with cold water, and a few books by my bed. I do not know when Aldric returns, but I am tired after my long day.

I pick up a small, flat, slightly browned biscuit and nibble. It is light but sweet, and tastes delicious. I finish that, and take the glass of ice water. I sigh, feeling refreshed and relaxed, as I lie upon the bed, waiting for my king. I don't recall ever having felt so relaxed in all my life and wonder if the scented bath was enchanted. As I lay back upon the silken pillows, I think of the time that I have spent here on Avalere. I have mentally resisted allowing myself to enjoy being here. At first, I could not reconcile what I knew of Avalere and my own desire for freedom and independence, cleanliness, and modern conveniences. But here, though I am the property of a man, subject to his dictates and my free will removed, I feel *alive*. My senses are awash in what surrounds me, my present circumstance a vivid reminder of how different things are here on Avalere. My skin feels soft, my body warm, and it feels nice as I close my eyes, allowing myself the freedom to smell, hear, and taste. I realize with both a sudden pang and wonder that I do not miss much about Freanoss anymore. What I miss now above all is my own autonomy. If I were to stay here on Avalere, would I ever reconcile being mated to the Warrior King? And on Freanoss—*was* I truly free?

But haven't the Avalerians harmed my people? I was told that they came to my planet of their own accord, stealing from our rich natural resources. My very presence here is due to their theft, and yet... I no longer believe those claims to be true. I am unsettled. The room is warm and I have experienced oh so very much today. I close my eyes and rest my head against the soft pillow. It is dark, the blanket warm, a fire flickering in the grate to my left. I feel lulled by the scent of my bath. With much on my mind and heart, I close my eyes.

I am in the forest by the Wise One, and there are people following me at my heels. I cannot see their faces, but I feel them. I feel *him*. I am on my knees, and the rain begins to fall, cold, biting rain unlike what we ever experience in Freanoss. I dig feverishly through the leaves, as I know it's here, I know I left it, my communication device. If I could only find it. And then I see a gleam of moonlight hit my bag. With a gasp, I throw off the wet leaves from the pack and quickly move to use it. I must be quick, before those in pursuit of me find me. But the moment my finger hits the button, I hear him.

"Little one." His voice is deep, the husky tone halting me in my feverish movements.

No one until him has ever called me *little one*. My eyes shut tight, my breath coming in gasps, as I feel his enigmatic pull.

He is so strong.

But he owns you.

He cares for me.

Only as your property.

He makes me feel alive. He protects me. No harm shall come to me if I am his.

But you are not free.

Then his voice comes lower, stern, but there's pleading in his voice now. "*Carina.*"

I turn to him, and he is already by my side, his touch tender as he reaches for my neck, rubbing his fingers along my skin. He looks at the device in my hand and sadness flits across his features. He frowns, trying to be stern. His hand on my neck tightens, and he grips the back of my head, pulling me to him as his mouth crashes on mine. His lips move in time with mine, his tongue exploring and plundering.

It is then that I wake with a start, and realize the room is completely darkened. He is above me, invading my senses, one hand wrapped around my waist, and one around the back of my neck. It is late evening, and my king has returned. He pulls his mouth off mine and whispers in my ear, "You were dreaming, my sweet. What were you dreaming about?"

I cannot tell him. I merely place my hands on his broad shoulders and grip him as his hands span my waist, his eyes probing. Though I don't respond, he is distracted suddenly as a stream of moonlight falls on my tunic. He sits up, reaches for something on the table beside the bed, and there is a flare of light as he strikes a match. Candlelight flickers. His eyes roam my body as the light brightens the room, joining the flickering of the fire at the grate, and then he returns to me, sitting on the other side of the bed and pulling me to him.

"Lystava has bathed you?" he asks. I nod my head as I snuggle up on his chest. If I am to only have this last night with him, then I will enjoy it, every minute, his strength and power.

"Yes, my lord," I murmur.

"And you ate, little one?"

"A little, my lord," I say, allowing my fingers to roam the breadth of his large, muscled chest, then lower to where his stomach flattens.

He growls low. "Does my sweet have an appetite of a different nature to be sated?"

I moan low, a mere purr as I nod against his chest, heat already pulsing between my thighs just being near to him like this.

One of his large hands travels to my tunic and he plays along the edge, raising it. I squirm at his touch, arousal pooling at my core, as he tugs it up and reveals the lace-edged undergarments. He gives an appreciative growl and explores the edge with one large, rough finger. The touch is exquisite; I am immediately aroused.

"You were dreaming," he repeats, not a question but a statement. I nod, my body tensing. Will he probe more? I offer no details.

"Your body tenses," he says gently, oh so gently, his thumb running over the silk center of my panties. He flicks over my tender mound and my breath comes in shallow gasps. I want more. I want it *now*. I want *him*.

"My lord," I whisper.

"What did you dream of, little one?"

I close my eyes and shake my head.

"She wishes not to tell me," he murmurs. "Then it is likely something that would earn my disapproval." The lowness of his voice combined with the flicking of his thumb makes me moan out loud. I want more pressure, and no more touching along the edge of the fabric but *beneath*.

"Is that true, little one?" he asks. "Were you dreaming of something of which I would not approve?" I do not respond. His fingers flex on the edge, then dip to my thighs. I yelp as he gently pinches my inner thigh. "Answer me," he commands. "Was it about another man?"

Shocked at his question, my mouth drops open. "Certainly not, my lord."

He smoothes his hand on the outside of my leg, gently moving from the top downward, toward my knee, then back up again, traveling to the innermost part of my thigh, as one hand wraps around my leg so the tips of his fingers graze the edge of my bottom. His voice is stern. "Did you disobey me in your dream?" he asks.

I hesitate but finally blurt out an answer. "Perhaps," I said. "I am not sure."

He pauses, his hand drawing circles on my thigh. "Perhaps," he repeats. "Hmmm. In your dream, did you try to get away from me?"

I turn my head to the side and merely nod. I do not wish to deceive him but I feel strangely guilty, even though it was only my dream. He would not punish me for a dream… would he? To my surprise, his finger reaches for my panties and gently pushes them to the side, one finger exploring my folds. My back arches, my legs falling apart wide open.

"Your honesty will be rewarded, Carina. And I'll not punish you for wanting to leave me." His voice softens, as he leans down and kisses the uppermost part of my thigh. "It is natural to want to be home," he says, his voice lowering as his mouth finds his way to my navel and he kisses me there. "I *will*, however, do everything I can so that you no longer *wish* to leave my side." He braces himself up and over me, lowering his mouth to my legs, his rough, bearded jaw tickling my thighs. He kisses the silk of my panties right at my mound. My hips jerk, my back arching, and I am already near release. Ever so gently, he moves the silk to the side, revealing my sex to him. Slowly, his tongue flicks out and he laps lazily at my mound. His tongue hits my bud, my hips jerk, and I gasp, but he immediately pulls away. He sits up, looking at me with that wicked gleam I've come to recognize as dangerous.

"You wish for me to pleasure you with my mouth," he says. "I certainly will, my sweet. But first, you must be prepared." He is standing, walking away from me, and I feel bereft. What has he done? Has he taken me to the edge like this, only to leave me here? And haven't I already been prepared for this by being bathed by Lystava?

He leaves the room, and I feel as if the warmth has gone out, my heart thundering in my chest. My fingers urge to explore the wet folds he's left pulsing with desire, but I know that if I do, I will be punished. I squeeze my thighs together. Somehow, if I ignore my desperate need for him, I can handle this, this exquisite torture. I close my eyes and count backward from ten, then twenty, then I recite my given number and I.D. *R-482. Carina. R-482. Carina.*

I hear his footsteps approach. I sit up, opening my eyes. In his hands, he has two things: a steaming mug and a gleaming silver razor. Over his shoulder is a soft white cloth.

I push myself back on the bed, away from him.

What is he prepared to do?

"Come here, Carina," he orders simply, coming to the side of the bed. He places his mug and razor down, and leans close to me. He brushes a strand of hair back from my face, and pushes my thighs apart.

"Do you trust me?" he asks. I look into his eyes, and I don't know the answer. This is a man who has whipped me, taken me as his, and confined me to his quarters. He's insisted on my utmost obedience. But he has also raised a sword in my name, prepared to slice the head off a man who kissed me, ready to kill another man who harmed me. I belong to no one but him, and if he has his way, I never shall.

This is the man who wiped away my tears, held me to his chest while I wept, and *named* me. I am his Carina, his little one. He stands above me with a gleaming razor demanding to know if I trust him.

"I don't know," I say.

Though his eyes harbor a touch of sadness, his lips quirk up. "So brave," he whispers. "So honest."

He stands between my legs, his eyes never leaving mine. "It is my desire that after this evening, you trust me all the more. Bend your legs at the knees, and keep them still," he says.

I obey, while his fingers grip the edge of my panties and remove them. I am now bare to him, embarrassed that I am not fully clean-shaven. He places the cloth on me, and I gasp at the feel. It is steaming hot, but not so hot it is painful.

"I must ready you," he whispers. I stare at him as his dark eyes challenge me.

"Yes, my lord," I whisper.

He removes the cloth and tips a small bottle into his hand. A smooth, creamy liquid seeps onto his palm. He smoothes his palm over my sex. The liquid is warm and smells like vanilla. His fingers massage it into my skin, then one finger dips between my folds. I gasp as he rakes upward, my nerves suddenly vibrating.

"Already wet," he growls, now grinning at me, his eyes heated. The light of the candle flickers on the silver handle of his razor. My eyes widen as he holds my gaze. I can hardly breathe for the anticipation.

"You came to me bare," he says in a voice like a low purr. "You came to me shaven. As the air of Avalere fills your lungs and the fire of my home warms your limbs, your body returns to its natural state." I squirm at his words. "Allow me to make you bare again," he says, with a pause, before he says, "*For me.*"

I swallow, my mouth suddenly dry. Before I even know what I am doing, I nod, a quick bow of the head, my breath catching in my throat. He bends down to me, his warm, strong body pressed close against mine. "My sweet, *trust me.*"

"Yes, my lord," I whisper. His lips brush my forehead. Before I can move, the sharp edge of the blade is on the sensitive skin at the top of my thigh. Down, down, he drags the blade. I feel the slow but painless scrape along my moistened skin. I draw in another shaky breath as he dips the blade in the cup of warm water and wipes it on the cloth, then returns to me, his brow furrowed in concentration, making him look stern and foreboding. I grip the edge of bed.

He takes the blade and again draws it along my skin. I feel the pull and then the smoothness. Removing the blade, he runs a thumb along the smoothed skin there. My sex throbs with need, but he gives me merely the lightest touch before his blade returns. He opens my folds and swipes the blade so slowly, so gently at the very edge, removing every bit of roughness. I close my eyes. He is so near me now that I can feel his breath as he bends over his work, alternating presses of the warm cloth and soothing liquid before the cool scrape of the razor. So slowly, so gently, he works. I squeeze my eyes shut, breathing in, then out.

"Good girl," he croons. "You will be rewarded for your obedience and trust, little one."

With every scrape of the razor, every touch of his hand, my pussy aches, the heat of my sex pulsing with every touch of his finger, until I am near ready to climax.

"I can smell you," he growls. "I need to taste you, to see

if my work has been done well."

He places the razor in the mug and lays the cloth next to it, dropping to his knees in front of me. He drapes one of my legs over each of his shoulders. My legs tremble. Though I am warm, I am shaking as his mouth and rough whiskers graze the soft skin of my inner thigh.

"So sweet," he whispers, then pauses, his gentle gaze capturing mine. "Relax, little one," he says. "You've done so well." Leaning in, he flicks his tongue along my slit. I moan out loud, fisting the blanket, the feel so exquisite. He pulls my sensitive bud into his mouth and sucks, then releases me, circling me with his tongue, slowly, up and down, as I close my eyes and sigh. I can hardly bear it.

"My lord," I murmur. "*Aldric*."

He growls. The king likes when I call him by name, here in the recesses of our room. I am building to release, and if he tells me this time I cannot climax, I know I will *die*. He swirls his tongue on my nub, flicking then sucking, alternating the wicked, exquisite torture until I can hardly bear it. My hips are straining so that he must hold them in his firm grip as he laps and sucks, lazy, powerful strokes of his tongue that undo me. My nerves are on edge, so taut I'm going to lose my mind.

"My *lord*," I gasp. "I… I—" I don't know what to say. My body is humming with need, shocks of ecstasy flooding my senses, but I know I haven't yet reach the cusp, my need still not sated, the release before my climax more delicious than I thought possible. He eats at my sex hungrily, his whole mouth taking me in, then he moves back and licks again before he flicks against my most sensitive parts, my hips rising to meet his mouth. To my shock, the fingers grasping my thighs shift, and before I know what is happening, he plunges one into my core as he sucks hard.

"May I?" I beg, a near sob with desperation, and he moves himself back from me just long enough to growl, "*Yes*," before his mouth comes back to my sex. My body thrums with a climax so powerful I scream his name, waves of pleasure flooding my senses. I do not realize at first that the scream I hear is my own, I am so consumed with the vivid, intense release. I finally settle back down, utterly exhausted, unable to lift my head or limbs. I realize he is cleaning me, wiping me with a damp cloth, then drying me before he lifts me in his arms and tucks me under the blanket.

"Drink, little one," he says, holding a cup of water to my lips. I obey, unable to do anything but what he says. I am utterly exhausted.

"My lord," I say weakly, unable to move, as the spasms of pleasure have weakened me. I cannot move.

"No more speaking, Carina," he orders. But how can I not speak? He has brought me to ecstasy, but thinks nothing of his own pleasure.

"But I—" I begin, but a quick, hard swat from him has my mouth clamping shut.

"I said no more speaking," he reminds me, wagging a stern finger at me. I merely nod. "You sleep now, little one," he urges. "I leave early in the morning. In my absence, I expect that you will obey those I have set as your watch."

I nod.

"Lystava will oversee your needs. My men will be stationed here to attend to everything else."

I frown. He raises a stern brow. "I expect your obedience, Carina. You know this."

I nod.

"Tonight, take your fill of me," he says. "Now rest."

I have no idea what tomorrow will bring, but I am prepared. I know what it is I must do.

• • • • • • •

It is the absence of his strong, warm body next to mine that wakes me. I pretend I am still sleeping as he moves nearly soundlessly around the room. I wait until he leaves the room a moment to relieve himself, and I look about. It is easy to locate an extra pillow. I slip out of the tunic I am wearing and quickly locate a simple tunic I can wear for the purposes of travel and work, a more rustic one. I quickly sneak back under the covers and pull them up over my shoulder as he comes back in the room. I yawn, and shift a bit on the bed.

"Are you leaving now, my lord?" I whisper. He comes quickly to the bed and reaches for me. I allow myself to feel the strength of his embrace one last time.

"Yes, little one. You rest now."

I nod, pretending to be half asleep. "My head hurts," I lie. "I am going to rest as much as I can today."

"Then I shall not bother you," he says. He has fallen for it. "I shall return as soon as I can. Remember, in my absence you obey those I have left to watch over you."

"Yes, my lord," I murmur sleepily. "I am..." I yawn for emphasis, "so tired."

With another gentle kiss, he tucks the blanket around me. "I shall instruct them to allow you ample rest before disturbing you," he says. "In my absence, you will be allowed access to the library and gardens. Enjoy them, and take this as a time to rest. I will return."

I nod. He leaves the room. I listen attentively, my own instincts now on high alert. I can hear him meeting with his men in the hallway, the low, murmured voices. Someone will be coming in the room to stand guard any moment.

Quickly, I drop to the floor, lifting the extra blanket and fashioning a decoy on the bed, pulling the blankets high enough so that none of my hair would be visible if I were indeed the one in bed. I crawl on all fours, crouched down, and lift the edge of the carpet. For one brief moment, I fear the key has been discovered, before I feel the cold metal graze my fingers. I crawl to the open door between my room and his. In my room, where Lystava bathed me, is the narrow passageway that exits to the garden. The door, as I suspected, is now locked tight. I slip the key in, turn the handle, and push the door, then shut it behind me.

I am in the garden now, the chill of the morning air causing me to shiver. I have seen several servant robes in the shed in the garden, hung there to be worn when a servant needs greater coverage in the morning, or when the rains fall. I grab the robe, pull it on quickly, and pick up a basket. Now I could be mistaken for merely a servant, gathering eggs or milking the animals in the stables.

Just a short distance away, I hear the men assembling at the gate. There is a large mass of men, and I see him, my king, the tallest one with the broadest shoulders, sitting upon his horse at the very front of the line. His chin is lifted, his regal face drawing the attention of the crowd. I allow myself one moment to admire his strength and power, beautiful to behold, as all the eyes of the men assembled in front of him are now on him. There are servants flanking him on either side, and this is how I will disguise myself, so that I am not seen. No longer wearing the king's blue, I draw no attention to myself as I quickly fall into line with the servants traveling by foot.

They begin processing, servants holding flickering torches in the cool darkness of early morning. There is little talk, but murmured voices, as we go deep into the forest, past the home of the Wise One, past where I had left my bag and device, deeper still to where the portals between worlds lies. They are heavily guarded, and it is often discouraged to allow travelers en masse, but today there is an urgency.

"Fall in line," a man says, holding a hand up to the servants I travel with. I must pretend I belong here. I watch as the soldiers go first, in groups of three, then the servants who attend them line up. There are fewer going than I had originally thought. It seems the others are merely escorts.

Panic begins to rise. Perhaps it is best I hide, then access the portal alone, but decide I can best hide my identity if I pretend to be one of them. I watch as a small group of servants directly in front of me enters the passageway for the portal. Eyes are suddenly on me. I discreetly stick a foot out, tripping one, who falls to the side, on her arm. She yelps, and her companion helps her up.

"So sorry," I mutter, but the man in charge herding the servants to the portal is growing impatient.

"Ten!" he shouts. "Ten at a time!"

Confusion reigns as I planned. Ducking my head, I quickly step toward the group entering the portal, just in time. He counts rapidly, then waves his hand at what looks like a small silver button. I have made it, the chaos behind me making the guard grow impatient. Immediately, the world around me darkens, quiet descends, and we are being transported. My heart beats an excited rhythm, now that I've made it thus far, my deception near complete. When the silvery gleam of our transportation begins to wane, my eyes adjust to Freanoss.

I must keep my bearings, my head down, as it is every bit as dangerous for me to be seen now as it was before our departure. There are dozens of soldiers and only a small group of servants, so I quickly step to the left, pulling my hood up. I duck to the side and walk quickly to a stone wall that separates the Nature Habitat from Production, two distinct locations on Freanoss. At first, I know not where the king is leading his people, but I suspect his sister will be at the holding station. I move quickly, ignoring the desire I have within me now to run to my king. I must keep him from knowing I am here.

I am unsettled here on Freanoss. There is no one here for me. Unlike the vibrant land of Avalere, Freanoss now looks so sterile, so bare. A pang of remorse hits me, but I push it away. I have work to do.

I duck behind a half-wall between the Habitat and Production, and from where I stand I can see the Avalerian commanding officers. We have not yet been approached by Freanossian soldiers. It seems we have caught them unawares, as the officers are preparing to advance upon the holding station. Their position now confirms that the king's sister is indeed where I suspected.

Ahead of me, I sneak quickly behind two robed servants, and scurry to where I can be hidden within the confines of the holding station. I step quickly in front of two soldiers whose backs are turned, and race through a doorway at the station.

I crouch behind another half-wall in the room where she is being held. To my surprise, I see her right away. She has the same fierce eyes and dark skin as her brother, though her brown hair is ragged and unkempt. They have hurt her. Whatever residual feelings I've had for the Freanossians flee at the sight of her, clearly abused. Fury makes my hands shake as I recall the mantra of my people:

We are one body. We are one people. Together, we will conquer darkness and rise as one.

It was a lie. It has all been a lie.

One man comes into the room and slams the door. I crouch behind the lookout tower, trying my best to be sure I am unseen.

"They have come for you, *Princess*," he spits out. "I know not why the Avalerians think so highly of someone of little worth like you," he scoffs.

"I am the princess," she says through gritted teeth. "Of course they come for me."

My own memory of when the Freanossians did not come for me fills me with remorse, but I shove those feelings down. I am not here to return to Freanoss. I am not here to even mourn what once was. I am here because I will aid my Aldric.

Just a short time earlier and I'd have agreed with this guard that such archaic notions as *Princess* and *King* were useless, but now I only see him as a bully. My king would destroy this weak, pale guard. How could I have ever felt allegiance to Freanoss? I look around at the sterile room, and out the window at the barren lands, so empty compared to the lush forests and gardens of Avalere.

"They approach," the guard says with a wicked smile. I wonder that he does not look afraid. The Avalerian warriors are trained in battle. They are stronger, fiercer, and the guard seems outnumbered. At his station, there are only two other guards, and a casual glance below does not show he is heavily flanked. But then the reason for his smugness becomes apparent.

"He has fallen for our trap," he says. "Whereas your people rely on brute strength and force, we have far more reliable methods."

The princess's eyes widen slightly, though she still does not show fear.

"When we rid your precious Avalere of your king, you will know we are not to be trifled with."

"We never trifled with you," she says.

He merely shrugs. "Then the king's death is but a cautionary measure. You have what we need, and we will take it." He scowls. Lies, all lies. I was told that *they* were the ones stealing from us, when the opposite was true all along. "Your barbaric ways are useless to those of higher learning and purpose."

My stomach churns with his words because it was not long ago that I believed them myself. To my right, my eye catches a small box of weapons—knives and tasers, the choice weapons of Freanoss. I take one of each, and tuck them into the band at my waist.

I hear a clatter of noises, and look out from where I stand. The Avalerian soldiers are here, and my king rides tall and proud in front of them. My heart thumps.

Don't go, I want to warn him. *It's a trap.* My breath catches in my throat. I do not wish for him to be harmed. He *must not* be harmed. I watch as the soldiers are led to the door nearly unencumbered, until a guard steps out in front. They exchange a few words, and my king lifts his head and hand in warning. His large hand falls, cuing the attack. His men charge the building, but mere seconds later, a blinding flash knocks them all from their horses. I know this weapon, not merely a blinding light but nerve stimulators that cause intense pain.

I watch in horror as his men grip their heads and stomachs, the pain from the Freanossian defense crippling the Avalerians. How will they rally? But my king is already up, mounting his horse again. He rides on, and I lose sight of him. I creep along a dark corridor to where I can watch. I need to get to him. I need to find him. To a Freanossian, the nerve stimulator would be crippling, but it appears the Freanossians have underestimated the fortitude of the Avalerians.

I go toward the sound of clashing metal, down a stairway that leads to the entry hall. I gasp as Aldric enters. He has dismounted from his horse and is brandishing his sword.

"Stand back!" one guard says, standing in front of him, but he ignores the protests. Though they seemed prepared to take him under protection while he was handicapped, it appears their plan is not working. I gasp as a guard shoots a taser at him, but still, he deflects the beam and charges them.

"Where is she?" he growls. "We do not wish to declare war on Freanoss if we are given what belongs to us. My sister is here, and you will return her safely. The fabricated accusations of Avalerian theft are no longer useful to you; neither is holding my sister hostage. Give her up."

The soldier frowns. "You have what belongs to us, too, do you not?"

The king glares. "She no longer belongs to you," he protests, and I suddenly realize they are talking about me. "She broke the law and is subject to ownership by me. She is also aware that you did not come for her, and had no interest in recovering her."

"Oh, we had an interest in recovering the woman," says the man with a leer. "She had one of our communication devices. They are rare, you know."

The king's eyes flash, and I fear he is going to cut the man's head from his neck, but he ignores the insult. I swallow, my eyes shutting briefly, absorbing the pain.

"What you *don't* know is that she's come," says the guard. "She is here, the woman of Freanoss you claim as yours, and because she has left your planet, she is free to return to Freanoss, if she chooses."

The blood runs cold in my veins. How do they know?

The king looks furious. "She is here?" he whispers, momentarily taken off guard.

"Certainly," the guard says. "Did you not know she would come to aid you? We thought perhaps she was ordered by you to come."

The king scowls. "Unlike the cowards of Freanoss, we do not order our women to do the work we are too weak to do ourselves," he growls. He raises his voice. "Carina!" he shouts, calling to me.

I am known, my presence no longer a secret. But I will not come. I will not betray my position to the Freanossians while my king still needs me.

"She does not have to obey your bidding, *King*," scoffs the man. "She has returned to her people."

And with that, my king has had enough. He charges the man, who ducks and misses his charge by a mere fraction of an inch, as they attempt to shoot him again. He somehow deflects each laser.

I must get to him. I scurry down the stairs, no longer caring who sees me. I can defend myself if need be.

"Carina!" the king says, and with the momentary attention diverted from the men he's attacking, his eyes go to me. The distraction is long enough for one man to hit the king with a blunt object, some type of club. I scream with rage as my king suffers the blow. When I reach him, I take the taser I have stolen from the room above and shoot it directly at his assailant, who crumples to the floor. But before I can shoot again, I feel someone's hands on me, fingers wrapped around my neck. I try to scream, but my words are frozen. With a shout of rage, Aldric slashes at the man holding me. With a gargled scream, the man falls to the floor, stained with crimson blood.

"Hit the silver cable!" I shout to Aldric. "It disables their hold on your men!"

The guard to his left screams in rage and shoots, but he deflects once more, slamming the butt of his weapon on the silver cable I know holds his men. Moments later, the soldiers of Avalere enter. The weaker, more cowardly men of Freanoss crouch behind columns and chairs as the fierce warriors of Avalere attack, their weapons drawn.

I can hardly bear to watch as man after man falls, slashes of swords and clinging of armor ringing in the small room. Now that the main weapons of Freanoss have been disabled, the Avalerians have the clear advantage.

"Come!" I shout to Aldric. "I know where your sister is, and you must get her while you can!"

He follows me, quickly coming to my side, grabbing my hand while we mount the stairs. "You reckless, disobedient little girl," he says with a growl. "When I get you back home with me, I will punish you so soundly you won't sit for a week."

I thrill at his words, though I clench a bit at the promised punishment.

When I get you home.
Home.

We come to where his sister is being held. The cowards who were holding her fled when their devices were disabled. She stands when Aldric enters the room, her eyes widening in shock.

"Come," he orders, grabbing her by the hand, and tugging her along with me. "The two women I love more than life itself," he growls. "Putting themselves in harm's way. Better to be tied to their beds than allowed freedom to roam and hurt themselves." His sister's eyes meet mine and we smile even as we run.

Aldric calls his men to him. There are no more Freanoss soldiers remaining standing. He raises his sword, and they prepare to regroup. "Battle has not ended," he says, but I shake my head and tug his hand.

"No, my lord," I insist. His eyes look at me, narrowing but curious. "That is not the way of the Freanossians. As…

with me," I say, faltering, "a fallen soldier of Freanoss is a nonentity. The powers that be will remove their existence from the records and hide this battle. They will not attack, as they know they have lost. They will retreat, now that you have clear victory and have reclaimed your sister."

He scowls. "How do I know this to be true?"

I raise my chin. "You don't. You only have my word for it." But I know that what I say is true. The Freanossians have no fierce loyalty like those of Avalere. They only wish to progress, and progress at this point will mean wiping this loss from memory and expending no more energy or time on battle. He must believe me. I need him to trust me, as I do him.

"Very well," he says, and my heart soars. He commands his men, and they all march in formation back to the portal. It is time for us to return to Avalere.

He believes me, and I am going *home*.

Everyone lines up and Aldric lifts his sister upon a horse one of his men holds by the reigns.

"You," he says, shaking his head at me. "You will answer for this."

I scowl at him. "For saving you?" I say.

His eyes narrow. "For putting *yourself* at risk. For *disobeying* me."

I freeze. "And what if I wish to not return?" I ask.

He pauses, before turning to his soldiers and commanding Idan to take everyone back to the portal.

"We need a moment," he says, pulling me away from his men. He pulls me close to him and lifts my chin with the tip of his finger. "What is this, Carina? Do you wish to stay here on Freanoss?" His eyes are hurt but honest, probing me. "My little one, you came to me as my property. I have been harsh with you, but it was for your own good, for your own protection. This is how my people show their mates that they have value."

His voice drops. "And if you choose to stay with me, I will continue to be who I am. I will treasure your allegiance to me. I will never allow anything to harm you. But I no longer wish to force your allegiance. If you desire freedom, then I will allow you to go." He pauses. "My Carina, I release you of your obligation." He turns and looks back from where we just came. Freanoss. "But after we leave, the portal between the two worlds will be closed forever."

I gulp, looking up at him. My momentary bravado fails me, now that I am so close to him. My throat is tight, my palms sweaty, as I reach for him.

"Aldric," I whisper.

He takes my hand to his mouth hungrily, kissing each tip of my finger. "I do not wish to have you with me caged, Carina. I wish for you to be with me of your own accord. I am freeing you, little one."

Free? Is there freedom on Freanoss? Where I mean nothing to anyone? Where my own human inclinations have been stripped from me? Freedom is merely an illusion. This I now know. I shake my head.

I didn't know what it was *like* to belong with anyone, *to* anyone… until I belonged to him.

"And if I go with you?" I whisper.

His eyes heat, his nostrils flare, and he pulls me to him so tightly it hurts. "Then I will vow my allegiance to you all the days of my life," he whispers. "I will protect you, and lead you, and demand your obedience to me as your lord." He leans down and kisses my forehead. "But you will do so as my freely chosen mate."

I close my eyes. "Take me with you," I whisper, allowing myself to feel the warmth of his embrace, bathed in the knowledge of how precious I am to him. My heart yearns to be close to his.

"I love you, my sweet Carina," he says, and at his words, I know now that the ways of the ancients have awakened in me the first feelings I have ever had.

"And I love you," I answer. He grasps the chain at my neck, still locked from the moment he placed it on me. He pulls me to him by the necklace and twists it, kissing me hard. He leads me back to his men and lifts me onto his horse with one arm, positions me so that I am in front of him, he behind me. We ride on to the portal, and I do not look back.

CHAPTER NINETEEN

Aldric

"Although I must confess this is one of the loveliest flowers I have ever seen, I am *almost* prepared to forfeit such beauty to be rid of the pesky flies," Carina says, slapping her hand at the air to ward off the insects. She is lying belly-down in a field of violets and dandelions, gracefully picking the long-stemmed yellow dandelions in a bunch. I've just sent my servant back to the castle with our basket of lunch remains, and am enjoying the time alone with her.

In the past week, I have enjoyed her company immensely. Somehow, her last time on Freanoss gave her the ability to let go of the residual claim she had on her home planet. I have made it my mission to convince her that the choice she made was not one she will come to regret.

I have taken her to the marketplace, walked her through the gardens in the morning, and brought her swimming to the ocean's edge. I delighted in her shrieks of glee as the waves carried her up, the gentle saltwater with a mild enough undertow that the Avalere people often take their children to the beach. She picked out beautiful linens I was happy to have fashioned into scarves and tunics for her. She is bedecked in jewels, and even now wears a soft pair of leather thong sandals, a real luxury on Avalere as we rarely wear footwear, but the shells of the beach cut her tender skin and I had the sandals fashioned for her. I have commanded that anything she wish cooked for her be brought to her on platters, her favorite tea be brewed at her command, her every need attended to. My servants adore my Carina and are eager to please her. She is demure, graceful, and kind.

I gesture to the flies. "It is because you are too sweet, little one," I say, kneeling next to her and smacking at the flies with my own hands. They scatter, and we are left alone.

She frowns, but she looks playfully at me. "Do even the flies obey you, my lord?" she asks, a coy smile playing upon her lips.

I lie on my back in the grass, reaching for her, and she squeals as I draw her over me so that her body is flush against mine.

"Even the flies."

"Do the birds of the air obey you?" she asks, as my hand reaches over the curve of her bottom and cups her warmed backside, the heat of her skin reminding me of the spanking I gave her earlier that day. She took her due recourse a week ago, for having disobeyed me and risked life and limb going to Freanoss. Though she hasn't been punished since, she thrives under my firm hand, and I leave a frequent sting on her skin to remind her that she belongs to me. Even now, as I squeeze her warm backside, she wiggles on me with arousal. My cock stirs under her in response.

"Even the birds obey me," I say.

Her eyes twinkle as she leans down and kisses my cheek. "And what about the beasts in the forest? Do even *they* obey you?"

I smile at her, running my hands through her beautiful lengths of hair.

"Even the beasts of the forest," I say with mock sternness, enjoying her squirming above me. "Everything and everyone obeys me, Carina, or they suffer my displeasure. This you well know," I say, with a pointed squeeze of her shapely bottom.

She flushes. "Must you always grope me so?" she asks, but I can tell she is pleased. Our lovemaking after I spanked her this morning has left me only momentarily sated, and she is every bit as eager as I am.

"Always," I say to her, lifting and flipping her so that she is below me and I on top. "And you obey me because I love you."

She sighs, and her face finally breaks into the wide, open grin I love. "Impossible barbarian, savage that you are," she says, her hand running down my bare chest. "I love you."

I stop her mouth with mine, and show her exactly how savage I can be.

THE END

STORMY NIGHT PUBLICATIONS WOULD LIKE TO THANK
YOU FOR YOUR INTEREST IN OUR BOOKS.

If you liked this book (or even if you didn't), we would really appreciate you leaving a review on the site where you purchased it. Reviews provide useful feedback for us and for our authors, and this feedback (both positive comments and constructive criticism) allows us to work even harder to make sure we provide the content our customers want to read.

If you would like to check out more books from Stormy Night Publications, if you want to learn more about our company, or if you would like to join our mailing list, please visit our website at:

www.stormynightpublications.com

Manufactured by Amazon.ca
Bolton, ON